DOUBLE WEDDING

Double Wedding

A Regency Romance

Alix Melbourne

OPEN ROAD
INTEGRATED MEDIA
NEW YORK

ISBN: 978-1-5040-9432-0

This edition published in 2024 by Open Road Integrated Media, Inc.
180 Maiden Lane
New York, NY 10038
www.openroadmedia.com

DOUBLE WEDDING

PROLOGUE

1798

Althea, Lady Chalford, known in London as the woman who had everything but didn't deserve it, allowed a tiny furrow in her brow to mar her otherwise perfectly alabaster complexion.

"I am not sure that I want to read this letter before I've had my chocolate, Gordon. It is from Walter, and you know his letters are never anything but demands for money. Perhaps you had better read it first."

Her husband, a handsome man with black hair and gray eyes, some ten years her senior, read the letter and handed it back to his wife.

"I think you had better read this one."

Althea's golden hair—still the same color, though she was now over forty—cascaded onto her shoulders in a profusion of curls, and as she read the letter she twisted it around her jeweled fingers, a sure sign of annoyance.

"Lord! I cannot believe he is our child! He has now managed

to ruin the only intelligent accomplishment of his wasted young life! He is a fool, and she is a ninny to let him get away with it!" She slammed down the china cup.

Gordon did not expect very much from his rakehell son, and in part blamed it on his mother's spoiling of him when young. She had never denied him anything, but when she saw later that he preferred young women to herself, she became as cold to him as she had once been loving. So Gordon could not blame his son completely for the way of life he had chosen. But of course, divorce was a drastic remedy, especially when there were children to bring up.

"They do not suit. She will never be able to put up with his philandering. What would you have them do? Perhaps she might remarry. . . ."

His wife's violet blue eyes—the reason he had married her—had turned to ice.

"There has never been a divorce in either of our families! And everyone will know quite well that it is Walter's fault! I can imagine how the children will be brought up—either ruined by Walter's profligacy, or turned into milksops by her smug righteousness. We may be certain they will not turn into anything we would approve. And that they should decide on this divorce without consulting us! That is quite enough! If they wish no *interference*, I shall be only too happy to stay away, and I never see those children! And I do not want anything left to them or their parents if it can be helped! Why support such disgusting behavior?"

"It does seem unfair to penalize the children for what the parents have done. And who can say how they will turn out? They are mere babies."

Althea concentrated her violet gaze on him.

"Gordon, you will *not* help them! I will not allow it!"

Her husband nodded his head. She knew that he loved her a great deal, and was afraid of her bad moods. He would do nothing about it. . . .

She would have been surprised to see him in conversation with one of his attorneys the next morning.

He was a quiet man, but he had his own convictions. His wife had made his life miserable, and he still loved her. But that did not mean that he could not oppose her. He was resolved to do something for those poor, poor children, and to do it in such a way that his wife would not know until he was beyond her reach, in the true sense of the phrase. Some day this inheritance might be very important to his grandchildren, and it would certainly teach Althea a lesson she needed to learn.

He left his attorney in a jubilant frame of mind. Oh, he would give a great deal to be around in twenty years when what he had set in motion came to pass. It would be very interesting to see what the beautiful Althea would do.

CHAPTER ONE

It was a very apprehensive gentleman who made his way over to Langley Manor on a warm spring day. Normally Drew enjoyed riding through the lovely Sussex landscape, but today he could think of nothing but poor Cama.

Camilla, Lady Green, Cama to her friends, had been exiled to the country by her doctor, who had seen the serious signs of exhaustion after a hectic social season, following on the sudden death of her husband in a carriage accident some six months earlier. Cama had attempted to keep up her usual pace, since she was a political hostess of some standing, but her health had given out. Her friends, Drew among them, feared that she would not recover, that her natural vivacity would not return, so strong was the impression created by the listlessness of her last days in London. Drew wondered what two months in the country had done for her, if anything.

She had been a good friend to Drew from the first moment he arrived in London to supervise his family's vast holdings and dabble on the Exchange, where he discovered he had a talent for finance. Cama had forced him to take part in the social whirl, telling him he would turn into an accounts ledger if he did not take some relaxation once in a while. But now she was the one who had deserted society. Her friends in London had loaded him down with letters and messages.

It had been at his suggestion, after the doctor's pleas had finally broken through her obstinacy, that she had come down to his county and settled in Langley Manor, which was a few miles from his own home, Drew Hall. But what if the rest had not helped? What if she were no better?

The butler led him into the parlor—Langley Manor had no drawing room—and Drew steeled himself. But the woman who came to greet him seemed to have grown ten years younger in two months. She looked magnificent. Cama had a strong profile and fine dark eyes—the lashes of which, her enemies swore, were dyed to match the chestnut hair, which at her age must have certainly owed part of its sheen to a chemical preparation. Whatever the cause, she was a strikingly handsome woman, and her powers of attraction were legendary, or, Drew corrected himself, perhaps not so much legendary as historical. . . .

She kissed his cheek and led him to the sofa.

"My *dear* Drew," she said in that low throaty voice, "you warned me that life here would be *slow*, but you did the neighborhood an injustice! Life (if that is the word I want) here is positively deadly dull!"

"That may be, Cama, but you look a thousand times better. Your doctor was right—a change of scene, some rest—"

"Darling, don't talk such balderdash! I would have recovered anywhere. Time was the healer, not this disgusting fresh air. But I certainly cannot imagine anyone in Sussex getting anything *but* rest, given the social life in the area."

They had tea, and Drew passed on all the messages, and had the morocco case full of letters brought in.

A good hour was passed in questions and answers about the

doings of their friends and enemies before Cama turned her dark eyes on Drew with a severe expression on her face.

"And you, dear boy, what have you been up to? More business in the City? Saving the prince from bankruptcy? How you can manage to find commerce so fascinating is quite beyond my understanding. Such a handsome fellow, wasting his time in all those meetings. I invest, and then I forget all about it. Much easier, really."

Drew laughed. "I foresee a tome entitled *Lady Green on Finance*. An absorbing study, I should wager. . . . But really, Cama, have none of the neighbors been over to see you?"

"All of them, and a colorless lot they are—though there is that family of redheads. *They* are colorlessly colorful."

A slow involuntary smile spread across Drew's face.

"Ah, then, you have not met Sir Walter Abingdon! I heard today that he came back from abroad some months ago."

Cama sat bolt upright. He had her complete attention.

"The rake? The one who spent his youth in the company of Lord March? I had no idea! No one mentioned him, I did not even know he lived nearby. He must be quite a wreck by now, after the way he's dissipated himself—and his money." Cama's fan began to flutter rapidly.

"Black Walter—that is what we used to call him—is not approved of, and is therefore not mentioned as one of the attractions of the area. He returned some months ago. I have yet to see him myself. But I shall go and pay my respects—we are actually old friends; that is to say, we once were friends."

Normally his hostess would have interrogated him on this last point, and he was surprised that she did not do so now; he looked up and saw that she had sunk into a reverie. Drew smiled. The poor-Camilla-stuck-in-the-country of a moment ago had been transformed into the Camilla of London, the female Machiavelli of the drawing room, expert intriguer, and, some maintained, provocatrice. What was there about the presence of Black Walter in the neighborhood to cause this reaction? Perhaps the summer ahead would be more interesting than he imagined. . . .

Lady Green gave herself a little shake. "Really, Drew, I believe that the solitude has quite driven me mad. Imagine, taking an interest in that wretched creature, Walter Abingdon! Nothing more tedious in the world than a rake in old age. But tell me, what shall we do this summer—you are to be at your estate more often, I take it—do you have any ideas?"

"Good works. Take blancmange to the sick, reread Bunyan—"

Cama shuddered. "I suppose this is what my doctor wanted—buried alive in Sussex with an impudent wretch reading me *Pilgrim's Progress*! Oh, it's going to be such a bore!"

But Cama had never been more wrong in her life, for at that very moment, hundreds of miles to the northwest in the city of Bath, a young man was approaching the door of number ten, Laura Place.

CHAPTER TWO

The boy looked at Laura Place approvingly: a right proper kind of place where the gentry lived. He lived in the country outside of Bath, and until now he had never ventured as far as the covered bridge which led to the little four-sided diamond that was Laura Place. It was lined with impressive buildings, and number ten boasted as elegant an exterior as any of them. He felt very important in his role of courier, even if it was just for his old aunt.

He let the brass knocker fall, and a moment later a very tall, rather forbidding person opened the door and favored him with an interrogative glance.

Colley's jauntiness drained away at once. He muttered something in the direction of the butler's waistcoat.

"Speak up, young man."

"I *said*, sir, that I have a message for Miss Mariotta Abingdon."

A large white-gloved hand was extended in commanding fashion. Colley drew himself up. "No, sir. They said I was to give it to the lady herself. No one else."

"Booth, can you tell me where my book might be?" called out a feminine voice from the next room.

"It's here in the hall, Miss Mariotta," came the reluctant answer. "And there is someone here who wishes to see you."

Colley tried to make the most of his five feet two inches, and desperately tried to look older than his twelve years. How dare this butler person try to intercept a letter when the addressee herself was in the next room! But Colley forgot his indignation when he saw that the young lady was giving him a really lovely smile.

"How very exciting! I have never received a message by hand from anyone!"

She took the letter and began to read, which gave him an opportunity to get a better look at her. He thought she was beautiful, but even he, with so little experience of the world of fashion, was struck by the soberness of her dress. The house and the butler proclaimed wealth, but Miss Abingdon was wearing a very countrified gray dress, one which did not in the least set off the wearer's black hair and cherries-and-cream complexion. It did, however, echo the gray eyes fringed with heavy dark lashes. But the paisley shawl which was carelessly draped around her shoulders seemed to show that the young lady did have some sense of what was in style. A mystery, thought Colley; he would have to ask his aunt about it.

Any number of Bath's most eligible young men could have explained the mystery to him. Miss Abingdon's dress, like her limited social circle, was dictated by her mother, who seemed to have adopted all the customs of the Quaker movement but the religion itself.

Mariotta broke off her reading and asked how her old nurse was.

"My aunt is not very well, miss. My mother is very afraid. . . ."

Mariotta looked at him sympathetically. "Yes, I was there several weeks ago. I collect from her first paragraph that she has given up hope herself. . . . Well, I must thank you for bringing me this letter, Mr. Wilson. Nurse often talked of you. I am sure she felt better knowing that you would deliver it to me."

Colley thought that he would like to hear her call him Mr. Wilson all day. He made his most elegant bow and left.

Mariotta was saddened by the news: Nurse Brown had been her own nurse, and had been part of her mother's family for almost fifty years. As a sign of favor her mother had sent her current favorite to see to the old lady's spiritual wants. But Mariotta privately thought that Reverend Colebatch was not what was wanted in a sick room.

The letter was long and appeared to have been written with great difficulty. Mariotta wondered that Nurse had not dictated it to her sister. But as she read on she understood: this letter was to be seen by no one. Mariotta read on with growing amazement, finally running upstairs to her room to read the rest in privacy. Nurse Brown was confessing:

> Now that you are twenty-one almost, and I may not live to see another spring, I must tell you. Forgive an old woman for not telling you earlier. I remember those dreams you had. . . . You must forgive your parents, it was what they thought was best. They loved both of you. I only hope that your sister may be as kind a person as you are. She lives with your father, near Lewes in Sussex, at Chalford Manor. You were separated at an early age, when your parents divorced. I am tired now, I cannot write more. Tell no one, especially not your mother. Perhaps you can write to your sister. Her name is, I remember, Diana. Please remember always your loving,
>
> Nurse Brown

At first Mariotta was stunned. But then her common sense asserted itself. It was all very romantic of course, but it was almost certain that poor Nurse had written this in a state of delirium. She had no sister, could not have. But there was her father's address . . . and a name . . . surely that was all a bit too specific for delirium. . . .

The next few days she could think of nothing else. Somewhere in Sussex there was possibly a girl who was her sister. If only she could ask her mother about it.

But Cecily, Lady Abingdon was not a person one could interrogate. Just the mention of her former husband's name was enough to give her an attack of the vapors.

Mariotta knew her mother to be a woman of high principle, genuinely unworldly and gentle, somewhat vague-minded at times, but essentially well-meaning. But for a young lady who loved clothes, music, and plays, this monastic existence was trying. Whenever she tried to talk to her mother about it, though, she found herself confronting a poor weak creature on the verge of tears at the ingratitude and callousness of her only child. Her mother made her feel guilty about her every secret desire.

Despite Lady Abingdon's absentmindedness, her maternal instinct served her well: whenever Mariotta transgressed, she seemed to discover it immediately.

If Mariotta were to merely hint at the curiosity she naturally felt about her father, her mother would burst into tears. Therefore, she did not ask.

Her mother's sister, Aunt Susannah, had once explained to her niece the full tragedy of that ill-advised marriage.

"Your mother did it to spite her parents, who were quite against the match. And your mother had quite a few other fish on the line, but chose Walter. . . . Well, he was quite the handsome heartbreaker, of course. And your mother thought she could change him. But he insisted on behaving just as if he were a bachelor, and Cecily was stunned. He actually thought she would put up with it all if she loved him. But of course she didn't love him. She was just a silly girl, mad for the first real rake she'd ever seen. And when she was pregnant and got so interested in all the evangelical sects, he couldn't endure being home. Not that I blame him. All those very odd people around from breakfast to dinner! He thought they were only after her money— and of course only he had the right to live off her! Forgive my frankness, child, but you should know, otherwise you'll think your mother was always such a poor-spirited creature. But she wasn't. It was the shame of the divorce that did it. . . . She thinks she has to give up all pleasure to make up for it. Her parents made her feel that she, not Walter, was really the guilty party, marrying without their approval."

If only Aunt Susannah were not away in Germany with her diplomat husband, she might tell Mariotta what the mystery meant. . . . The only thing she was sure of was that the timing was wrong: her parents had separated when she was only one year old. And they had only been married for a year and a half. It was not possible that another child could arrive.

Perhaps nurse had been delirious after all.

Days passed and she began to brood, bringing up memories from her childhood. She remembered various moments when she had felt unaccountably sad or happy—perhaps it was related in some way to this possible sister. And those dreams of herself . . . she had heard of such things; people who were related sometimes did sense each other's thoughts, moods. But without any real information Mariotta could not keep dwelling on this event. Gradually the idea of finding out became buried under the weight of visits and dinners and lectures, for it was May, and even in her mother's set there was a tacit recognition that it was the heart of the social season.

She and her mother, and her mother's favorite divine,

Reverend Colebatch, were walking through Sydney Gardens one afternoon, Mariotta admiring the grottoes and thatched pavilions, her mother agreeing with Reverend Colebatch that it was indeed a sad spectacle to see all these persons who had come here only to display their new clothes. Mariotta heard a familiar voice call out to her, and she turned and saw a tall dark gentleman waving at her.

She stood still and looked at him, a delighted expression on her face.

"Jack! Whatever are you doing here? When did you arrive? Why have you not called on us?"

"Business. This minute. No time. There, that answers your questions. Heard about a horse that could win here, and I had to come and see if it was true. I was over to Laura Place and they told me you were walking in the gardens."

He paid his respects to Lady Abingdon and inclined his head in the direction of Reverend Colebatch, who was looking at him in clear disapproval. Jack quickly took Mariotta's arm and led her a good ten paces in front of her mother—in sight, but out of hearing.

"A rather dashing fellow," said Reverend Colebatch slowly. "Did I understand that he frequents racing circles?"

Lady Abingdon was put on the defensive. "Well, yes, he does, he owns a string of good horses. I am sure I see nothing wrong in it if one is not exclusively occupied with the gambling side. . . . Jack's family is most respectable, they have vast estates in Scotland—"

"A Presbyterian country . . ." Reverend Colebatch obviously felt no other comment was necessary. The Reverend Colebatch was rigidly Church of England, and felt that any other sect was not deserving of respect. Lady Abingdon, who had dabbled in many religions, held no such views, but Reverend Colebatch was a great power in Bath and Wells, and she did not wish to get in his bad books, so she said nothing of the very energetic Scottish preachers she had heard.

Mariotta and Jack, deep in conversation, were happily unaware of the dark thoughts being entertained behind them. Mariotta regarded Jack as one of the family, since he was the brother of her closest friend, the former Mary Campbell. Her mother knew this, and therefore did not worry that a *tendre* might develop between the two.

Most mothers would have worried: Jack Campbell was tall, dark, and blue-eyed, and his mustache, grown during his service in Spain, reinforced the impression of a handsome fellow made to break female hearts.

"So, Miss Abingdon, when may I wish you happy?"

"Jack, don't be so ridiculous! You well know there is no one of any interest in my life except you, and you are here so seldom that I perish for want of human conversation!"

"Ah, the Reverend Colebatch does not provide such conversation?"

Enchanting dimples appeared. "No, his conversation is most decidedly *divine*, not human."

"I am really very sorry that I have to go down to Kent tomorrow, or I would introduce you to some of my racing friends who live in Bath, all of whom are quite un-divine."

Mariotta's voice dropped to a whisper.

"Kent? Where in Kent precisely?"

"Near Tunbridge Wells. Going to see Robert Charters and his newfangled stables. Why, did you wish to come?"

"Very unkind of you, Jack. You know mother won't let me go five miles from Bath! No . . . it is just that I have some important business in Sussex, near Lewes. Would that be very far from Tunbridge Wells?"

"Ten or twenty miles at most, I should think. Nothing for a good horse, which I shall have. Not that you are worthy of such sacrifice," he teased. "But you have my curiosity aroused. Why can you not write?"

A slightly devious look put him on guard.

"No; the truth, Mariotta. I can see you are planning to lie."

She gave a laugh and said she was not sure he would believe the real truth, but that she would tell him.

Fifteen minutes later they were well out of Sydney Gardens, making their way toward Laura Place, trailing behind the substantial form of Reverend Colebatch and the slender one of Lady Abingdon. And Jack had learned everything.

"Well, you were right. I can hardly believe it. And you think that if I drop in on your father something will become clear. . . . I just don't know. . . ."

"You will take a message from me. You will say that my mother has kept me from him—which is certainly true. And that I wish to know how he goes on."

"And then I casually ask him if there's a daughter about the place! No, it won't do."

Mariotta lowered her lashes. "A gentleman who took part in negotiations for the Iron Duke must know how to handle these things. . . . You will not ask about Diana, if there is such a person. You will merely ask to be shown around, so that you may describe the estate to me. Chalford Manor—sounds as if it's been in the family for a long time. The rest I leave up to you. You will know what to do. I have confidence in you!"

"And your mother cannot be told?"

"Never! She would read me all of Jeremiah if she had any idea! Oh, Jack, Bath is so dull. Mama's friends are all a thousand years old, and if you were to meet the one young person of our set, Jonathan Cabe, you would understand why I long for just a bit of excitement! Perhaps you will find out something, perhaps not, but at least you will see my father."

Jack Campbell often took a cynical view of the female sex— he had had too many easy conquests prompted by his fortune— but he felt nothing but compassion as he saw the stricken face of his friend. Jack wondered about the foresight of a mother who had buried this twenty-year-old beauty in such a life.

Mariotta had not been brought out; she had no truly eligible suitors; she had not one decent fashionable gown. Lady Abingdon, understandably enough, had turned her back on the world which had caused her such grief in youth. But did she have the right to keep her daughter from it as well? His resolution wavered.

The huge gray eyes looked at him imploringly.

"All right, I will do it. We'll discuss the details after dinner, when your mother starts talking about religion with Colebatch."

CHAPTER THREE

Jack made his way down to Lewes in easy stages, with a stop of several days in London. He paid a visit to his uncle, and attended a rout at which there were any number of eligible young ladies. But Maryanne, Leila, and Sally were all so predictable. They thought him handsome, charming, and they were quite willing to fall in love with him on the spot.

"What do you want?" asked his Aunt Rosa in irritation. "You are quite the handsomest fellow they've seen. You have great wealth. Why should they *not* fall in love with you? They are all well-bred girls, they would do it in the accepted manner, and make you very good wives!"

His uncle inquired as to whether Jack was setting up a harem.

"That is not what I mean, Cedric! And you know it!"

Jack stretched out his very long legs and leaned back. "I just don't want it to be so damnably easy. I have the illusion that someone might like me specifically—that a thousand others would not be capable of arousing precisely the same degree of affection. But I suppose I ask for the impossible. Give me another month, aunt, and if I see nothing better, you may start the round of parties, dinners, and picnics again. I shall be obedient, I assure you, and ready to fall for the prettiest girl at Almack's."

Aunt Rosa looked quite pleased with this plan, but her husband gave a derisive snicker, which quite annoyed her.

The ride down to Tunbridge Wells was pleasant, and Jack forgot to worry about his matrimonial plans as he considered the possibilities of Robert Charters's mare and his stallion mating to produce a horse that would win every race in England.

A few hours of conversation with Robert and he had almost forgotten his promise to Mariotta, but the next day he woke with the nagging sense that he had forgotten something. Then he remembered, and made inquiries about the fastest road to Lewes, and managed to get there before tea.

Lewes prided itself on several noteworthy attractions, and considered itself far superior to that frippery seaside resort of Brighton, which was only eight miles away. The natives liked to mention their genuine ruin of a Norman castle, Anne of Cleves's House, and Firle Place, a mansion from the fifteenth century.

But the inhabitants were not too cosmopolitan to exhibit curiosity about a stranger. The tall Scotsman who was staying in the Pelham Arms was immediately noticed. The local girls made a point of spending an entire afternoon at the Lewes Lending Library, located next to the Pelham Arms, indeed, in the same building. The Scotsman smiled at them from the bay window, but, disappointingly, that Was the extent of his attentions.

Jack had made up his mind to find out what he could before he bearded the lion in his den.

"So, you going out to look at Black Walter's place? Didn't know he had any horseflesh worth looking at . . . but he is a cunning one, you never know," said the bearded innkeeper, one Sam Tupper. "Hasn't paid his bill here for months. That poor young girl corned and paid it last, so mortified she were."

Jack set down his tankard and asked if that was the housekeeper he was speaking of.

"No, no, it be his daughter, Miss Diana. Terrible life she has. Him with his women, his gambling—no one proper or decent will receive him. But she's not like him. The poor girl."

The next morning Jack set out for Chalford Manor, some five miles from town. It was very pretty country, and he enjoyed the ride. The approach to Chalford Manor was well kept, indicating that at least some things were taken care of. The house itself was an immense gray stone building, imposing, but not really attractive.

Jack was welcomed by an ancient butler who was everything he should be, surprisingly enough. He was shown into the study, a pleasant room with views of the garden. The first impression was one of taste and elegance, but closer inspection revealed signs of decay. Jack noticed the spots on the rugs and drapes, and loosened plaster around the ceiling moldings. He guessed that the servants did their best, but that money for real repairs was lacking.

He was kept waiting for a good twenty minutes before his host arrived.

"Mr. Campbell?" asked the gentleman as he entered the room with a quizzical expression. "I do not believe that we have met."

At first Jack was unable to answer. The man facing him was of his own height, and he bore a startling resemblance to Mariotta: the same eyes, the same dark hair. The face, to be sure, was lined with too many late nights of drinking, but when he smiled, as he did now, it was stunning how much he looked like his daughter. Not that he was in the least feminine—it was the shock of seeing a successful male version of what had only existed in a woman. . . .

"You are come from Scotland, I suppose?" The voice was deep, well-bred.

Jack regained his composure. "Yes, I came down to see Robert Charters—you must know of him—"

Black Walter immediately became animated. "Yes, yes, I am a friend of Old Q's, you know. I take a great interest in racing. Had horses of my own some years back. . . . And what prompted you to do me the honor of stopping by?"

Jack found himself reluctant to begin what was certainly going to be a difficult interview. But he took a breath and began, thinking of Mariotta.

"It is rather a delicate situation. Your daughter, Mariotta, is an old friend of mine, and through sheer accident she found out where you lived . . . and she has the idea she has a sister . . ."

Black Walter had put his hands over his eyes.

"Hadley, is there any brandy left?" he called to the butler from the door of the library. "Bring it then!"

He turned back to his guest and gave an audible sigh. A trifle theatrical, Jack thought.

"I knew it had to happen! Cecily is such a fool, you know. She wouldn't give them up and I certainly wouldn't—they were the only things in my life I could really call my own. So she agreed that we'd each have one, but her condition was that they should be kept separate—I might *infect* both of them, you see. Infecting one didn't matter so much."

Jack was bewildered. So it was Mariotta's own sister, and not, as he had begun to think, a child born on the wrong side of the blanket to Black Walter, and then adopted by him. . . . But how was it possible?

The answer to his question knocked gently on the door and then entered.

"Here is my daughter herself. Diana—Mr. Jack Campbell has come to bring me a message from an old friend. He will only be here a short while."

Jack understood that the girl was not to know, but he was surprised that Black Walter bothered to lie. Jack was about to say something appropriate and found himself confronting a pair of gray eyes just like those he had last seen in Bath. He was unable to stifle his reaction in time. "Identical! I cannot believe it!"

"What does he mean, papa?"

"He means that you bear an uncanny resemblance to one of your mother's cousins, with whom Mr. Campbell happens to be acquainted." He was as calm as could be. He invited Jack to spend the day, but Jack refused, saying he had to get back to London, where there was to be an important horse auction.

The talk turned to horses, in which Diana also seemed to take an interest, and Jack was able to observe her a little.

A twin. But different. For one thing, she was well-dressed. Black Walter at least had seen that she had the clothes she needed. And her hair was cut short in the current style—the resemblance would have been even more incredible if Mariotta did not wear her hair in long plaits, coiled behind her ears. . . . And Diana was a very different sort of personality; that was obvious from a brief acquaintance. This twin was composed, thoughtful, not at all easy to read like her sister. Mariotta was bursting with life, but this girl was like a volcano under very tight control, and there was a wary expression in her eyes, utterly unlike the carefree and ingenuous Mariotta's. Diana was civilized, that was the word, as if she had learned the lessons of polite society which Mariotta had never been taught. He could not tell whether she believed her father's story. Probably not, he decided; but she would not be able to do anything about it—the world was conspiring against these sisters. He felt powerless to do anything—the girl was not approachable, and Black Walter did not leave them alone, naturally.

He enjoyed his talk with Black Walter a great deal, since his host was a past star of the turf and had taken up with one of the major figures of the racing world, Old Q, when he was a mere twenty years old, and the master himself was seventy. The stories he told of his friendship with the old roué were quite unsuitable for a young lady's ears, but Diana seemed quite able to take it in her stride, even going so far as to remind him of some of the funnier stories. She had a cool and cutting way of depressing her father's pretensions, and Jack began to have the peculiar conviction that she was the parent and Black Walter the child.

There was another facet of her that he found interesting: she treated him as if he were merely a friend of her father's. There was utterly no attempt to engage his interest, and he could almost believe that she did not find him attractive in the least. This, he had to admit to himself, was slightly irritating.

He took his leave of the Abingdons, promising that he would pay a visit when he next came down to see Robert Charters.

The thought of Mariotta's disappointment bothered him as he rode out the gate, but he comforted himself with the fact that he had at least found out that there was a sister—and certainly Mariotta could arrange to write her. . . .

He was halfway to the main road when someone riding a chestnut waved him down from a side path. He stopped, recognizing Diana Abingdon. She must have taken a shortcut through the woods.

"Please, I must speak with you. Let me ride with you as far as Lewes." She was out of breath, and there was an urgency in her voice.

"That is five miles. Won't your father be worried?"

She shot him a satiric smile. "Father does not worry about me. I worry about *him*. With reason. I have complete freedom—of that sort anyway."

"And what sort do you not have?" He asked curiously.

She looked at him levelly. "I lack the freedom to have any sort of financial security; I lack the freedom to predict my father's behavior from one day to the next; I lack the freedom to pay any bills we have. Does that answer your rather impertinent question?"

He knew he had been wrong to ask her anything so personal, but he rather thought a girl who rode alone with a man she hardly knew would not be upset. She seemed to be reading his thoughts.

"Don't you think we should set off? You are thinking that this is improper. I am accounted quite a good horsewoman, and often ride alone; the neighborhood is used to it by now."

They rode for a while in silence, and then she suggested that they stop by a stream which was screened by a thicket of trees.

"This will do. Now, Mr. Campbell, I would like very much to know what you were really thinking of when you said the word *identical*."

He thought he saw the ghost of a plea in her face, which made it much more like Mariotta's, and he abandoned all ideas of lying to her.

"But your father does not wish it, you know."

"His wishes concern me as little as mine do him. Oh, I love him, but he is really impossible . . . but that is not our subject."

"You seem to know something already."

After a moment's hesitation she confided in him. "I have had dreams, since childhood, about a girl. Sometimes she was hurt, and I felt the pain. . . . If there is such a girl, if she is not just the dream of a lonely child, but a real sister, I think I have the right to know."

Not such a cold little thing after all, thought Jack.

"Well, I shall tell the story exactly in the order it happened. . . ."

When he was finished she was silent for a moment, then she shook herself and got up.

"You know, I think I am jealous of Mariotta. I have spent so much time traveling that nothing seems so wonderful to me as staying put in one place. And Mariotta has a respectable home. She is not subject to the scenes we have here every day. . . ."

"You might be surprised. Mariotta would certainly envy your life. She is dying of boredom, or so she always says."

Diana was surprised. "She is actually unhappy? Our mother mistreats her?"

"Not what you would call mistreating . . . but there are aspects to her education which have been neglected, shall we say, and she is allowed virtually no freedom. Her mother entertains only the serious young clergy and the wealthy old bachelors and widowers."

Diana laughed. "I should dearly love to meet one of those wealthy old bachelors! Here I see nothing but dashing young men come to consult my father much as you have done."

"And you have no interest in them? I was always under the impression that women generally preferred a handsome man." Jack was teasing, but there was an edge to it. He was well aware that she had not been interested in him.

Diana looked at him, much as he might have looked at a horse. "Yes, you are a very pretty fellow, Jack Campbell. But my father was just such a dashing heartbreaker, and look what he has come to. No, I require strength and solidity in a man. I have no illusions about love; I have quite outgrown such childish things, I hope! You are certainly one of the most handsome, engaging fellows I have ever met, but you could never interest me, even if you wished to, which, of course, is unlikely. You see, I am forewarned and forearmed."

This was said in a lightly mocking tone. Jack was ashamed of himself for letting it bother him, but he felt his irritation rising.

"I am deeply hurt, Miss Abingdon. I am great friends with your sister, and I thought . . ."

"Oh, that does not mean I would not like you as a friend! I am sure that you would make a capital friend."

Jack found that this attitude on the part of a beautiful young lady did not precisely please him. The more he saw and heard of her, the less she reminded him of Mariotta.

They rode the rest of the way in virtual silence, but when they reached the Pelham Arms Diana asked shyly if she might send a letter to her sister with him.

"I shall be most happy to deliver it," Jack said in a formal tone.

He waited while she hastily scribbled a note after asking the innkeeper for the paper and wax.

"Thank you very much," she said, smiling at Jack.

The smile was the same: The dimples were there after all. It was the first smile he'd had from her.

"You will never know how grateful I am that you decided to tell me. I am in your debt. . . ."

He was startled to see that tears were forming in those cool gray eyes, a sight which completely upset his estimation of her character. It was really too bad that he would most probably never see her again. . . . She was a genuine mystery.

He went back to London and spent a few days with some

fellows he'd known at Oxford. When he took his leave of his aunt and uncle, Aunt Rosa asked him whether she should start planning some dinners for his next visit.

"No, I don't think so," he said absently. "Somehow I think I'll give it more time."

Cedric once again irritated his wife by producing a most unbecoming snicker.

"He'll find his own, Rosa. I did, and I wasn't *too* unsuccessful at it."

Jack laughed at them and told them he only wished his marriage would be as happy as theirs.

CHAPTER FOUR

Since it was a Friday afternoon, Jack knew where he would find Mariotta: at Meyler's, looking at all the new books and magazines that had come in. He found her poring over a French fashion journal with half the female population of the town looking over her shoulder. But she caught sight of him and gave him a meaningful glance. He went outside and walked in front of the Pump Room, which was next door.

"Oh, Jack! Where shall we go? Shall we walk? No, I guess mother would find out. Let us go to one of those nooks in the Pump Room."

They did, and found themselves a place on a striped sofa in the least populous corner of the room. Mariotta was all aglow with excitement and seemed to be unable to sit still.

"Jack, I see by your face, you've something wonderful to tell!"

"Only if you'll let me! Now, what do you wish to know first?"

"What she looks like."

"You have only to look in a mirror."

"You mean she looks a great deal like me?"

"Oh, she does not smile so much, and she is better dressed, but she looks exactly like you. And her hair is cropped."

"Stop joking, Jack. What do you mean precisely?"

"I mean, my dear child, that she is your twin. Your identical twin, from what I could tell."

Mariotta sat in a state of shock, unable to react, not noticing the acquaintances who said hello or nodded from across the room. Finally she seemed to come out of a trance, and she began to fling a thousand questions at Jack. She too, it turned out, had had the dreams of a girl. . . .

Jack told everything in great detail, with the exception of the conversation about handsome men. He felt no need to go into that.

After they had analyzed everything as much as time would allow, he remembered the letter, which he handed over to an eager Mariotta who read it on the spot, so great was her curiosity. After she read it she folded it and put it in her reticule, her eyes dancing in the old familiar way.

"Well?"

"Oh, she sends her best regards and hopes we will find a way to meet someday. . . . I shall write her back—she provides me with the address of an inn where she can receive mail. I shall have to make similar arrangements. Mother would never let me receive letters from her, and Booth would be sure to tell. Can you conceive of such unnatural parents! Of all things, never to have told us anything. So stupid, really. We might have met somewhere, quite accidentally, and then what?"

"I suspect that is one of the reasons you have never been out of Bath, and Diana has never been *in*."

A few days later Jack took his leave of Bath and promised Mariotta that he would be back in two months after his affairs in Scotland were arranged.

"And what are these vague matters in Scotland? Do you have a secret, Jack?" Mariotta was only teasing, but he reacted very seriously.

"Yes, there is, you wretch, and you had better just forget everything about it!" He left a girl burning with curiosity, which would serve her right for being so observant.

Mariotta went back into the house and sat down, giving a sigh of relief. It had really been very hard not to tell Jack. But Diana had made it clear that absolutely no one was to know.

In her letter Diana had said that she would waste no time on emotions—surely her twin would know what this meant to her. Rather, she put forth a plan: she would pretend to be going to a friend in London, but instead she would go on to Bath, and put up at an inn on the outskirts of the city. She would send word with a messenger that Mariotta should look for a Miss Jean Smith in the Pump Room. This would mean that Mariotta should go to the Orkney Inn.

Mariotta spent the next two weeks in anticipation, but nothing happened, and she had almost allowed herself to give up hope when a boy came up to her in the Pump Room, after being told which lady was she. The boy quickly said that Miss Smith was hoping that Miss Abingdon would meet her in the Pump Room the next day.

She was unable to sleep that night due to the excitement. She thought of what Jack had said about Diana's being well-dressed, and bitterly regretted that she could not wear her one good dress to this meeting—her mother would notice if she did.

Mariotta's high spirits were somewhat lowered the next morning when she looked out her window: It was raining torrents. And she would have to walk over to Pulteney Street before she could hire a sedan chair. . . .

The sedan required the entire sum of her weekly allowance, but she was so grateful to be out of the wet, sitting on its velvet seat, that she could not regret the money.

The Orkney Inn proved to be a small but neat hostelry a little outside of the city. When she walked in the hall the innkeeper welcomed her warmly and bade her sit by the fire.

"You be the sister, I warrant," he said. "There is a great likeness between ye."

At first Mariotta was alarmed. Surely he would see that they were twins. But she realized from his remarks that he thought no such thing. Perhaps Jack had exaggerated the resemblance.

A few moments later when she was led into a private parlor she had' her answer.

The girl by the window was dressed in the height of fashion in an elegantly simple cream gown trimmed with cherry flounces, with kid boots to match. Her hair was curled and cut in the latest crop, and from top to bottom she was a perfect illustration out of the pages of *La Belle Assemblée*.

Small wonder the innkeeper had not noticed that they were twins. Mariotta was in her old brown merino, wearing jean boots, with her hair as usual in two heavy coils behind her head, the weight of the hair having combatted its natural tendency to curl.

Diana stared in silence.

"It is the strangest sensation," she said finally, "but surely I am not so beautiful as you!"

Mariotta began to laugh. "Much more so. But is it not immodest of us—we are twins, after all. What is true of one is true of the other as well!"

They went over to a mirror above the fireplace and examined themselves.

"The hair," said Mariotta, "that is really all that sets us apart. And the clothes, but that can be fixed."

"So can the hair," said Diana thoughtfully.

They began to talk in a rush, completing each other's sentences, discovering that the dreams they had were based in reality—Mariotta had once had a nasty fall from a horse, for example, and Diana had been violently upset at the same time.

As they talked Diana found herself listening to Mariotta's voice in fascination—so that was how she sounded to others! And Mariotta in her turn examined her sister's graceful movements. It was an eerie sensation, for although they were familiar with their mirror images, a three-dimensional copy was quite different.

In the middle of a sentence one of them would stop and stare, so strange was the feeling of looking at one's exact double.

They agreed that their parents had been quite wrong to keep them a secret from each other.

"And then there is grandmother!" exclaimed Diana. "She knew of course—she has always treated father badly, and now I can see why."

"Have you ever seen her? I did once, but I was too young to remember it."

"No. But I know she is a great lady. She has a house on Cavendish Square, three estates and so on. She was a great political hostess, I believe. Perhaps one day she will acknowledge us. . . ."

Mariotta began to tell her sister how she detested Bath and longed for something different.

"So Mr. Campbell was right! You really dislike your life here. . . ."

"And what did you think of Jack? A very handsome man, so all the ladies generally think."

"Yes, he is. Do you have a—"

"Special affection for him? No. It is strange, but he is exactly like a brother to me. I cannot think of him in that way. We are merely the best of friends. But how is it that father let you come here? Does he know?"

"He thinks I am in London visiting friends. He thinks nothing of letting me traipse around the country with nothing but a groom and maid. I have told my groom that I have a friend in Bath whom I must see—he disapproves, but he is silent. My maid is still in London; her mother there is not well. I tell you all of this for a reason, as you will see."

"Oh, lord, Diana! It is so late! Mother will be wondering where I am!"

Diana took a deep breath. "Well, I suppose you will think me quite mad, but I must tell you anyway. When I first thought it up it seemed quite easy, but now . . . My plan is this: we will change places, change lives."

Mariotta's mouth opened to speak, but nothing came out.

"But Diana," she finally said breathlessly. "People would discover us!"

"Of course it is possible, but I have given it all a great deal of thought. We would only do it for one month. Surely we can do it for that long. At the end of that time we might very well be found out. . . . You think it impossible? Well, it was only a dream—"

Mariotta shook her head, her eyes shining. "No, no, read my mind, twin. I think it quite wonderful. But how? I am at your service, but just look at me!"

Diana reached over and ruffled her sister's hair.

"Look. You will simply have your hair cut and done in London. That is all it will take. And you will have my clothes, remember. As for your mother, I shall simply tell her that in a moment of depression I had my hair cut. I will manage her anger. You will start by telling her you are going to have your hair trimmed—and you will come here instead. Everything will be ready."

Mariotta began to have the feeling it was going to happen. They decided that they would make lists of the most important people that they would have to recognize—and the places they belonged to. Luckily Diana's circle was very limited, due to the fact that she and her father had returned to Chalford only three months earlier. And Mariotta could describe all of their close friends—or rather, her mother's close friends—in five minutes.

"We cannot worry about everything," said Diana. "If we do not know someone who seems to know us, we must be calm and simply nod. A lady may forget a recent event, for example, one may be feeling unwell—there are a thousand ways to prevent discovery. And no one would be suspicious—we are so alike, after all."

"And we shall try to explain everything away—but if we can't, we shall just confess."

"Oh, no," said Diana, "I don't like that part. Better would be to deny it all, and then get in touch with each other—we must make arrangements for that. Then we can simply switch back and no one will ever know."

"I suppose that's possible. But you must realize that it is possible someone will simply know immediately. You must be prepared to confess, if need be."

Diana still didn't like the idea of being caught, but she agreed that it was something that might happen.

Mariotta's eyes were dancing. "But Diana, how will you endure my life? There is a toad known as Jonathan Cabe, for example, mother's favorite divinity student."

"Don't worry, I won't accept him, or anyone else—and neither should you. Nothing we can't get out of easily."

"Well, Diana, you'll have to wear these clothes—you can't get out of *that*."

"We'll see," said Diana airily. "Perhaps Mariotta will suddenly develop an interest in fashion. . . ."

"But mother does not believe in Outward Display. You can't imagine what kind of lecture on Vanity you'll get."

"I suppose I can't, but it doesn't matter. I'll get it, not you. And I have a feeling that I will be able to deal with mother . . . and perhaps you will do better with Black Walter. . . . A change may make the difference. We won't have each other's habits of behaving with them."

Mariotta was half out the door when she remembered that Jack would be coming back to Bath. What if he came early? He would certainly know the difference.

"I plan to be you—more animation, eagerness. I can imitate high spirits . . ."

"Life with father is so hard?" Mariotta took her sister's hand in hers.

"Not precisely. I think that I am merely so tired of it all . . . the selfishness . . . the weakness. . . . I have no strength anymore."

"Perhaps he does not need as much as you give him."

"You'll see, you'll see."

"Life with mother may not be an improvement."

Diana smiled a tight little smile. "Of course, but at least the roof won't leak in the picture gallery, and the repair won't wait for a year! And the servants are probably paid on time."

Mariotta thought having a picture gallery so romantic that the leak hardly counted.

CHAPTER FIVE

Diana woke the next morning and wondered if she had dreamed the meeting with her sister. She had set out on this adventure in a spirit of anger at her father. But now she was wondering if she had not gone too far. Her better self was condemning the way she had dragged a perfectly innocent party into all this. She would have to give Mariotta one more chance to get out of it.

The event which had driven her to this was her father's new plan to have her marry one of his old friends, Carlton, Lord Drew. Her father worshipped him, and he was undoubtedly just such a rake as he. Diana had never met him, and never wanted to. But her father would find some way to push her into this man's company, and it would all be so awful! She would have to tell Mariotta all about it, she could not let her go down there not knowing. . . . If the exchange were abandoned, she would have to go to London and throw herself on her grandmother's mercy. But she would not go home. She had had enough.

Mariotta arrived in a sunny mood. She would not listen to any objections—she would handle Lord Drew—it would be wonderfully thrilling—Mariotta would throw herself in the Avon this minute if she did not get to go. When the distressed

Diana suggested that they forget the entire scheme, two large tears rolled down Mariotta's face.

Diana was shocked. "Mariotta! Pray, do not cry!"

One gray eye smiled out from behind her hand.

"I am really good at that, aren't I? I am not really crying, Diana, but if I thought you really meant to abandon the plan, I might start in earnest. I don't care what father is like as long as he doesn't beat me—"

"Don't be silly, father doesn't do anything of the sort, but I hardly think Bath could prepare you for life at Chalford."

"Enough, my sister—how nice to be able to say that word. You are a miracle, and so is this plan! Jonathan Cabe is about to offer for me, I can tell. And he has a mouth like a frog!"

Mariotta seemed to regard this as the ultimate argument, and would listen to nothing further.

"And you do not want to marry this rich old man, Lord Drew?" asked Mariotta curiously.

"Of course I wish a rich husband—after a life with a proverty-stricken rake, you would too! But I do not wish one who is a friend of my father's and just such a gambler as he, no doubt. Rich men do not stay rich long that way. I want a nice, unimaginative man who will provide me with security—and no excitement."

Mariotta repressed a smile. "Well, Bath should suit you right down to the ground. Nothing imaginative about our bachelors and widowers—at least in my mother's set. I have heard that there are any number of wonderful daredevils, if one is allowed to seek them out. But I never have. They are not in the Pump Room, though, that I can swear."

"I must warn you that Black Walter is capable of betting on anything, just like Old Q. And he has the devil's own temper."

Mariotta looked thoughtful, and for a moment Diana

wondered if she had finally dissuaded her. But her pensiveness was caused by something else.

"I have sometimes felt that I could be very angry. . . . I have always restrained it, our mother is far too fragile, she has nervous attacks . . . but I think I must have inherited his temper. I often feel like doing *violence* to people."

"If you have been able to restrain it, I doubt that you really have Black Walter's temper. He never lets anything stop him. But enough of this. If you are determined, let us begin by exchanging our rings. Did you tell your mother you were having your hair trimmed today?"

"Yes, but it was a struggle. She got a headache, and this time I took advantage of her sickly state. I have drawn a picture of your coiffure to give to the man in London."

Diana was busily packing up her jewelry case. "Now, let me think. Here is your money. Marmaduke—he is both groom and driver, and invaluable—we must not let him see us together, and you must wear this hat over your hair."

But the result was unsatisfactory.

"Here, sit down," said Diana. "I am going to cut your hair enough to fit under the hat."

Mariotta felt apprehensive, but she conquered her fear. What must be done, must be done. She looked at the results ten minutes later.

"One thing you will never make, Diana, is a ladies' hair-dresser!"

"Oh, it will do. See, the hat covers it, and I've pinned up the ends. They do look dreadful, don't they."

Mariotta giggled. Her hair had been butchered, but now she was wearing a beautiful traveling costume for the first time in her life. And it was wonderful.

Diana looked at the transformed Mariotta with approval:

The blue dress with its matching cloak looked lovely. She herself was a bit of a dowd, dressed in Mariotta's old green muslin, but already she felt wrapped in respectability, and that made up for it.

They said goodbye.

"Are those real tears this time, Mariotta?"

"Yes, yes. It seems terrible to have to separate so quickly, when we have only just found each other. . . ."

"Somehow I am sure that we will be together. After all, in three and a half months we turn twenty-one, and we receive something from grandfather's estate then. Perhaps we could live in London together, who knows?"

"Yes, but mother says it will be very small. But there is your rich husband—he could take care of the both of us!"

"If you have not found your own rich husband."

Mariotta shook her head. "I doubt I shall. In my experience wealth makes a man boring (excepting Jack of course). I want adventure, a young soldier, something like that, travel, you know."

They kissed and went different ways: Mariotta out to the coach where Marmaduke was waiting; Diana back into the inn. Diana waved at her sister, already leaving in the coach, and turned back to her room. Her heart was pounding. A new life had begun, from this very moment.

Diana arranged to take a hackney into the city, and was surprised at how excited she was at the prospect of seeing fabled Bath.

She entered the city from the direction of the road to London, and she was able to admire the Paragon Buildings and many other impressive facades before the driver turned onto High Street and then on to the Pulteney Bridge, which she thought enchanting, spanning the Avon as if it were a Venetian Bridge of Sighs transplanted. And then they were in Laura Place, which was obviously an area where the wealthy and respectable would live. When she was standing on the pavement she looked at the wonderful sweep of Great Pulteney Street, which stretched out from Laura Place, in the direction of Sydney Gardens. This would be a wonderful city for walks, despite the rather steep hills. She would enjoy it, she thought.

Feeling more nervous than she had expected, she let the door swing open in front of her.

The butler noticed nothing but her new coiffure, which he admired in a very polite way. She quickly went up the stairs to the right bedroom and collapsed on the bed in relief. It seemed a miracle. She had entered her mother's house, something she had dreamed of a hundred times when they were stranded in Europe, without funds or friends. She had always thought her mother's house must be a haven. And so it seemed now.

The room was furnished simply, but everything was clean and well cared for. There would be no leaks in this roof, and there would be new bed linen made when the old wore out.

There was a soft knock at the door.

"Come in."

A round-faced woman smiled at her and closed the door conspiratorially. This must be Mrs. Oakes, the housekeeper.

"I thought I'd warn you. Lady A. has invited that Cabe to dinner again."

Diana groaned. To have to deal with him on her first day!

"Now, you always groan like that, Miss Mariotta, but I've told you, it's not good for your voice. My mother always said a lady should speak softly and never make unpleasant noises! . . . I must say, Miss, that coiffure is lovely. Such a difference it does make!"

Diana was amused to think that she and Mariotta had the

same involuntary reaction to Mr. Cabe. Perhaps this would help Mariotta at Chalford as well. . . .

Diana washed and changed for dinner, somewhat afraid of what might happen when she saw her mother for the first time.

Diana went down to the green salon. A small woman was sitting at the writing table, finishing a letter. Diana was unprepared for how petite her mother was, and felt like a giant beside her.

"Dear! Your hair!" said a soft voice in falling accents. "It is so . . . extreme. Is this really the effect you wished? I thought it was to be merely a trim, surely?"

Diana sat down on the chair opposite and tried to look upset.

"Yes, it was, but the hairdresser was carried away! He insisted that this would be much better, and really it was too late—he had already cut off the back!"

Her mother compressed her lips in a long-suffering smile. Then she began a lecture on Vanity, saying she hoped that this new coiffure would not turn her head as it did so many girls these days, etc., etc.

Diana used this time to study her mother, while affecting a suitably cast-down expression. Lady Abingdon could really have been quite attractive if only she would have done something with herself. Of course the sandy hair and freckles would never be considered beautiful, but the features of the face were quite lovely. It must have been a trial living with a daughter who so much resembled a hated husband. Diana wished they had inherited their mother's mouth, a finely sculpted thin-lipped one, instead of their father's wide mouth. Her mother was wearing a gray serge, suitable, Diana thought, for a saint on the way to the pyre. Not that Mariotta's closet held much that was preferable. Something would have to be done. Even respectability would admit of a little more gaiety.

Diana forced her mind back to the lecture at hand.

"One gives into earthly pleasures at the expense of one's soul, so the Reverend Colebatch assures me. I should not like that to happen to my own daughter. What is inside a head is far more important than what is on it!"

Diana had never heard anything like this in her life. She listened to it much as she might have listened to the discourse of a learned Muslim about his religion—as an exotic and interesting thing. She resolved to read a few of her mother's favorite religious tracts so that she would be better able to converse in this house with these people, who talked about things her father didn't even think of. She began to wonder what in the world had ever made her parents marry in the first place. Ridiculous! It could only have been love; there could be no other explanation.

She assured her mother firmly that if she had been brought up correctly—which she knew she had—how in the world could a new hair style lead her to the Wrong Path?

Lady Abingdon was a little fuzzy about this, and unable to give a clear answer—either way she condemned the upbringing she'd given her daughter—and finally said that she was sure Mariotta would think about all of this when she said her prayers.

Before dinner Diana took the opportunity to familiarize herself with the house.

Everything in it was as it should be, from the dragged-brush work on the walls of the library to the silk-hung drawing room, to the Chippendale furniture, to the collection of porcelain dishes in a mahogany cabinet. But the general effect was somehow cold; intimate touches were lacking. Anyone could have lived in this house. On the other hand, she reminded herself, here there was no feeling of dampness and no creditors knocking at the door. She would no longer have to worry about those things.

What she did have to worry about sat next to her at dinner. Also present was a rather tedious friend of her mother's, Mrs. Willow.

Mr. Jonathan Cabe was a tall, slender gentleman with a bad complexion and a nasal voice. His mouth, as Mariotta had sworn, was froglike. He also expressed dismay about the loss of her lovely long hair, and Diana suspected that her mother had suggested he mention it. He made several awkward and elaborate witticisms, based on quotes from the scriptures, but Diana could not quite understand them. She did, however, understand that he too was afraid she was about to plunge into Vanity and Excess. A little of this went a long way. Forgetting her role momentarily, Diana undertook a depression of his pretensions.

"Why, Mr. Cabe,"—here she fluttered her long lashes— "I suppose this means that you are *trying* to compliment my appearance. I must be looking very well indeed if you are going on so about Vanity! Do you mean to say that I have reason to be vain?"

Mr. Cabe grew flustered. "No! That is, yes! Of course you look well—you always look well. I sincerely hope you did not think I thought otherwise!"

"She is teasing you, Jonathan," said Mrs. Willow coldly. "Mariotta is so playful, you know."

But Diana's flirtatious smile had caused Mr. Cabe to turn red, making her realize that Mariotta must never have flirted with him. Poor Mariotta must have put up with a good deal in silence, judging by the surprised look her mother was giving her. But really, this Cabe was unendurable! And Diana would be happy to rid Mariotta of him, even at the price of Lady Abingdon's anger.

The rest of the meal passed quietly enough, but after everyone had taken their leave Diana began to understand Mariotta's reluctance to oppose her mother.

Lady Abingdon called her daughter into her room. She was lying in a dejected pose on the sofa, a damp cloth on her brow, her maid Smithson bustling around muttering darkly about "attacks." Sighing heavily, the invalid asked to be given some weak tea.

"Dearest," she began in a faint voice, "you know how I value dear Mr. Cabe. . . . I am horrified . . . yes, *horrified*, to even think that a daughter of mine . . . might have wounded the sensibilities of such a fine young man. It has quite overset me . . . one of my brain spasms is coming on; I can feel the headache beginning . . ."

The pale blue eyes had tears in them. Mariottawould have no doubt fallen to her knees and begged forgiveness, but Diana could not do it. She was experienced in the ways of hypochondria and had a keen instinct for separating the real illness from the false. Her mother looked as strong as a horse. Diana had seen her appetite at dinner. . . .

"Perhaps you should go to the Pump Room with me tomorrow," said Diana brightly. "I know that at your age these digestive problems can develop into serious afflictions."

Her mother looked up sharply. "What do you mean, at my age?"

"Of course I do not mean to say you are *old*, mamma. Of course denying one's age is a sign of vanity also, I believe. . . . But I am persuaded that a course of the waters would help you. Strange that one who looks so healthy, and eats so well, should suffer so."

Lady Abingdon waved her hand, indicating that this viper of a daughter might leave the room.

The next day Diana persuaded her mother to come with her

for what was her first trip to the Pump Room, although her mother had no suspicion of this fact.

The day was lovely, so they decided to walk. Diana was wearing a dreadful dark blue calico, and her mother was in her eternal gray, but even this could not keep the daughter from enjoying Bath.

Diana was a great admirer of the pale golden Bath stone of which most of the buildings were constructed. In the morning sunlight the city seemed to glow, the weather was gentle, and she was very glad to be there, walking beside her tiny, delicate mother.

The Pump Room was something of a disappointment. It was terribly tame, Diana thought. It was carpeted and decorated with chairs and tables like any public room, and in one little window embrasure was the fountain, with a woman who gave one a cup. The water was vile tasting, which meant it must be good for you, but Diana refused a second cup.

Of the various people who came up and greeted them, only one made a real impression on Diana. This was Mr. Huntington, a widower of fifty-five or so. Diana made it her business to find out as much as she could about him, because it was clear that he admired her mother's seriousness very much.

It did not take Diana long to evaluate Bath society and her mother's place in it, which was a rather peculiar one. By birth and breeding she was considered above reproach, but her dress and her serious scholarly interests marked her as something of an oddity. But she was a wealthy, respectable widow, and it was clear to Diana that any number of gentlemen were ready to pay her court if she would give them the slightest encouragement—but she did not.

After giving it some thought, Diana began her campaign. She started teasing her mother about her suitor, Mr. Huntington.

"Whatever do you mean, Mariotta! I have never encouraged him in the slightest! I see him at the abbey on Sunday and in the Pump Room, now that you insist we go there, but I cannot imagine he has the slightest interest in me beyond mere civility. What are you imagining, child?" Her mother narrowed her myopic eyes, justly suspicious.

Diana absently twisted her rings. "Well, I suppose it is merely wishful thinking on my part. He is such a thoroughly nice man, lonely for a woman in his life, I think. And it is really too bad if a creature like that Mrs. LeFanu is going to end up mistress of Ardwell! And he has shown a particular attention to you, whatever you may think."

Lady Abingdon sat up. Mrs. LeFanu was one of her oldest enemies, a rather vulgar widow who played cards till dawn—for money—and rarely showed her face in the abbey.

"You cannot be serious! She is most unsuitable! What would his children say if they knew! I cannot credit it! Mrs. LeFanu!"

Diana looked remorseful. "Oh, I had not meant to upset you, mamma. But the LeFanu has invited him to dinner, and he has gone. If no more suitable person invites him, one must expect him to go to her table. After all, his children are gone, he lives alone. And it must be quite hard on the poor man. He does so love company, and gaiety."

It took a few moments for Lady Abingdon to absorb the horror of all of this. She knew the children and liked them both, and had nothing but respect for the family. And she knew that what her daughter said was true: Edmund Huntington needed company.

"I am, of course, not the slightest bit interested in Mr. Huntington," she began at last, with Diana hanging on her every word, "except as a friend, of course. I detest women who throw themselves at any eligible man, but I do not see why we could not invite him here for a simple meal. We might, perhaps, have one or two other friends as well—Mr. Cabe, Mrs. Willow— and I think it might make the man feel he had some real *friends* in Bath."

Diana tried not to look too interested. "A wonderful idea. But why a simple meal? I am quite sure Mrs. LeFanu gave him something quite out of the ordinary. We could show him something quite elegant. I might be able to find something in those French cookbooks cook has."

Lady Abingdon looked at her as if she were mad.

"You? You have never set foot in that kitchen! When did you start?"

"Oh, I have been preparing myself—I expect to marry *some* day, after all." Diana realized that this was a very dangerous moment. But Lady Abingdon's famous instinct failed her here, and she did not interrogate further, seeming quite satisfied with the hasty explanation. She said that if Mariotta wished to try her hand at preparing a menu, she was happy to let her.

Diana was delighted. She would use this chance to make permanent changes in the kitchen. The food served every day was of good quality but unimaginatively prepared—the vegetables consistently overcooked, the meat a trifle dry. Diana was used to better—Black Walter demanded good dishes from his cook, who loved him and stayed even when she was not paid for years.

This hurdle passed, the next was the problem of dress. Diana had fallen in love with a lovely lavender chip hat displayed in one of the Milsom Street shops, and went in and told the proprietor that she wished to buy it, but not just yet. Diana had the money, but she knew Mariotta would never have been able to make this purchase. A few days later she brought up the question with her mother, who seemed frankly shocked.

"I know you never think of such things, mamma," explained Diana patiently, "but there are those who would think that we do not have the money to dress well. I know you care little what the world thinks—and you are right—but if I am to find a suitable husband, I do not think it would do. . . . And really, why give Mrs. LeFanu reason to say you are after Mr. Huntington's fortune? I realize this is all very blunt of me, and terribly vulgar, but I do think it is time."

At first her mother was angry and ready to have a headache. But gradually the force of her daughter's argument was felt. She protested, however, that she did not in the least know how to buy clothes anymore—she would not wish to look a fool—who could advise her—

"Oh, I have found an excellent woman on Milsom Street. She has her shop, and I have ascertained that the very best families go there. . . . She will help us. You must not be angry at me, but I find it sometimes irritating to see my own mother in clothes which do not set off her looks, especially when she is quite superior to many of the other ladies who peacock around the Assembly Rooms. I realize you are not frivolous, as, alas, I am, but it would indeed make me happy to see you dressed as you should be."

Lady Abingdon was stunned by this seemingly artless speech, and she could not take offense. Flattery was not unpleasant, even to her. She agreed to at least look into the shop on Milsom Street.

Diana knew it would be quite a battle, and she elicited help from Mrs. Small, the shop's proprietor. She went to that lady a day ahead and warned her of the problems involved.

Lady Abingdon's friend Millie accompanied them to Mrs. Small's. It was touch and go—the prices being so much more than Lady Abingdon remembered—until she put on a blue satin evening gown embroidered with silk rosebuds and knots of silver twist. This dress brought out Lady Abingdon's coloring to best advantage, which even she realized.

"It is so very expensive," murmured her mother, "do you really think? . . ."

"I think that you will make Mrs. LeFanu look a dowd, and that Mr. Huntington will embarrass you with compliments!"

"I'd like a brighter color myself," observed Millie, ignoring Diana's warning glance.

"No, not for Lady Abingdon," said Mrs. Small. "She has light blue eyes, and this shade is right for her hair as well. And may I say that her ladyship has a wonderful figure, as does her daughter."

After all this Mrs. Small had no difficulty in gradually convincing her client to purchase an entire wardrobe. And then she suggested that her ladyship's daughter might need something.

"Oh, yes," said Lady Abingdon, flushing. "I am selfish! Of course, she has nothing suitable either!"

And so the lavender gown and the chip hat made their appearance. Her mother, suddenly young again, began to say that Mariotta must have this dress, and that, and this manteau, and soon they both had creditable wardrobes. Diana began to feel guilty about her manipulation of her mother, but she comforted herself by thinking that after all her mother did have the money. . . .

Mrs. Small implied that a discount would be provided, given the number of things chosen, and she carefully never named the actual price. By the time everything was delivered it would be too late, everything would already be the correct size. . . . Diana resolved to smooth over that possible catastrophe.

Mr. Huntington responded to the dinner invitation with

flattering speed, and begged permission to bring along his cousin, Mr. Richard Trelawny, who was planning to settle near Huntington in the Bath valley.

Lady Abingdon found out everything she could about this Trelawny, and a certain light dawned in her eyes. Richard Trelawny was a bachelor of forty, with an independent income, and a good name. Perhaps, if Mariotta were not inclined toward Mr. Cabe, this might be a suitable match. . . .

Diana said that it would depend on what sort of man he seemed, but certainly she would be cordial to him.

The day of the dinner arrived at last, the price of the dresses forgotten, as mother and daughter saw how wonderful each looked. Diana took charge of arranging her mother's hair. Her mother was capable of being competitive. The matter of Mrs. LeFanu had made this clear. Lady Abingdon, afraid that she could not really compete in the fashionable world after being out of it for so long, had avoided it completely. But when Diana had shown her that she might compete and even win, in a manner of speaking, she became excited and delighted with the idea.

Diana fervently prayed that the evening would be a success. Otherwise it would be back to dinners with Jonathan Cabe and his colleagues. . . . Diana had managed to persuade her mother not to invite Mr. Cabe, saying that he would very likely disapprove. Her mother agreed without a murmur. Instead, Millie and William Kean—her husband was up for the month from London—were to be the only other guests. Millie dressed eccentrically, but her husband was the complete gentleman, according to Lady Abingdon, and would be an asset at the dinner.

When she was satisfied that her mother was looking her best,

Diana went to make her own hasty toilette. Jenny, her maid, came to assist her. When she was dressed in the white crepe gown with the blue silk trimmings and a blue ribbon threaded through her curls, Jenny stood back to take a look. Diana turned to look in the mirror, and Jenny suggested she wear the diamond drop earrings.

"A good idea," said Diana, who had not the slightest idea what they looked like. "Would you get them, please?"

Their eyes met in the mirror, and Jenny looked at her with an air of being puzzled. Then she walked over to the bonheur-du-jour which was under the mirror and pulled open the top drawer and got out a small box. After a pause which seemed to last forever, Jenny took out the earrings and put them on Diana's ears.

"You do look lovely, miss," said Jenny in a normal tone of voice.

Diana cursed her own stupidity. She should never have agreed to wear them. Perhaps Jenny would think that she was daydreaming about the evening to come?

Diana managed to calm her fears before she went down, but she made a resolve to be more careful. Everything had been so easy until now, her confidence had misled her. . . . If she were capable of such stupidity, what of Mariotta, who was entering a potentially far more dangerous world. And at that moment, as she had that thought, it seemed to her that she could hear Mariotta saying not to worry, that everything was going well at Chalford. It was a most peculiar experience, and Diana sat back down on her bed. Had she imagined it? No, it was so specific, so *real* a sensation. Mariotta had spoken to her, in a way, she was certain of it! Perhaps now that she knew Mariotta, those formerly vague feelings, those dreams, would all turn into something more like communication. . . .

And with this somehow warming conviction, Diana made her way downstairs.

In the drawing room Diana found a talkative company, already quite at ease with each other. Mr. Huntington, a ruddy-complexioned man with distinguished gray hair, was talking about his favorite subject—flowers. He had brought Lady Abingdon a sample bouquet from his greenhouse and was favoring her with a detailed description of how they were produced.

His cousin, Richard Trelawny, was introduced, and Diana was pleasantly surprised. He looked to be forty or so, and had the style of an experienced gentleman of the world. There was something calm and reassuring in his manner, which Diana liked immensely. She was not able to talk to him for more than a moment because Millie Kean wished her to be presented to her husband.

"William, this is the same little girl you saw last year. Now hasn't she grown up?"

Mr. Kean, a man of about sixty, gray-haired and thin, had a very merry smile, and he said he did not see anything so different—a prettier hair style perhaps, but that was all.

"The one who has changed is Lady Abingdon! Just look at her, blooming like a girl!"

It was true. Lady Abingdon, emboldened by the many compliments she had already received from Mr. Huntington and the Keans, was glowing with happiness. And the blue satin dress was the final touch which made her seem a different person.

At 6:30 dinner was announced, and the party proceeded into the dining room.

"It seems that we are left with each other," said Richard Trelawny with a smile. "But I confess that I hoped it would be so."

Diana smiled in answer and took his arm. She liked every-thing she saw—the calm brown eyes, the assured manner, the elegant evening clothes, which were neither too overdone nor too conservative. It was as if Fate had sent her answer to her desire to meet a respectable, reliable man. But of course she must not jump to conclusions. First she would see if he had any conversation.

The dining room was glowing with candlelight, the mahogany tables were shining, and the first course looked wonderful.

The turtle soup was pronounced astonishingly subtle, the procelain admired, and the wine drunk in moderation.

It was really too bad that Mr. Trelawny was placed across from her, Diana thought; but at least he could drink to her, raising his glass and looking directly at her, with great seriousness. This was almost as pleasant as hearing his very well-informed comments on the subjects raised by the others.

Edmund Huntington loved the theater, it turned out, about which Lady Abingdon knew very little; and in her anxiety to shield her mother from having to reveal ignorance, Diana found herself discussing things which Mariotta would certainly not have known. Just as she realized this and resolved to be silent, Millie's husband William asked her where she had seen the actor Kean last.

"Oh, I am very afraid I have misled you," said Diana in confu-sion. "I have only heard of his performances, from my friends and from reading. It is of course not the same thing."

"Remarkably sound views you have all the same. I doubt you would change your mind were you to see a performance of his Lear." Mr. Kean quickly changed the subject, for which Diana was grateful, and she encountered a smiling glance from Mr. Trelawny, clearly intended to make her feel better. He was a thoroughly nice man; she was certain of it.

The menu was a great success, especially with Millie Kean. Diana suspected that poor Millie had been afraid that the food would be as dull as it was every day at the Abingdons'.

Instead the company was treated to turbot, roast chickens, ham, tongue, roast quail, a salade Italienne, and some excellent Bordeaux and Madeira.

The dessert course offered a choice of tarts, jellies, and cheese-cakes. Since it was all her own doing, Diana was very proud every time someone commented on the food and drink—Lady Abingdon understood nothing of wines, but Diana knew a great deal about them, thanks to her father's taste for it. It had been wonderful to order all of these things and know that the bills would be paid on time—a very different feeling from the dread her father's parties had always inspired. . . .

Lady Abingdon was as proud as could be of the way her daughter behaved, and told Millie later that she would never have believed that such a child could turn into an adult so quickly.

But Millie, observing the way in which Mr. Trelawny all but monopolized Mariotta after dinner, was uneasy. Richard Trelawny was all that was correct and civil, but there was a gleam of arrogance whenever he talked to her, which she could not like. But of course Mariotta was looking wonderfully beautiful this evening, and behaving with great charm and tact. No wonder Mr. Trelawny bid fair to lose his heart to her. Millie decided that it would be best to keep her comments about Mr. Trelawny to herself and her husband. It was just possible that a marriage might come about, and it wouldn't do to have made remarks of a negative sort. . . .

For his part, Mr. Trelawny was delighted with Mariotta Abingdon, who was even more beautiful than his cousin had led him to expect. And the fact that the girl would inherit a decent amount was also pleasant to contemplate. He could not help but wonder, however, how that harridan Millie Kean came to be a friend of the family. She was overdressed, overjeweled, and underbred, as he later told Mr. Huntington. But his cousin did not agree—he thought Millie a capital sort of woman, and said she told wonderful stories of Bath habits.

After dessert the party had moved back to the drawing room, Lady Abingdon explaining that since it was such a family party, the ladies would not withdraw.

Since the cart bearing the claret, port, and Madeira followed them into the drawing room—at Diana's request—the party became very sociable, with the two older couples gathered around the sofa, and Diana and Richard Trelawny at the window seat, examining the china cabinet.

Diana thought Richard easy to converse with, and deduced from his conversation that he was an essentially serious man, concerned about the people on his estate, touchingly fond of his sister Caroline, and very much impressed by his cousin Edmund Huntington.

"Edmund's estate, Ardwell Park, is a model for us all, Miss Abingdon. The reforms he has instituted to the benefit of his people . . . his wonderful succession houses, his botanical feats . . . he is quite an accomplished man. Of course his love of amateur theatricals is his weakness—but every man has one, does he not? He is so proud of his little theater, and really, it is very impressive, accurate down to the last detail, everything one could want. He had it finished not two months ago and is *burning* to put something on. But you know, despite his wealth, he is not ostentatious; his hospitality is sincere. And you know, I think hospitality which springs from the heart is very different from that which springs from ostentation."

"I think," said Diana slowly, "that having a friend such as

you say such things is the best recommendation a man may have."

Before the party broke up, Mr. Trelawny asked Lady Abingdon if he might take her daughter out driving the next day in his barouche. Lady Abingdon gave her permission graciously, since Mr. Huntington had already engaged her to go and look at some lacquerware with him, saying he desired a feminine opinion. This was quite an unexpected development. Lady Abingdon had not been out driving with any man not her relative for almost twenty-two years.

When everyone had gone, mother and daughter had a very pleasurable, if elliptical, conversation in which they each made it clear that they were more than happy with the evening's events.

Diana went to bed convinced that after less than a month in Bath she had found the man of her dreams. But when she woke the next morning she remembered a dream of a dark man with a mustache, riding over a plain in pursuit of her. But perhaps this was really Mariotta's influence—and for the thousandth time Diana wondered how her sister was, and whether she was finding whatever she had really wanted out of this exchange.

CHAPTER SIX

The journey to London was a wonderful adventure. Mariotta was taking her first trip to the metropolis in her own coach, driven by an expert coachman. The trunk in the back was full of lovely clothes, and the trip seemed all too brief.

In London there was a great deal to do in a short time, the first order of the day being to get her hair cut by the celebrated Jerome before Diana's maid Cora saw her present state.

Jerome clucked over the hastily lopped off ends, but when he finished he was satisfied and Mariotta was delighted.

It was really too bad that she had to be in Chalford in a matter of days—there was no time to see the sights of London. Here Mariotta faced her first real test: the maid Cora. Mariotta was certain that it would not be long before this sharp-eyed young woman discovered the truth.

Cora greeted her warmly and exclaimed that she was looking so much happier. Bath must have helped, and how was her old school friend, Miss Leigh?

Mariotta was able to handle all of this easily enough, and said that Bath had been very enjoyable, a remark which almost made her laugh aloud.

In great good humor—Cora's mother was on the mend, and she had seen her old beau—the two young women started the journey down to Lewes. The weather was uncommonly fine, and it was hard for Mariotta to suppress her enthusiasm for the beauties of the landscape rolling by, the excitement of coach travel, and the very good meals they had at the inns.

Mariotta gave some serious thought to the problem: she knew she could never keep up the imitation of Diana for long. She was much more impulsive, unrestrained. There would have to be an excuse, a reason to be her ebullient self. It did not take her long to hit on the very thing.

As they were nearing Chalford, Cora asked her if she thought her mood would continue to be so gay at Chalford.

"Oh, yes," dimpled Mariotta, "there is a reason, you see . . ."

Cora smiled smugly.

"I knew it, miss! So there *was* a young man at Miss Leigh's! A brother or some such, I'll wager."

"I shall say nothing, Cora, but you are free to think as you choose. . . ."

This conversation would have repercussions, Mariotta knew Cora would certainly let the other servants know what had changed Miss Diana.

They drove up to the entrance of Chalford Manor at about four in the afternoon. It was still sunny, and Mariotta fell in love with the grounds crisscrossed by dappled walks and horse trails. The house was very impressive, but a little forbidding, just as Jack had said.

The staff greeted them warmly, making Mariotta feel at home immediately. In her response to them she betrayed herself, however, since she did not know that Diana was very restrained about such things.

It was immediately noted, and belowstairs Cora was

questioned closely. Cora confessed all, and told them that she was delighted to see Miss Diana gay for once, instead of weighed down with the responsibility of running Chalford, for everyone knew that Himself was about as responsible as a baby chick.

Mariotta wandered through the house after changing in her bedroom. The housekeeper suggested that she take a nap, but she was far too excited. Her bedroom had once been quite beautiful, with its marble-manteled fireplace and molded ceiling; but the rose-colored velvet hangings were sadly discolored, the carpet was worn, and the entire room seemed damp. She was about to request a cheery fire when it occurred to her that the household might not have extra firewood for an afternoon fire, at a warm time of year at that. She would have to be more careful, Mariotta reminded herself. These things were taken for granted at Laura Place, but Chalford was obviously straining to keep going.

The house had been intended for elegant entertainments, that much was clear. It had some fifteen bedrooms, most of them unspeakably decayed; there was a billiard room which showed signs of use; and the library, full of wonderful-looking morocco-bound volumes, looked as though it had not changed a bit since it had been built a hundred years earlier.

But she was shocked, she had to admit to herself, by the degree of disrepair everywhere. Everything was as clean as possible, given the problem, but cleanliness could not make up for peeling plaster and wet spots, rugs worn to shreds, and the fine satin wood furniture covered with stained silks.

The portrait gallery was just as enjoyable as she'd expected, but it made her a little sad to think of what these elegant people would have said if they had seen what had become of their once lovely estate.

She was slowly descending the main staircase when her father came through the front door.

"Back I see!" He called up to her with a smile.

"Yes, a very nice trip."

Jack had warned her, but Black Walter's physical similarity to herself and her sister stunned her at first. She had never had such a sense of being someone's flesh and blood before; it was somehow upsetting. She was used to not looking like her mother, to being independent in a sense. But here he was, so obviously her father, the source of her. And unlike her sister, he was *a very* male version.

The dissimilarity in temperament became clear rather quickly.

"So, you had a nice time? Well I had rather an awful time, trying to raise some money for various things we need. The scum wouldn't give me a cent." He laughed harshly. "The bankers are afraid I might seduce their wives, you know. It's happened . . . the prosy fools, so worried about their reputations—and mine!"

He continued on in this vein throughout dinner, during the course of which he drank a bottle of Burgundy. Mariotta had never seen anyone drunk before, and the spectacle was fascinating to her.

Her father seemed to be a man buried in selfishness, and very anxious to shock the "proper" people he came in contact with. Mariotta could not wonder at a banker who would not trust him; it was only common sense. A desire for his own destruction seemed strong in him. As he drank, his manners turned nasty, and he began to rail at a fate which left him unable to provide for his daughter.

"I am a fool, to have loved women, given up everything for them . . . and now Loulou. Well, Loulou will be worth it, I'll shove her down their throats!"

Mariotta had the definite feeling that Loulou was not someone her mother would want her to meet, and she wondered just what Black Walter's plan involving this person was.

"Well, Diana, would you like to lay odds that I'll get Loulou into Almack's? Come, bet on it.

"No, I do not think I shall. And I don't have anything to wager with in any case."

This answer did not please Black Walter, and with an oath he threw the decanter to the floor, where it shattered, staining the walls with wine.

She was unable to conceal her horror at this behavior.

"Ah, a few days away and you have become unaccustomed," he sneered. "I disgust myself, you know. Well, you needn't be subjected to these boorish manners of mine, my dear daughter. I have already indicated the way out: marry Drew."

Mariotta stood up, enraged.

"How dare you speak to me like that! I shall marry whom I choose, and all the smashed decanters in the world won't decide the matter! You are indeed a boor, sir, and have been at the bottom so long you have forgotten how a decent man behaves!"

It gave Mariotta great pleasure and relief to give vent to her feelings; but then it struck her forcibly that her twin would not have reacted so violently. In hesitation she stood at the door to the dining room.

Her father stared at her for a moment, as if she had said something startlingly original. He set down his glass.

"What is this, daughter? Temper? I should send you to London more often. . . . You actually seem to possess some of the family spirit! Bravo, my dear, you are well in the way of becoming a true Abingdon at last!"

Mariotta's nose went a trifle higher in the air.

"If it means behaving as you do, father, I should rather become more like my mother!"

She had touched a nerve. He did not like this comment at all.

"Your mother? Your mother, that provincial little creature forever moralizing? You would die of boredom, or do as I did—run away!"

This was so singularly appropriate that Mariotta smiled, puzzling her parent even more.

When she finally went to bed, Mariotta counted over the many mistakes she had already made. Something would have to be done to explain this change of personality. . . .

She let drop a series of remarks over the next few days, all of which would have induced even a very stupid parent to conclude that his daughter was in love. Mariotta began to feel safer after this—everyone knows that love can change a person greatly.

"You will be receiving something from your grandfather's estate soon," said her father one evening. "Your birthday is little more than a month away."

"And you have no idea of how great or little this inheritance might be, father?"

He shook his head, and then gave her a sad smile. "My dear Diana, if it *were* a great deal, I should try to get some of it from you; so it is best I do not know."

"Gambling?"

"Gambling," he answered with the sad conviction of a man who knew his own weakness. This was Black Walter in a good mood—sober.

Robert and Millie Cushing, Diana's friends of only a few months, were just as nice as she had said they were. Immediately recognizable due to their flaming red hair, they were high-spirited and active. They were full of news: Lord Drew was at his estate with his nephew; Camilla, Lady Green, a legendary hostess, was over at Langley Manor, recovering from a serious illness. In return for this intelligence, they wanted their friend to tell them all about her trip to London. Mariotta tried to be vague, but she did hint that she had met a gentleman who was worthy of her interest. This seemed to satisfy them, but Mariotta began to wish that there were such a gentleman: he would serve both the purpose of explanation for the change in her spirits, and as a deterrent to Black Walter's plans for her marriage with Lord Drew.

The first weeks at Chalford passed quickly. Mariotta and her friends went on picnics, attended the small assemblies in Lewes, and went shopping in Tunbridge Wells. The assemblies were very provincial when compared with the gatherings in Bath, but Mariotta found them far pleasanter, especially since she was now wearing lovely clothes and taking part in the dancing her mother had objected to.

Country living seemed wonderful to her, and one afternoon Mariotta dressed herself in some old clothes and went out berrying in the woods. Moving from bush to bush led her onto neighboring property unawares. Tired and warm, she unloosened her bonnet and lay down for a moment to rest under a willow by the river.

Some twenty minutes later she awoke with a start and found herself being kissed by an unknown gentleman.

He quickly let her go and tried to assume a contrite expression.

"I am very sorry . . . but no, not so *very* sorry," he said with a charming smile. "I am afraid that I yielded to a strong impulse."

Mariotta was looking into the bluest eyes she'd ever seen in a man's face. He was very blond, very tall, very well-proportioned, and even in his fishing clothes, he looked elegant.

"Well, since I am also in the habit of yielding to impulse, I suppose I must forgive you, Mr.—"

"Gerald Drew. This is my uncle's land, you know. You are, technically speaking, trespassing."

"You are related to Lord Drew, then?"

"Yes. My uncle, in fact. Miss—"

"Abingdon, Diana Abingdon. Your neighbor."

"A neighbor! How lucky Drew is! We are just down to take a rest . . . haven't been here in years . . . had no idea there were such charming sights in the vicinity."

"Yes, the country is particularly beautiful at this time of year," said Mariotta, blushing from the intensity of his regard.

"That, too," he murmured. "But come, Miss Abingdon, let me help you up."

Mariotta had met very few really handsome men in her life, excepting Jack, and she found herself staring in the most improper way, quite unaware of how very beautiful she herself was looking.

He asked if she were a bit dizzy, and smiled at her so frankly that she decided in an instant: she too would give in to an impulse.

"Mr. Drew, I have something to ask of you; it may seem mad, but I have a feeling that only you will do."

"Name it. Miss Abingdon, I am utterly at your service."

She took a breath and mentally begged Diana's pardon.

"Could you . . . would you pretend that we have met before— say in London, two weeks ago? Please do not think you must agree, but if it is not difficult, I would be so grateful!"

She looked up at him, her expressive eyes beseeching, and he could not bring himself to refuse her, although he knew it was all quite improper. Drew would be angry if he knew, but there was no reason he had to, and it did promise a bit more excitement than he'd expected when Drew had told him to come down to Drew House. . . . Such a pretty girl, even in those clothes . . .

"Of course, Miss Abingdon, I cannot refuse a neighbor. And I was near London two weeks ago, and could easily have gone into the city for a day. Certainly there is no one who could say that I did not. Will that do?"

"Oh, how wonderful! I knew you must be kind as well as handsome! I am so grateful!"

Her smile was almost enough to make him forget his reservations, but a quick vision of his uncle's face made him ask: "But are you going to tell me what this is all about? I think I rather have a right to know."

Mariotta looked guilty. She certainly could not tell him that it was to ward off the possibility of being forced to marry his uncle, a plan about which he certainly seemed to know nothing.

"If you must know, it is because there are . . . several gentlemen in this neighborhood who insist on favoring me with their quite undesired attentions. I know it was very wrong of me, but I made the mistake of declaring that my affections were already engaged . . . by a gentleman I had met in London. There. If you do not wish to be party to all this, I shall understand."

She smiled a little uncertainly, showing two charming dimples at each corner of her mouth.

"I consider it a flattering lie, Miss Abingdon, and I shall be happy to rescue you from unwanted suitors."

He walked her back to the path which led onto Chalford ground, and she found herself completely at ease with him. And he apparently felt the same, since he talked of his plans for the future.

"And so now I am enjoying my leisure, trying to make up my mind whether I want to go in for politics or diplomacy."

"Oh, I should think diplomacy," said Mariotta without thinking. "You would travel a great deal then, wouldn't you?"

"Yes. And you, I see, like to travel."

"Yes . . . that is—" Here Mariotta stopped. Diana had traveled widely, but *she* had never been anywhere. She would be hard put to describe any of the places Black Walter had been. She could say that she had been too young to notice very much, or that longing for England—no, none of this would do. She would have to avoid such discussions, that was all there was to it.

Her companion wondered why she had suddenly grown silent, and tried to put her at her ease by saying that he knew that his uncle and her father were old friends—some mysterious meeting had begun their friendship.

If he had tried, he could not have found a worse subject, Mariotta thought. But it was clear that he was completely in the dark about the marriage plans, and for that she could only be grateful. As was usual with her, she did not think about the possible consequences when his uncle found out that his nephew was said to be enamored of Walter Abingdon's daughter.

When they reached the path, Gerald promised to call on her and her father the next day.

"With your uncle?" Mariotta inquired as calmly as she was able.

"Oh, no, Drew finds visits a dead bore. I doubt he'll be over until next week to see your father. Right now he's dancing attendance on Lady Green over at Langley Manor. The rest of the time he's doing things with the bailiff about estate repairs, dreadfully tiresome stuff, you know. And I actually found him buried in some old Greeks the other night. A man could go mad in the country, that's what I think."

Mariotta was heartily thankful that this prospective suitor would not be over for a week. By then she would have made it clear to everyone that Gerald Drew, and not his uncle, was her preference. Diana would be so grateful. . . .

After dinner, when she was settled down with the novel she

was reading (one her mother would most certainly not have allowed in the house, since it was French), she was unable to concentrate on the heroine's terrifying predicament. Her mind kept drifting to Gerald Drew. She kept remembering the bright blue of his eyes, his open smile, and engaging manners. . . . Indeed, he was just what she had always dreamed of: a dashing young man, out for adventure. But, she reminded herself, she was here as Diana. Could she permit herself to entertain any serious feelings for him? On the other hand, she could allow herself an agreeable flirtation until the time was up. Then things would end of themselves . . . and if they didn't, perhaps they might meet at her grandmother's house. At this Mariotta smiled. She was so silly! She did not even know her grandmother as yet, and here she was making plans to use her house for a meeting with a young man.

The next day Mariotta spent in the garden, supposedly helping the gardener repair some of the damage done to the flower beds by a storm the week before, but actually waiting for Gerald to ride up.

It was a warm June day, and Mariotta enjoyed being out in the sun; but it was very hard to keep her mind on what Caleb Walker was telling her to do.

The longed-for sound of a horse riding up the drive came at last.

"That'll be what ye've been waiting for, I'll be bound," said Caleb smugly, taking her tools away from her. "Best go in and make yourself pretty."

Mariotta shot him a surprised glance, and then laughed.

"No use fooling you. I'll help tomorrow, I promise."

With that she was off to the house, running as fast as her skirts would let her. She ran up the back stairs and into her room, calling Cora as she passed the sewing room.

She washed, and then Cora was there, helping her into her most charming morning dress of pale rose.

"It's him, isn't it?" asked Cora.

"Yes, oh, yes!"

"Well, you do look lovely, I'll say that. And what is his name, might I ask?"

A glowing Mariotta told her, but did not stay long enough to see her reaction.

Cora raced down to the kitchen to talk to cook, and Mariotta moved almost as quickly to the drawing room where her father was just about to send for her.

"Ah, there she is! My dear, I see you have an acquaintance at Drew Hall! Very pleasant! May I offer you something? Hadley, bring some refreshments, please!"

Black Walter was all amiability, but Gerald seemed hardly to notice, so busy was he in admiring Miss Abingdon. If he had thought her very pretty before, in her berrying clothes, he had to admit now that he had been blind: the girl was a beauty, a diamond of the first water. . . .

Mariotta was engaged in much the same activity. Gerald in his fishing clothes had seemed extraordinarily handsome, but Gerald in well-cut riding clothes and glossy boots was a hero out of the most romantic novel.

Black Walter was the ideal chaperone for two people on the verge of falling in love. He enjoyed hearing himself talk, and he did not require any but the most perfunctory comment, which, in this case, was precisely what he received.

Gerald did manage to make Black Walter understand that he much admired his daughter, but Mariotta was afraid that her father was taking all of this as attention due the woman who might soon be Gerald's aunt. She knew that she would have to be prepared for a real storm when it was discovered that it was the nephew who was her choice; but she felt that she was up to handling her father—certainly more than Diana would be. In any case, she promised herself as she smiled into Gerald'd eyes, the matter would be settled before Diana returned. It was the least she could do for her sister.

Gerald rode back to Drew House in a pleasant daze, and began immediately upon his arrival to tell his uncle all about this raving beauty stuck out here in the country.

"She is really so beautiful, then?" asked his uncle skeptically, unwilling to believe that Venus was in Sussex.

"Oh, yes, but that is not even the chief thing about her—it is her spirit! She has a kind of dash few women possess, and she's not afraid of what people think either!"

"Sounds very like her father," said Drew dryly.

"Oh, no, not like Black Walter! Much better, knows how to behave, as if she had been brought up well, instead of with Abingdon's duns and light women."

Drew lit his cigar and then sat back in his wing chair, blowing smoke at the ceiling.

"Poor, poor Black Walter. I really must get over and see him . . . but I rather dread seeing what he has become. He was once very kind to me, and we share certain interests. . . . And after all, I am in his debt."

Gerald asked how this could possibly be true.

"Oh, he was not always as he is now. Once he was the most wonderful gambler. Generous, had that light touch, fortune's darling. I was a young cub of twenty, didn't know my way around the ivory-turners. To make a long and very ordinary story short, I found myself in over my head. And he was having an incredible run of good luck at the same table. So he bought my vowels and tore them up."

"He tore up your I.O.U.'s? I can hardly believe it!" Gerald thought of the obvious decay of Chalford Manor and shook his head.

"Nor could I, I assure you. Never let me pay him back, only laughed at the idea. But now . . ."

Gerald sat up. "Tell you what, Drew, give the money to the daughter! A secret—that way the fellow won't waste it on roulette or drink. That house could use repair—I could see it. And she'd make sure it was done, I'm sure of it." Gerald was quite thrilled with his own acumen and nobility of spirit.

It took a bit of persuading, but Drew was finally brought to see that this would really be the best way of paying back the debt.

"And Abingdon's pride could be spared," Gerald pointed out. "Diana can give him some story of receiving money from a relative—she's very inventive—and he doesn't even have to know it's from you. You have no way of knowing that he'd accept the money if you offered it directly, do you?"

Drew saw the truth of all this, but he saw something else as well: Gerald was much taken with Diana Abingdon, a state of affairs which was quite undesirable, considering Gerald's present situation. . . .

Drew spent that evening looking through the estate books, but in the back of his mind he was worrying about Miss Diana Abingdon. The next morning he paid a call on Cama.

He found her gazing pensively at a newspaper.

"I cannot imagine," she said languidly, "how you can have the cheek to call on a lady of my age before noon! Do you realize that it is *ten o'clock*?"

Drew's hazel eyes narrowed. "Now what is this, dearest? You know you look ravishingly in the morning toilette. You have been up for hours, what can have put you in this mood? Let me guess . . . the gazette . . . London news . . . it must certainly be Lady Quennel."

A tiny and quickly suppressed smile was visible behind the delicate teacup.

"Well, you are certainly gifted. . . . Perhaps you should go to fairs, tell fortunes. You would do quite well!" snapped Cama ungraciously. "But of course it is Lady Quennel! She has taken over all of my plans, such a bold-faced thief! You remember my plan for the Venetian breakfast by Wendell's pond? *She* has done it. And gotten a good many interesting people too. I do not think I can bear to see that harpy at another of my soirées."

She had a plotting expression in her dark eyes, and Drew was unable to keep from smiling. She defended herself.

"I know you think it funny, wretch! But in my world the battles are fought with such things—and even you must know that the things at stake are a good deal more serious than Venetian breakfasts! Cabinet posts can be decided if the mix of guests is right . . . but you are here for something, aren't you. That air of having just ridden over on a whim doesn't fool me."

"You wouldn't be so bad at fairs yourself. Yes, I have a little worry . . . that might become a big worry. . . . Gerald is under the spell of Black Walter's daughter, who is supposedly quite lovely."

Cama very deliberately set down her cup.

"How very interesting. I should love to see a child of *his*! I can hardly believe she survived her childhood with that man. But why are you worried? Gerald is handsome, well-bred, surely it is time he settled down?"

"Yes, but that is precisely the problem. He is about to become engaged to a very nice girl by the name of Leila Grayson—perfect in all respects, and wealthy to boot. But they are not able to announce the engagement yet, because her father is still in Italy—a diplomat. When he returns all will be settled."

Cama was puzzled. "But what is the problem? A little flirtation can mean nothing in these circumstances. . . ."

Drew sighed, and brushed back his hair distractedly.

"You do not know Gerald. No one knows Gerald as I do. He is charming and handsome, true; he has talents which permit him to swim where other men might sink. But he has great weaknesses as well."

"Raised by women," said Cama sagely.

"Exactly. All of them blind to his faults. All he asks is to be loved and admired, fed and clothed, and he is amiability itself. But if he ever has to face any hardship, he is unable to deal with it. Unpleasant things are assiduously avoided. He is prepared for nothing but success. But this is all apart from the problem: he is shockingly susceptible to the fair sex. If you *knew* the entanglements I've gotten him out of!"

Cama was looking very interested. "You mean, he might actually . . . have serious intentions concerning Diana Abingdon?"

"Oh, without a doubt. And leave it to me to explain everything to Leila. And you must admit, any daughter who had spent her life with Black Walter must be ready to leave home. And who could blame her?"

"Not I. But Gerald needs money, does he not?"

"Oh, yes. He knows about as much about finance as a rabbit. If he marries a sensible girl, all will be well—Leila would handle it all. But a daughter of Abingdon's . . ."

They both considered for a moment, the financial acumen of Black Walter.

"Really, it is not possible," said Cama. "You must do something. . . . Actually, I have an idea—"

"I have gotten one of my own. But let me find out how serious it all is first. I'll go and see Abingdon, and get a look at her."

But that very afternoon a messenger came from Scotland. There was a question about the cargo. This drove everything else from his mind. He would have to go to Edinburgh and arrange for a new crew and captain.

Drew quickly wrote a note to Camilla excusing himself from dinner the next day, but promised that he would be back within the week.

But it was a full two weeks before he returned.

Gerald did not regret his uncle's absence. He occasionally felt a twinge of conscience over Leila Grayson, but by the time he had spent a week with the delightful Miss Abingdon he was unable to remember what his fiancée looked like.

Black Walter was satisfied with the new Diana. He was seldom interested in anyone but himself for very long, but he looked up periodically and saw that his daughter was going out riding, on picnics with the Cushings, and in general spending a great deal of time with Drew's nephew. This surely augured well for her reception of Drew, he told himself. The boy would talk about his uncle, and Diana would gradually become interested. . . . And when Drew returned from his trip all would be decided. For once he did not feel like an inadequate father: he was managing very well, and the girl was looking happier every day.

Mariotta lay by the Chalford stream one delightful afternoon and let her book fall to the grass. She really could not concentrate on Pope's Belinda when her mind was full of Gerald. It was wonderful how they seemed to agree about everything, needing no words, really, but only looks to convey their understanding. She had never known anyone like him—of course, she had never really known any man but Jack—but she knew that he was someone extraordinary, the man of her dreams. He, too, was bursting to travel, have adventures. And he wanted her to be by his side. . . .

She imagined herself as a diplomat's wife, wearing a lovely gown, smiling at him across the table. But here the daydream abruptly fragmented. How could she be anything to Gerald, when she was unable even to tell him her real name?

She had known him for three weeks now, and she had had many opportunities to tell him, but she was not able to do it. He would look at her with his clear, honest, blue eyes, and tell her that she was the most enjoyable girl he'd ever met, the only one who knew how *to have* fun, so frank, such an unusual female. How could she tell him she was nothing but a deceitful impostor? Gerald would not understand. All the qualities he prized in her would be seen in the harsh light of deception.

And the month would all too soon be up. Mariotta tried not to think about all of this. She repressed her fears and comforted herself with the idea that Diana would think up something. Perhaps Gerald need never find out.

"I wonder, dear Diana, if you are as happy as I? I think you are, I feel it . . ." Mariotta laughed at herself for having spoken aloud, but it did seem to her that she felt her sister being happy.

CHAPTER SEVEN

But Diana was far from happy. Jonathan Cabe was holding her unwilling hand.

"Miss Abingdon—Mariotta—I have long had it in my heart—"

With horror Diana realized that this quite repulsive person was about to propose. She quickly moved over to the window seat and sat down on it, turned to the street so that he would not be able to see her face.

"And now I must ask: Do you think, could you . . . could you think of . . ."

Despite his frog mouth and boring conversation, Diana could not help feeling sorry for the nervous young man, so she finished his sentence for him.

"Consider marriage? No, my dear Mr. Cabe, I could not. I find that I am not ready, just yet, to leave my mother. You must forgive my frank answer, but I know you to be a gentleman of excellent understanding. But some women are perhaps not meant for marriage. . . ."

Diana wondered that a bolt of lightning did not strike her down on the spot for telling such a lie, but it was really the only way to spare Mr. Cabe's pride. She could not very well tell him the truth, which was that he was simply not suitable for her, and Mr. Richard Trelawny was.

Mr. Cabe dropped her hand as if it were a red-hot chestnut.

"I am very sorry, to have made unwelcome—"

The beautiful Diana smiled dazzlingly and told him to pretend that it had never happened; they would merely go on as before. Mr. Cabe was so grateful for this attitude (he would not wish to find another place for Sunday dinner) that he barely noticed how quickly he was walked to the front door.

Diana went back to the window seat and looked out on the rainy square. She noticed that people were pursuing their affairs despite the weather. The Widow LeFanu, immediately recognizable because of her favorite blue and red striped turban, was passing through to Great Pulteney Street. Diana hoped that Mr. Cabe would not stop and talk to the widow, known as one of the most illustrious gossips of Bath: even if you were determined to tell her nothing, she still managed to worm something out of you. And it would not be pleasant if Mr. Trelawny were to hear that Miss Abingdon was not in favor of marriage. . . .

Her mother still had hopes for Mr. Cabe, and she wondered how long it would take her to hear of the refusal.

After dinner Lady Abingdon sent for her daughter.

Lady Abingdon was bent over a book, and at first did not seem to realize that her daughter was in the room. Then she gave an imitation of being surprised, pulling herself away from the power of the book.

"My dear, I did not realize you were here! Such a style! Bunyan!"

Diana was amused at the idea of her very literal mother reading *Pilgrim's Progress*. Lady Abingdon saw her daughter's half-smile and thought it referred to something else.

"You smile, child. You feel victorious after rejecting a

wonderfully accomplished man! Greek, Latin! Knows them as well as his own tongue! A serious, solid person. I cannot congratulate you on such an action. I would have thought that your upbringing, your education would have made you the ideal mate for such a young man."

Diana was not sure how to respond, aware that Mariotta would have to live with the results.

"Well, I suppose it is no good trying to fool *you*, mamma. The real reason for my refusal is not what he may have told you. It is that my affections are already pledged to another."

Lady Abingdon let her Bunyan drop from her lap and sat upright.

"You cannot mean Mr. Campbell! Tell me it is not so! He has not a shred of spirituality! I will allow that he is a very handsome fellow, but you were not brought up to judge by appearances!"

Diana got a glimmer of how to manage it.

"I suppose you are right," she said morosely. "He would never do."

"Yes, quite. I hope that as your mother I may influence you in this matter. You have been greatly sheltered, you know, and I never dreamed that Jack—well, that is, I may have considered him correct as a friend, but surely you can see that Mr. Cabe is greatly his superior."

Her daughter's large gray eyes seemed to be sadly beseeching, and Lady Abingdon broke off to ask if she had already given her heart to Jack Campbell.

"No, it is just that I have not yet told you the truth. . . . There is someone else, but it is not Jack. And while this person lacks Mr. Cabe's religious interests, he has other qualities."

Diana looked down at her lap, as if in maidenly confusion. Her mother looked distraught, a litany of unacceptable names running through her mind.

"Who is it, then, my child? Please tell me, and then we shall puzzle it all out."

"It is Mr. Trelawny. He has been so kind, and I could not help but feel affection for him."

Lady Abingdon's pale face showed relief. She had expected far worse. She had always deplored Mariotta's impulsivity (a quality taken from her father, unfortunately), but Mr. Richard Trelawny was exactly the perfect husband for her. He would see that her high spirits did not lead her where it had led her father. He would know how to handle such an impetuous wife.

Certainly Jonathan Cabe would have been ideal, from her point of view, but she had to admit that Trelawny was a very good second choice. And there was a good fortune there, not that it signified, but it was nice to know her daughter would be taken care of.

Lady Abingdon could not suppress a certain pleasurable feeling at the idea that she would be able to deal the Widow LeFanu a blow. That lady had been pushing Miss Southey at Mr. Trelawny for six months, and had predicted a match. It would be satisfying to prove her wrong.

Unaware of the precise nature of her mother's musings, Diana was nonetheless certain that she was happy. Now all that was needed was Mr. Trelawny's proposal. She had no doubt that he would eventually come to it, but it would be better if it happened quickly, before Jack Campbell was due back in Bath, before she wrote to her sister again.

She went to bed that night thinking of everything. When she thought about marriage to Richard, Diana felt a quiet sense of secure happiness. He was a charming, civilized man. There would be no surprises with him, which was exactly what she desired.

When she next saw Richard, in the Pump Room some days after Mr. Cabe's proposal, it was clear that gossip had already informed him.

They sat down at one of the tables.

"I have heard about poor Jonathan," said Richard, a slight smile playing around his mouth. "My heart breaks for the poor fellow. For some reason he thought you would share his living in Whitechurch. I could have told him otherwise."

"Oh?" Diana was a little unsettled by this remark.

"My dear Diana, you do not strike one as a curate's wife, particularly *that* curate."

Diana raised her chin. "There are some very fine men who are curates, Richard, some who would be a good husband for any girl."

"Perhaps. But I doubt that you would like the life. I cannot see you pinching pennies and doing good works."

Remembering her life with Black Walter. Diana thought that she knew more about pinching pennies than anyone of his acquaintance.

Trelawny was continuing with his teasing, and Diana found it slightly annoying.

"And did you really tell the poor wretch that you had no interest in marriage? And he actually believed it?"

Diana found this impertinent, if correct.

"It matters little if you believe it, Mr. Trelawny, as long as Mr. Cabe does!"

He found her sudden haughtiness charming. "So now it is *Mr. Trelawny*. Forgive me, your majesty, for I have erred. Am I to understand that you wish to live with your mother forever? I confess that I had sometimes imagined that you wished nothing so much as to leave the house on Laura Place."

Diana looked so annoyed that he knew he had struck home.

"And what would you suggest I do about it, if that were true?" asked Diana only half humorously.

He took her hand. "I would do what you think I would: I would ask you to marry me."

His eyes asked the question, and she bowed her head in assent. It was done.

"When shall we announce our engagement?" he said, still in a conversational tone of voice.

"I am not sure." Diana thought rapidly. "It seems to me that we shall have to wait—until mother is over my refusal of Mr. Cabe." *And I have time to tell Mariotta*, Diana thought to herself. Her future here was so uncertain, and she was almost sure that Mr. Trelawny would accept her explanations for the charade—but she must do Mariotta the justice of telling her before she could read it in the *Morning Gazette*.

They walked back to Laura Place from the Pump Room in great good humor with each other. Richard Trelawny was glowing with a kind of warm happiness.

Lady Abingdon watched them walk through the square, and commented to Diana that everything was clear as glass.

"But we must not tell anyone," said her daughter. "Think of how it would seem to poor Jonathan."

Her mother looked guilty. "I had forgotten! Of course, we shall keep it among ourselves for a few weeks, and then I shall gradually lead him to accept the idea that you might be swept off your feet by someone else."

But a few conversations with the suddenly intractable curate showed Lady Abingdon the falsity of this belief.

"Of course Trelawny is *wealthy*," said Mr. Cabe when he confronted Lady Abingdon with the gossip about her daughter. "But never tell me that your daughter has any more than tepid liking for him!"

Lady Abingdon considered this a presumptuous remark, and answered coolly that the best alliances were often based on things more permanent than passion.

"Just so. Money, for example."

Lady Abingdon was angry at Mr. Cabe for an entire day after this conversation, and insisted that it was high time to announce the engagement.

Diana prayed that Jack would arrive soon, and said that they really could not announce the engagement to everyone in Bath without telling Richard's sister Caroline first.

"It would be sure to reach her if we did, and her opinion of me would suffer accordingly."

Her mother was finally made to see the truth of this, and Diana was able to breathe more easily.

Diana, successful in her plans for herself, now turned to the matter of her mother and Mr. Huntington.

Edmund was interested, that was clear. But Lady Abingdon had a bad angel who saw to it that every time her suitor began to talk seriously, she began prosing on about some point of religious doctrine. Edmund Huntington went to church every Sunday, made generous contributions to various charities, and had every right to consider himself a Christian gentleman, but he did not wish to hear about Original Sin over dinner.

Richard laughed at Diana's worries on this score.

"Why disturb yourself," he said one day as they were out walking in the hills around Bath, a little ahead of their compan-ions. "They will either make a match of it, or they won't."

"You do not understand. My mother does not know her own mind. She fills her days with so many unimportant things that she does not see what matters. She will be very unhappy when Edmund marries someone like Mrs. LeFanu, but then it will be too late! But she would be shocked if I told her to remember that Edmund is an ordinary man, and that she should not bore him with Original Sin!"

Richard looked at her curiously. "And have you always felt this way? Does your mother know that her interests are not yours?"

Diana gave him a frank look. "Ah, you are afraid that I am quite a heathen! No, it is not true, although my mother might turn anyone into a raving pagan! If I thought for one moment that her interest were serious, I should have nothing to say against it. But it seems to me that it is only a way of getting attention, without acting like a woman. She was in revolt against my father in the beginning, and now it is a role she cannot forsake. She did it all to repay him for his very shocking neglect."

"Something his daughter will not have to worry about," said Richard.

It was a few days later that Richard told Diana that his sister Caroline was coming to Bath.

"I am quite sure that you and she will become great friends," he predicted.

Diana understood that she would have to charm the sister. Richard adored this older sister, who was apparently a paragon of virtue. Caroline's chief interest was in horticulture. To prepare for this new friendship, Diana began to read books about botany, but found it very difficult to absorb. But she was determined to have at least some acquaintance with Caroline's passion. She began to visit the gardens, hothouses, and parks around Bath, in the hope of learning enough to be conversant on this subject. Really, Bath was certainly improving her mind: first religious dogma and now flowers. Poor Black Walter would think she had gone mad.

Diana returned from one of her research outings in the

company of Richard to find her mother in high spirits. When Richard had taken his leave, Diana asked her mother what had occurred.

"Nothing. Why do you ask?"

"You look like you are about to rise like a hot air balloon. What is that letter you have in your hands?"

"Such an honor! Most thoughtful, gracious! Mr. Huntington!"

"Yes? Mr. Huntington?"

Her mother was looking very happy, and Diana began to think that Mr. Huntington had already proposed.

"Ardwell Park," her mother finally articulated. "We have been invited to his house for a week!"

Considering her recent conversations with him, Diana was led to conclude that Richard had had a hand in this, so as to give the courtship a push. Ardwell would be ideal. . . .

The next few days were spent in plans. Clothes, of course, had to be examined as to their suitability. And Mr. Trelawny was engaged as their companion on the way to Ardwell.

Diana worried about Jack Campbell: he was due any day, and she must see him—there was so little time left! Finally she decided that Jenny, who was not going, would have to convey a message.

"Please tell him that he must manage to come to Ardwell somehow—if only to see me for an afternoon. It is very urgent. I know he does not know Mr. Huntington, but you can explain the situation, with my mother, that is. But please make sure Mr. Campbell understands that I *must* see him."

Jenny smiled slyly and said she would give the gentleman the message.

Diana left Bath mistakenly sure that she had foreseen every problem, and that she might now relax and enjoy herself. She was about to announce her engagement to the perfect man, and she would never have to go back to her old life. . . . Certainly the exchange had been good to her.

CHAPTER EIGHT

It had been years since Diana had enjoyed a stay on an estate comparable in any way to Ardwell Park. And even those few times when she and her father had been invited to a famous estate of Europe, she had never really been able to enjoy herself, for Black Walter required constant surveillance—was he flirting too much with the host's wife? Had he lost too much at cards, or, worse by far, won too much? Was he drinking to forget? These and a thousand other questions effectively ruined her enjoyment of elegant estates. But here at Ardwell she was free to relax completely. Whatever one might say of her mother, it was clear that she required no overseeing in society.

Ardwell Park was located at the southern end of the Widcombe Valley, just across the River Avon, in sight of Bath. But one could not have imagined a greater contrast. In Bath one tended to forget the countryside, despite the fact that it was visible in the distance. But here at Ardwell all was peace and tranquility, and Diana had the sensation of being deep in the countryside despite the distant outline of the city.

One afternoon Richard asked her to go for a walk.

"I think you will like the bridge down at the lake. Palladio, again, and very charming."

Diana thought the bridge lovely, and said that Edmund's park and flowers were enchanting.

"Yes, Edmund is quite an expert on these things. His hot houses produce all year long, but I'm afraid that only my sister Caroline enters into this passion enough for him. They go for hours talking of strains of roses. I am happy that you admire the estate. . . . Do you think you would be happy living in such a place as this?"

Diana was looking at the ducks and swans, and so did not see the concentrated expression on Richard's face.

"Yes, it has everything one could desire. Except the life of London, of course."

She looked at her companion then, and saw that he was flushed.

"I understood that you have never left Bath." he said stiffly.

Diana's heart began to beat quickly. Surely she should tell him? But her instincts warned her not to.

"No, I have not, but I read, and my friends have described the joys of town to me." Diana rapidly searched for a change of subject, and hit upon one sure to stop him.

"Richard, you did not warn me that Miss Coates has a *tendre* for you," she said recklessly.

This kept them occupied until they returned to the house to dress for dinner, and Diana could only thank her stars that she had noticed that poor Maria Coates, a quiet and charming lady of over forty, was unable to disguise her attention whenever Richard spoke. Richard laughed off the idea, genuinely unaware of this admirer who had known him for many years.

Maria Coates cost Diana a little twinge of guilt, however, as it passed through her mind that this woman was deeply in love with Richard, whereas she herself could offer him no more than affection and respect. But she comforted herself with the idea that he, at any rate, was in love with her, and not with Maria.

At the end of the first week both mother and daughter confessed themselves unwilling to leave such a congenial group of guests, and Mr. Huntington promptly invited everyone to stay two more weeks—he had a secret project they might all aid him in.

The project was quite a shock to Lady Abingdon.

"I cannot believe it, Mariotta!" she hissed to her daughter in a whisper as they were going to the drawing room with the other ladies after dinner one evening.

"What is it that upsets you? The idea of a play?"

"Amateur theatricals! I cannot credit it! Such an undignified thing! So unserious!"

Diana wanted to ask just what her mother had thought Edmund would do with his newly decorated theater—use it to exhibit his plants? But she used all of her tact to make her mother see this activity in a better light.

"Well, I quite understand. But you must see that it is an innocent desire, after all. He has that lovely little theater, with a real curtain, a real stage—he is obliged to use it. But you need not be in the play. You could help Edmund direct the rest, tell them where to move, how to speak, and so on."

Lady Abingdon said nothing immediately, but her face lightened. She, Lady Abingdon, would never *act*, but telling the others what to do—that was quite another thing. . . . And then, she and Edmund would be involved in the same work. . . .

Diana rose the next morning and went down to have her breakfast of boiled eggs and muffins. She sat down with a sigh of happiness, feasting her eyes on the sight of the six newspapers lying on the silver tray. Her mother took only one paper in Bath, and Diana had been feeling news-starved, and this visit had been a godsend. She was just starting the first paper when what appeared to be a blond whirlwind sat down across from her.

Enormous blue eyes surveyed her a bit blankly.

"Oh! I know—you are Mariotta! I am so glad to finally meet you!"

Diana waited for an introduction, but the girl made no moves in that direction, and instead began to consume a large quantity of bread and butter.

Finally Diana asked who she might be.

"Goodness! Quite forgot! You don't know me, of course! I am Gussie Storbridge—really Augusta, but no one would wish to be called *that*. We are neighbors of Mr. Huntington's. He has invited us to come and act in the play. We shall be here a week or two." This struck her funny for some reason, and she began to giggle.

Gussie kept up a steady stream of chatter, and Diana was completely unable to read her paper until the young lady's mother came in, introduced herself, and took her daughter off.

"Let Miss Abingdon have her breakfast in peace, child! You'd never know she was nineteen, would you? Such a child!"

Diana had to agree with that mentally. It was difficult to believe that this enthusiastic girl was only a little younger than she.

Mrs. Storbridge was a woman of some style and intelligence. That was apparent. The daughter was dressed in the best style, but she was such a sad romp that one could easily miss the beautiful clothes and the elegant figure. Diana heard bits of the mothers and daughters conversation as they left—all of it concerning her. She had to smile. There was a certain appeal in the girl's frank manner and indiscreet questions, a little of

Mariotta in her personality, perhaps . . . although Mariotta was not *silly*.

At luncheon, which was attended only by the ladies, since they wished to appear to lack appetite at dinner, Diana observed the mother and daughter once again.

Gussie was certainly vivacious and beautiful, but she understood only very simple things. Her mother was at great pains to explain things clearly to her, but Gussie's response was usually a dazzling smile and a change of subject. But the girl knew instinctively how to get on with people—she praised and complimented constantly. No, Diana decided, there was no need for her mother to worry. The girl would do well; that was as certain as her beauty. Many men looked for nothing more than a face and a degree of fortune, and Gussie had both. Diana, for her part, liked the girl and wished her well.

It was on this afternoon that Maria Coates suggested that they picnic by the lake. Gussie took up this idea and ran to Edmund with it, and he agreed immediately. The next afternoon, therefore, found the company walking down to the lake followed by a caravan of hampers.

Gussie was skipping alongside of Diana, thrilled with this novel way of dining.

"So, Mariotta—may I call you that?—it is famous that you may be coming to live in our neighborhood. Really, it will be so delightful! I will walk over to visit you, we shall do all sorts of shopping in Bath—mamma is not very good to shop with, she dawdles so . . ."

Diana looked at Gussie, bewildered. "Whatever do you mean, Gussie? My mother and I live in Bath and are not planning to change residences. . . ." Diana began to wonder if Edmund had said something about marrying her mother. . . .

Gussie giggled. "No, now don't be shy! I have heard that Richard is building at Werton, not three miles from here! And he must be thinking of a wife. And it must be you."

Diana was stunned. So this was what Richard had been thinking of when he asked her if she could live at such a place as Ardwell!

She walked down the lake in silence and sat under the willow. She had no intention of living in the country year round, and certainly not so close to her mother. After the exchange was revealed, she was certain her mother would be very disapproving of her daughters. But, of course, she would be able to persuade Richard to stay in town for the season. She was certain of that. She would manage to convince him. . . .

The picnic went very well, and the discussion centered around the plans for the play, which had not yet been selected. Unconsciously, Diana sought to keep her distance from her fiancé. She was surprised when he reproached her for avoiding him.

"No, it is merely that Mrs. Storbridge and Gussie are so amusing! I intended no slight to you, please be sure of that!"

She gave him such a warm look that he was placated.

The next day Richard found her in the garden and said he had a surprise for her. He led her to the drawing room, where a very thin gray-haired lady was sitting talking to Edmund.

"My sister Caroline," he said proudly.

Caroline looked up and gave a wide smile.

"So this is the *young* lady! How lovely she is to be sure! Richard, you described her inadequately, surely! Such eyes, such a complexion! But you do not take after Lady Abingdon? I have met her already—"

"No, you are quite right; I take after my father."

Richard nervously interrupted, saying that Mariotta was

really much older than she looked—about to turn twenty-one, in fact.

"My dear brother," said Caroline with a sweet look, "what have I said? She is beautiful and she must be good (else you would not love her). Dear Miss Abingdon, you are not upset that I call you *young*, are you?"

"No, of course not. My mother taught me not to worry about such things, in any case. She impressed upon me that spiritual values are what matter, not age, beauty, or wealth."

Everything about Caroline Trelawny was narrow and thin, giving her a somewhat oriental look, emphasized by her rather yellow complexion. At this remark her eyes narrowed until she quite looked like a Chinese empress, Diana thought.

Diana was forced to listen to a botanical conversation between Edmund and Caroline, one which Caroline seemed intent upon making as technical as possible, so that neither Richard nor Diana could follow it.

But Lady Abingdon came to their rescue by coming to engage Edmund in a discussion of possible plays. Richard and Diana took this chance to drift into one of the window recesses, where a little private conversation was possible.

"What did you think of her, Mariotta?"

"A remarkable woman."

"I knew you would like her! I wish you to become great friends. She has very graciously promised to show you through the orchid house here. She is quite at home there."

"That will be quite lovely, Richard. I so appreciate it." Diana wondered if she would ever be punished for this lie. Although a tour of the orchid house would certainly be punishment enough.

Arriving with Caroline Trelawny was Mrs. Storbridge's sister, Lady Quennel. Diana found it hard to believe that this enormously fat woman with the unpleasant expression could be the charming Mrs. Storbridge's sister. That she was a close friend of Caroline's was also hard to believe, on physical differences alone.

Lady Quennel was an unpleasant, gossipy sort of woman, and after a few days of her company, Diana began to wonder if Caroline could be as sweet as her brother claimed: surely her friend must indicate something about her. . . .

This opinion was confirmed after the tour of the orchid house. Caroline Trelawny, when her brother was not present, showed clearly that she did not like Diana. And when she talked about Edmund in a possessive way, it was obvious that she herself assumed that *she* would marry him. But it was also clear that Richard had not told his sister about the understanding between Cecily Abingdon and Edmund Huntington.

When they were playing a game of chess one evening after dinner, Diana asked Richard if Caroline and Edmund had ever thought of marriage. He laughed.

"Caroline! Never! She is very happy running my house, she has never been interested in any man, with the possible exception of me. No, they are merely great friends. Both so botanical, you know."

Diana said nothing. Either she was wrong, or the brother did not at all understand his sister. Caroline would find out how things were soon enough.

The amateur theatricals soon dominated the party's activities. The play had finally been chosen: *The Beaux' Stratagem* would be their first production. But there seemed to be no one who would, or could, play the hero of the piece. Edmund wished the part of the tavernkeeper, which was by far the most fun. Maria Coates and Mrs. Storbridge were set for two of the minor roles.

Mr. Storbridge would help with the scenery, and Caroline and Lady Quennel had volunteered to help with costumes and props. It was clear that the heroine would have to be either Diana or Gussie. There were no other young girls in the group. But who would be the heroes? Edmund knew that he could, in the end, talk his friend Richard into being the second lead, but he was quite inexperienced, and would never do for the main hero.

It was at this point that Diana received a note from Bath: Jack had arrived and would ride out to Ardwell, if Mr. Huntington would give his permission.

Diana read this and went to find Edmund with it still in her hand.

"We have our hero," she said confidently, praying that Jack had acted before. "Jack Campbell is an old friend, and a wonderful actor. If you invite him, we may certainly persuade him to join us!"

Edmund was electrified. "By Jove! Knew it! A miracle! But what does he look like?"

"Tall, handsome, quite the hero, in fact."

When Jack rode up in his high-perch phaeton Edmund saw no need for an audition: the fellow was perfect, as he told everyone within hearing.

Jack made his bows to the ladies, talked briefly to Lady Abingdon, and then asked for Mariotta.

"She is by the lake," said Richard. "I tell her she will get the sunburn, but she only laughs."

Jack had not really paid very much attention to Trelawny, but something possessive in the man's tone made him look up. A gentlemanly sort, slightly stiff, and what in the world could Mariotta be doing with him, if she was, indeed, doing anything?

Jack walked down to the willow and heard a voice hail him from the bridge. It seemed to him that she gave him a look of intense scrutiny, but he could not be sure later, because she quickly smiled, showing the dimples he liked so well.

"It is so good to see you. Jack!"

He gave her a brotherly hug and then stood back a bit to get a better look.

"You look much more grown up! A coiffure like your sister's—makes quite a change. I suppose it was my story of her that made you do it. Wonderfully becoming. What is this Trelawny to you? He seemed a trifle paternal, I thought."

Diana raised her chin and remembered what it was she didn't like about this young giant. "And just what do you dislike?"

"You look just like Diana when you do that, Mariotta! A haughty, prissy miss. Nothing wrong with him, appears to be a solid fellow. But he's not at all your type. Far too slow for you."

Diana made a strong effort to regain what she thought of as Mariotta's gaiety, and said that Trelawny had somehow earned her affection, but that if he, Jack, didn't like him, she would drop him immediately.

"No, no! If it is just one of your flirts! But what is this about a play?"

"You are needed. But I need you more—I desperately need to get word to Diana. There have been some developments in London—we are to get an inheritance, you know. In October. And I must arrange with her. Perhaps we shall meet in London—"

"And you dragooned me here to play post office. All right. But you don't need to give me details—your business, after all. Since Mary and I spent our youth putting on plays for our family, you did well to pick me. But I can only stay a week, no more. But I doubt you'll get an answer from Diana very quickly."

Diana was relieved. He was so agreeable, really. And she liked it that he did not wish to pry into her affairs.

She was surprised at just how glad she was to see Jack. No doubt because he, at least, knew there were twins, even if he didn't realize which one he was talking to. But his presence brought new dangers. He was much sharper than her mother, as she discovered when she and Richard were playing chess.

"You amaze me, Mariotta," Jack had murmured as he sipped his claret near them. "I never knew you could play."

Her chest began to tighten, her mouth felt dry. She had no idea whether Mariotta played any such games.

She flashed him a smile. "You do not know *everything* about me, Jack. May I not have a few secret accomplishments, develop new interests?"

His blue eyes scanned her face, and then he turned back to his drink. "Well, you have certainly developed some unexpected ones," he said, nodding at her partner.

Diana thought him the most exasperating man she'd ever met and took back all of her kind thoughts about him.

CHAPTER NINE

The situation in the breakfast room was precarious: Black Walter had seen Lord Drew at last, the night before.

Mariotta tried to remain calm. "I do not see how you can talk of an engagement, papa, when I have yet to lay eyes on him! No matter how much encouragement he may have given you—"

Black Walter slammed down his plate of ham. "Do you not understand? We shall have to sell Chalford any day now! If you don't marry Drew, there is no hope at all! Matters have grown serious! You are a silly little girl, but even you must be able to understand!"

"You should have thought of that before you went gambling our money away!" his daughter snapped at him.

The harsh lines around Black Walter's mouth deepened.

"Drew is all I could wish for you. A gentleman. He will make you a good husband, and he will save the only piece of the Chalford legacy I have left. Need I point out that I am perfectly able to place you in such a position that marriage to Drew would seem like heaven?"

Mariotta did not quite understand this last threat, but she assumed that in the past her father had done something truly despicable, and that Diana knew of it. Thoughts of sleeping potions and compromising situations ran through her head and she shivered.

"Have you no sense of duty?" her father raved on, banging the table for emphasis. "After all that I have done so that you should have decent clothes—"

But his words floated on air. Mariotta had turned on her heel and left as he dramatically addressed the window.

She stormed into the hall and began looking through the morning post, hoping to find something from Diana. But there was nothing from Bath. There was a large cream-colored envelope addressed to her, however, in what appeared to be a masculine hand. Instinct made her take it to the privacy of her room before opening it.

She opened the letter and a draft fell out. She picked it up and realized that it was for two hundred pounds, an incredible sum. The letter was mystifying. Lord Drew was repaying her father for some unspecified service. He did not wish the money to fall into her father's hands, however. He desired it to be used to restore Chalford as much as possible. He was giving it to Miss Abingdon, sure that she would know where it was best spent. His nephew Gerald had assured him that Miss Abingdon would understand the need to keep this entire matter to herself. He hoped to make her acquaintance soon.

Mariotta's first reaction was one of delight—now they would finally be able to repair the roof. But then, after a rereading, she began to get annoyed. The man was trying to buy her affection; it was all suddenly clear! Perhaps he assumed that the money would seal this dirty bargain between him and her father. The more she thought about it, the angrier she became.

She was unable to take action until after lunch, but then, as soon as she was finished with various housekeeping matters, she snatched her bonnet and began to walk through the woods to Drew Hall. She would return the money to that devious old man who was Gerald's uncle.

The walk did nothing to calm her temper. It was an unusually warm day, and by the time she arrived at the door of the rather imposing house she was regretting her decision to walk. She automatically took note of the excellent maintenance of the house and grounds, and admired the address of the butler who politely inquired as to her name and business with Lord Drew.

"I am Miss Abingdon, from Chalford. It is a personal matter."

He inclined his head sagely, and went off for a few moments. He returned smiling, and led her to what he called the Yellow Saloon.

The room was done in yellow and green and was very elegant except for its very casually dressed occupant. This person was wearing outdoor clothes, suitable for hunting, but certainly not for lounging about a silk-covered sofa. Lord Drew certainly had some unceremonious friends.

The man looked at her, an eyebrow raised in question.

"I have come to see Lord Drew," Mariotta announced stiffly.

"At your service, Miss Abingdon. I should have known you anywhere."

Drew regarded the lady with interest. She was undoubtedly very beautiful, even in her obviously exhausted state. He wondered what her smile was like. He was struck by the resemblance to the young Black Walter, which was remarkable, despite the utterly feminine incarnation. He noticed her shortness of breath, and realized that she must have walked over from Chalford—two miles—on this hot day. He rang for the butler.

"Smith, would you bring us some lemonade, please. I think we would enjoy that."

He looked at his visitor, clearly awaiting an explanation.

Mariotta was completely confused. The man opposite her was no more than thirty-five, and looked nothing like a contemporary, or even a friend, of her father's. He was of medium height, with light brown hair, and everything about him bespoke the well-bred gentleman. His intelligent-looking hazel eyes had a spark of humor in them, and on the whole he betrayed not the slightest touch of the rake.

But she was still resolved to say what she had planned to say. Appearances, after all, could be deceiving, as her mother always told her.

"I have come to return your gift, sir. I cannot accept it."

He was distracted by the arrival of an affectionate dog and did not answer for a moment.

"I am very sorry for that, Miss Abingdon, for I did so wish to discharge at least some of my debt to your father." He could not imagine how his letter could have been interpreted as insulting, but he saw that Miss Abingdon was truly disturbed.

Mariotta smiled ironically. What debt could this wealthy man owe her father, a man barely able to keep a roof over his head, even a leaky one...?

"I know nothing of your past dealings with my father, but I do not wish to enter into any agreements based on money."

Drew pushed back his hair with an impatient gesture.

"Agreements? What agreements?"

Mariotta was tired. The lemonade had not yet arrived. She became sarcastic.

"Come, sir, do you deny that you and my father have come to an agreement that I am to be married off to you—auctioned off?"

Lord Drew made a choking sound and began to cough, a direct result of having tried to suppress his laughter.

"*I* do not think it comic," said Mariotta.

Drew stood up and walked over to the window. He must get control of his mirth and not offend the child. But really! Black Walter was impossible!

"Miss Abingdon," he said finally, a little smile still playing about his mouth, "I have never discussed you with your father. I know nothing of any wedding. I believe that you have been led to believe something which is true only in your father's imagination."

Mariotta sat down suddenly, an expression on her face made up equally of relief, amusement, and horror.

"Lies. Oh, Black Walter, you wicked, wicked man!"

Mariotta smiled, and Drew saw the charming dimples. Poor Leila, how would she be able to compete with this girl, as wild and mobile as quicksilver? There was going to be a great deal of trouble. . . . But then a glimmering of an idea entered his mind. No, it would really be too base of him. . . .

The lemonade arrived, and very quickly the two of them were on good terms, and began to talk of many things unconnected to Black Walter.

Mariotta thought that Drew was really quite charming. She imagined that he was very successful with women when he chose to be. After her embarrassed apology he had managed to put her at her ease at once. She quickly fell into the kind of friendly banter she had always enjoyed with Jack Campbell, and thought that Drew might turn out to be a friend—although she did not think she would ever see him enough to make that happen. But all the same, it was nice to think it could. It made her feel a little closer to Gerald.

"Is Gerald going to be back soon from Lady Green's?" she asked, thinking of how surprised he would be that she had become friends with his uncle.

"Oh, he's helping Camilla move furniture. She's taken it into her head to make that place more the thing—but it's just a little country house, and that's all it will be. I think my Camilla is just bored, too much time on her hands. You should really go with me to see her, she'd enjoy you."

They went out to visit the puppies just born to his setter, a much-awaited birth, since the offspring were expected to be exceptionally good hunting dogs. The tiny puppies were with their mother in the back of an old coach, chosen for reasons no one could understand, as the location of the birth.

Mariotta looked down at the tiny balls of fur and tears came to her eyes.

"So beautiful! And tiny! I have never felt anything so soft. . . ."

"You have no puppies at Chalford?"

"Only two very old collies." Mariotta wanted to tell him that she had never seen a puppy up close before—her mother had always disliked animals in the house—but she thought it might seem strange in Black Walter's daughter. He had had dogs once, but had been forced to sell even them at a moment of financial crisis.

Drew watched her cooing to the puppy in her arms. Logic dictated that he do what he could to end anything that might be between her and his nephew, but he could not help but feel sorry for it: she was such a lovely girl, and now she was talking about Gerald in a style that made clear just how attached she was already. She was ascribing virtues to him he did not have. But that was the magic of Gerald: he appeared a hero, even to those who should know better.

For her part, Mariotta thought Drew a very easy gentleman to talk to—not that she had talked to so very many in her life that were under fifty! But she liked his humorous way of telling a story, and she thought that if only he would not speak of Gerald in that condescending way, they might be excellent friends. She could see that Drew was not saying everything he thought, and she did not like people who held back—why could they not simply say what was really on their minds? She did, after all. But on the whole, she thought the visit a success, surprising, considering the way she had felt during that hot walk. Her return was made vastly more comfortable by the loan of Drew's elegant carriage, complete with driver.

As he watched her drive off, obviously excited by the carriage and handsome team, Drew thought that accomplishing his aim would not be hard, at least in one way. It was clear to him already that Miss Abingdon deserved better than Gerald. There was no doubt that beauty like hers would be rewarded with a far better match as soon as the London ton made her acquaintance.

It was too bad, of course, for as soon as she spent a season at Almack's she would lose that engaging frankness, and the childlike enthusiasm which made her so fresh.

That evening Drew took the first step: He wrote a letter to Mrs. Grayson, inviting her and her daughter Leila to come and stay with him at Drew Hall. Gerald, he told her, was so very lonely without Leila that it made him feel that the best present he could give him for his birthday—a week away—was the presence of his fiancée and future mother-in-law.

Camilla, when he told her about the daughter of Black Walter, approved his action.

"My dear, if she has half the appeal of her father at that age, you had best get an entire wedding party down! When I think of how fascinating Black Walter was!"

Drew gave her an intensely curious look.

"Were you ever . . . interested in him, Cama?"

He was afraid that he had at last gone too far. Cama was remarkably free about such things, but there was a point beyond which she did not reveal herself.

But she smiled and shook her head ruefully.

"I almost married him, in fact. Think of it! But he was so passionate, you know. A great deal must be forgiven a truly passionate man. And he genuinely loved women. But my common sense saved me, and he went to the north and found poor Cecily, who understood precisely nothing about him. How does he look?"

"As if he had seen hell. I think he had rather a hard time of it in Europe. Diana seems lighthearted enough, but she is so young, she probably does not understand the things which weigh upon him."

"I cannot summon up any pity for the man," drawled Cama. "He has made his own hell, let him live in it."

"I understand that view, but I remember him as he was when he helped me . . . a generous fellow, you know."

Cama's dark eyes narrowed as if she were looking into the sun. "Yes, he was that. But the other side of that particular coin is thoughtlessness, heedlessness . . ."

Drew promised that he would bring Diana over to visit Cama soon. He said that he thought Diana's liveliness would cheer Cama and keep her from being quite so bored.

"She sounds a bit like medicine. I do hope she isn't."

"No, nothing like that! And after all, we have to give her something to replace Gerald."

"I hardly think I would do. You would be a better choice, Drew, if you weren't turning into an accounts ledger!"

CHAPTER TEN

The next few days Mariotta spent happily paying off accounts in Lewes and making arrangements for the repair of the roof. Drew had seen to it that the draft was cashed immediately in Tunbridge Wells, and had given her useful advice about the repairs. It was pleasant business to pay off a shopkeeper who had obviously long ago given up Black Walter as a bad debt. If only her father did not find out and ask the source of the money. . . .

This was unlikely, since Black Walter had left for London, telling his daughter that he had some minor business with his lawyer. The business was far from minor and had nothing to do with his lawyer. Black Walter went into the City, to the famed Garroway's. Garroway's appeared to be just another coffee house, but it was actually the center of the most important estate auctions in the city. The suave auctioneer dressed in black was the most persuasive of men, describing the delights of the mansion for sale.

Black Walter quickly made his business known to the appropriate person, specifying that Chalford must go on the market within two weeks, no earlier.

He made his way home the next day, feeling wretched. The

bills had finally come due, and the moneylender would not wait. And this moneylender was not interested in having a friend in society; he wanted only his money, and his alternatives were unpleasant. Diana would not be able to marry Drew quickly enough to help, and Loulou would never speak to him again if he asked for a loan. Loulou would marry him, that was certain. But not soon enough—she would want everything to be the most lavish, and, comically enough, the most proper.

He had met Loulou in Paris, where she had been on the stage, a tantalizingly attractive soubrette. She had married very well, her husband had died, and now here she was, in London, waiting for him to marry her. She was as common as she was beautiful, and the idea of making the ton accept her as his wife was appealing. But something kept him from going through with it, namely his daughter.

Diana would be horrified, he knew. He could already see the expression on her face. But, on the other hand, if he sold Chalford, she would be equally horrified. All he could do was hope that his luck changed at the tables before the house was sold. . . .

It was a rainy day, so Drew and Gerald decided to play billiards before supper.

"Diana is a lovely girl," said Drew idly.

"Yes, a stunner, isn't she! We have to get Cama to invite her for a dinner party. And her father too, of course."

"Of course," answered Drew dryly. "But don't you meet with her enough as it is?"

"Oh, no, she's been busy as a bee—all sorts of construction going on. She said you were her idea of the perfect English gentleman, by the way." Gerald looked at his uncle expectantly.

"Very nice. A bit remote, though, don't you think?"

Gerald's answer was forestalled by the announcement that a coach had appeared in front of the house.

"Are you expecting someone, Drew?"

Drew took a quick puff on his cigar and then put a ball in the side pocket.

"Yes, actually. The Graysons. Lord, don't tell me I didn't tell you?! I really am getting impossible, just as Cama says!"

Gerald put his cue stick down. "My God, Drew, what are you thinking of! Diana!" This was hissed in a style very unlike Gerald's usual smooth tone, and it was difficult for Drew to keep his countenance.

Drew showed his fine teeth in a smile formed around the ever-present cigar. "Thought of everything, my boy. My fault, I'll take care of things with Diana. No worries for you. Or do you intend to break off with Leila now, get it out of the way, so to speak?"

Gerald was about to say that he certainly would, when he reconsidered. Leila would be sure to cry; her mother would be arctic. Really, he did not like making people unhappy. Why hurry it? It would all keep. Better by far to do it by letter. . . .

Drew read his nephew's face and found what he expected. Very well . . .

Leila and her mother were in the hall, and they went to greet them.

Leila, attired in the most fetching traveling dress, was even prettier than Gerald remembered her. She was not beautiful like Diana, of course, but she had lovely ash blond hair and smiling green eyes. She was very small and made Gerald feel protective.

At first Gerald could find nothing to say; but then, under the influence of Leila's teasing questions he began to behave more naturally, and by the time dinner was over it really began to seem to Drew that nothing had changed. Diana Abingdon must be merely an exotic attraction, Drew theorized. And of course Gerald was unable to say, even to himself, what it really was that bound him to Leila. But watching the young couple play a noisy game of cards, he did not think his plan was going to be too difficult to put into effect. Of course it was ruthless of him, but he did not worry too much about that. He had to do what was right for his nephew's future—he stood in place of the boy's parents—and Diana Abingdon would have to be sacrificed.

A few days later Drew rode over to Chalford, ostensibly to talk to Black Walter. They had a drink and recalled old times, but there was an edge to Black Walter's humor that put Drew on guard: something was wrong, something was bothering him. This was so atypical—normally Black Walter was only bothered by affairs involving women—that Drew suspected it was some-thing very serious.

Before he left he managed to coax Diana into showing him the garden, in which he was not the slightest bit interested, as she well knew.

"Gerald sends greetings, but there is a *situation*," began Drew.

"Involving a woman?" Diana looked at him sharply.

"Well, yes. I might as well be frank: Leila Grayson and her mother have arrived."

The gray eyes looked up at him blankly. She did not have the slightest idea who the Graysons were. So much the better, he thought, recognizing at the same time that it was cruel of him even to give words to the sentiment.

"Sometimes," he began, "one has a prior *commitment*, and then something happens which makes one regret it. But one has to make a choice, hard though it may be." He looked down at her and saw an exasperated expression.

"Can't you be plain, Drew? Is this how you conduct your business? I dearly hope not!"

He was a little annoyed at that; he was not use to young ladies addressing him in that particular manner.

"Leila Grayson is the young lady to whom Gerald is considered engaged."

Mariotta stood still, in the middle of the path, turned to stone, her heart beating painfully. Her immobility lasted only a few seconds, however, and then she took a deep breath.

"What does 'considered' mean?" She gave a shaky laugh.

He had to admire both her intelligence and her self-control. She had immediately found the important word.

"Just that for family reasons it had not been announced. And now they have come to visit, and Gerald must either be civil, or risk an awful scene. He prefers to wait, and take care of the matter another way."

Mariotta did not want to think what she was thinking: that Gerald was a coward, that he wanted to do it by letter, tell this unknown girl he loved another—by letter!

"What is she like?" Her eyes begged him to say something negative, but he steeled himself to do what he must do.

"She is quite a lovely, charming girl, of a great fortune, but quite unspoiled. Her mother is charming as well, indeed, quite a remarkable family in general. . . . I am sorry I cannot say she is mean and ugly, like Cinderella's sisters. . . ."

Her cheeks were flushed, and she gave him a reproachful glance. "I should *never* want anyone to lie to me about such things! You have a very low opinion of women, I gather!"

He patted her hand and led her through the garden gate.

"It will be all right, Miss Abingdon. I shall take Gerald's place for a while, they will leave, and then the planned engagement will evaporate into air, leaving everyone free to do what they wish. Patience, my child, patience is all that is required."

Mariotta felt comforted by his self-assurance. "Yes . . . I

suppose it will turn out all right in the end. Lovers always must conquer obstacles, is it not so? But please, call me . . . Diana. I feel that we are quite old friends already."

He looked down into the rosy face and nodded. "But Diana does not suit you at all. . . . I think Cherry would be a much better name for you—the exact shade of your cheeks and lips, after all. . . ."

"You must have made a great many pretty speeches to be so proficient," said Mariotta dimpling. "And shall I call you Carlton?"

He made a face. "Never! Only my enemies do so. Drew, that is the name my friends use."

They continued to walk together, and began to plan how to manage the charade they would have to play.

"I shall act as if Gerald and I are merely friends," said Mariotta, beginning to see that at least this might be an adventure.

"No . . . I do not think that would do," said Drew improvising as he went along. "Certainly Gerald's true feelings for you would be obvious, especially to Leila's mother, a woman of some intelligence. No, I am afraid that I will have to be Gerald's substitute, and everyone can think that there is something between *us*."

Mariotta suddenly forgot her own misery enough to realize that Drew was getting himself involved with something quite unusual for a man in his position.

"Oh! I do not think I can ask all this of you. It is most unfair, it is not your fault, after all!"

Drew turned his eyes away from her concerned face. This artless, and completely untrue, statement made him feel a villain. But the game had begun, there was no going back now.

"Your scruples do you credit, Cherry, but Gerald suffers little from them. He is demanding that I help him during this very difficult time."

Mariotta was already busy justifying Gerald's actions to herself. "Of course, if Miss Grayson is so lovely a girl, he certainly cannot suddenly break it off; he must do it gradually, so as not to hurt her quite so terribly. . . . He is only being kind, I am certain of it."

Drew did not like this line of reasoning at all, but he decided to let her comfort herself with this idea for a while. He had done enough for one day.

"It is better that I do not meet Miss Grayson," Mariotta said when Drew was leaving. "I should feel sorry for her, you know . . . and a bit guilty, though I did not know of her existence. . . . I suppose Gerald would not have married her even if he had not met me; at least I hope so."

Drew was more touched by this than he would admit to himself, but on the ride home he cold-bloodedly planned the rest of the campaign, precisely as if it were a business maneuver.

The first days without Gerald were terribly empty, it seemed to Mariotta. Even the Cushings could not find a way to cheer her. She was so used to seeing Gerald almost every day, and now he had to be busy with the Graysons, managing to snatch only an hour now and then. But even when he came it was not the same, he was forever turning red at his own tactless mentions of his guests. She knew it was not something he could help—they were all doing everything together, after all—but she was a little annoyed by it.

As Gerald's visits grew fewer, Drew arrived more often, to play cards or quoits with her, and talk politics and scandal with her father. He became quite one of the family, staying for tea, and then gradually staying later and later until it was time for supper.

Mariotta felt entirely comfortable with Drew, and if she grew to expect his visits, and be unhappy when he did not come, she could tell herself that it was because he always brought news of Gerald. But the information he gave her about Gerald and the Graysons (who had extended their stay) made her uneasy.

Drew always began by saying that Gerald missed her "like the devil," but he would then describe all of the picnics and rides to picturesque spots in such a way that it was clear that everyone, including Gerald, had had a perfectly wonderful time. Sometimes Mariotta had the feeling that Gerald liked Leila Grayson a great deal, although not in the passionate way he loved her, and that there was certainly some kind of bond. . . . But she dismissed this thought. Gerald might be suited to any number of females, but it was she whom he loved, and surely that was all that mattered. And, in the end, she had to admit to herself that all of this had made not a bit of difference in the essential thing—she still loved him.

Drew watched his nephew with a certain hidden amusement. Leila was so open and artless in her affection, and the mother so warm and generous with her future son-in-law. Mrs. Grayson went on shopping jaunts to the Pantiles in Tunbridge Wells, where she found presents for everyone. Gerald was embarrassed by one obviously expensive gift, a presse-papiers made of Sienna marble, surmounted by a small golden fox. He was immediately taken with it, but felt he should not accept it, especially considering his plans to end the engagement. It made him feel low, a sensation very unfamiliar to a boy who had always justified his meanest act. But here he was caught. He should obviously refuse, or later return, such a gift. But he took it.

"It's the damnedest thing, Drew! I feel like a wretch. Perhaps I should get it over with, tell Leila now. . . ."

Secure in the belief that Gerald would never develop the courage to commit such an unattractive act, Drew merely directed the conversation to the subject of what kind of life the happy husband of Leila Grayson might expect. The contrast with what he might expect with Diana Abingdon was implicit.

Finally the Graysons took their leave, although Drew did everything in his power to make them stay longer. It was understood that the engagement would finally be announced, within the month. Gerald seemed to have almost forgotten Diana, and discussed with great eagerness when and how it would be done.

But that evening Gerald came to Drew in a depressed state.

"I'm a beast, Drew. I don't know what to do. Diana! What shall I do? I didn't even think—if she should see the announcement! And it is already too late. . . ."

This was the moment Drew had been waiting for.

"I think I know what to do. You leave it to me. But you had better leave—go to London, stay with your friends. Better if you aren't here. You have decided? Finally? It is Leila?"

Gerald looked shamefaced, and nodded his head.

Mariotta could not believe it, but there were actually two letters for her. The first, which she snatched up eagerly, was in Diana's handwriting.

It was a long, satisfying missive, describing all of the events at Bath and Ardwell in brief. Mariotta found much to amaze and puzzle her. Trelawny was surely too old, if he was Mr. Huntington's friend . . . and her mother, actually flirting! Diana had performed miracles. . . . The suspicions of the maid Jenny were certainly aroused; Mariotta knew her very well, and she was indeed a sharp-eyed miss. . . .

At last she had an address, to Ardwell in care of Jack. She began her answer immediately, describing Gerald and Drew, but leaving out the fact that she was finally in love. That would have to wait. And would Diana understand it? she wondered. This engagement to Trelawny seemed a very calculated thing, with very little real feeling involved.

She was absorbed in the task of answering this letter when a groom arrived from Drew Hall, carrying a message for her.

It was from Gerald, and it said that he was leaving for London immediately, and deeply regretted that he could not come and say goodbye in person. Mariotta collapsed into a chair, utterly miserable. She knew how to understand this: He must be in love with Leila Grayson after all . . . not to come and say goodbye, to leave without explanation. . . . All of that pointed to only one thing, his cowardice was now all related to her. He was afraid to tell her.

She spent a terrible night, tossing and turning, cursing her impulsiveness, reviling Gerald, dwelling on his faults. She began to think that she had been a little fool, falling in love with a handsome face. She had known so few men that she had taken this one more seriously than she should have. . . . She finally managed to fall asleep as the sun was coming up, too tired to think anymore.

Drew arrived the next day, ready to play the role of a sympathetic friend with a shoulder to cry on. He found the object of his sympathy picking flowers while the gardener made disapproving noises. She did not look as if she had been crying, and Drew began to wonder if the letter had been delivered.

"I have brought you two puppies, Cherry," said Drew. "Come and see which one you prefer."

She said nothing, but took his arm and led him away from the gardener, who was watching with open curiosity.

"Here, this is far enough. Oh, Drew, I've been such a fool!"

He was not expecting this kind of reaction.

"You mean, about Gerald?"

"Yes. Now tell me the truth, really, I shan't cry. He's going to marry *her*, isn't he?"

The gray eyes looked at him steadily. He took a breath.

"He does not know his own mind yet . . . but it is possible. . . ."

"He's a cowardly wretch, and I'm a fool. As soon as I heard of Leila I should have thought about what it meant that he hadn't told me about her. *You* had to do that for him!"

She was magnificently angry, Drew thought. The sparks were flying from her eyes, and she looked like she was ready to kill Gerald. Very good. Half his aim was accomplished. With Gerald's help this was going to be quite easy.

But a moment later the anger dissolved in unwilling tears, and Drew let her use his shoulder. Now he was on familiar ground, and he told her a carefully edited version of the truth, and did everything he could to make her conclude that she was well rid of his nephew.

"Your jacket . . . I am so sorry, I don't usually cry. . . ."

"It will survive. Now come and see the pups."

The dimples made their reappearance.

"You think I am a child, to be distracted from a broken heart by puppies! Well, I am almost twenty-one, though I am sure that the puppies will indeed help!"

Drew was very happy with the results of the day, and he prayed only that his nephew would not, as he so often did, change his mind.

Mariotta spent a very bad week. But then, with visits and projects she began to feel that life held some promise as well as sorrow. And she was aware that Drew made a difference—when he came to visit things seemed much brighter.

Black Walter watched these visits and said nothing, but drew his own conclusions. The only question was whether he should write to Garroway's and have the house taken off the market.

He sat at his desk one afternoon, composing a letter to Garroway's, explaining that there were reasons which required the sale to be delayed, when he was interrupted by an old friend. He left the letter on his desk and went off to Tunbridge Wells to see what promised to be an exciting boxing match.

Mariotta was spending the day examining the repairs, to see if the leaks were really all taken care of. She made her way into the library finally, and noticed the letter out, obviously unfinished. She was about to put it in the drawer, but her curiosity won out, and she read it.

She was stunned. The shabby elegance of Chalford, from its leaky roof to its peeling portrait gallery, had become very dear to her; and she could not imagine her father living anywhere else. His debts must indeed be huge for him to do this! How could he have let matters go so far! She remembered Diana's description of her life, and she had her first glimmer of what longing for security lay behind her sister's assured manner. It was inconceivable to the daughter of Cecily Abingdon that a man who had started with a decent fortune should have wasted it to such a degree, and now found himself without a roof over his head!

She looked around the library and tears began to roll down her cheeks.

It was at this inconvenient moment, when she was both tearful and badly dressed, that the butler announced Drew.

She made an effort to repress her tears and wipe away the traces. She rose to welcome Drew, who was carrying a bouquet of his rarest flowers. She thanked him and then burst into tears.

"First time my flowers have produced tears," he said. "Would you tell me what it is that has you in this state?"

She calmed herself with the idea that Drew would know what to do.

"Look at this letter . . ." she whispered, fully aware that she should not be showing her father's letter to anyone.

He read it quickly and gave a whistle, brushing his hair back with a restless movement.

"The old boy is really under the hatches this time. . . . And you did not suspect it?"

"No . . . that is . . . he did act upset some weeks ago, but it passed quickly. What shall I do?"

Drew looked down at the pale little face, and the eyes which were still full of tears, and impulse overcame him.

"I shall investigate; you shall say nothing, do nothing. I think I know someone who will lend your father enough to take care of the debt."

"But he will merely run up new ones."

"Not if it is known that he does not have the deed to his own estate."

"You mean . . . to find a buyer who would let him still live here?"

"That's it, Cherry. Then everything will be taken care of."

She looked at him with such shining gratitude that he almost told her not to be grateful; he was no hero, but a man out for himself. But he held his tongue.

He sent a man to London with orders to immediately make the high bid for Chalford, before Black Walter's letter could reach there. The rules at Garroway's were that without written notice, the house must be sold on the terms agreed to initially.

Drew felt he had finally paid the debt he owed to Black Walter, but a voice in his head nagged at him, pointing out that he was doing everything to bind Diana to him, and not out of the noblest of motives.

CHAPTER ELEVEN

Lady Abingdon had been having a perfectly wonderful time at Ardwell until the arrival of Caroline Trelawny. After a few days of watching Caroline dominate the conversations at dinner and demonstrate her superior knowledge of botany, to Edmund's pride, Lady Abingdon began to see what her daughter said was true: Caroline Trelawny was certainly interested in Mr. Edmund Huntington. Lady Abingdon's first reaction was to go to her room with a headache whenever it seemed that Caroline was about to lead the way to the greenhouses. Then she began to absent herself from other things as well, until her daughter came to talk to her one afternoon.

"Dear Mariotta . . . so nice of you to come and see how I am. . . . My headache is quite shocking. . . ."

"I see . . . of course you know that everyone is rehearsing for the play today. Caroline has finally chosen her part, the role of Mrs. Sullen."

Lady Abingdon sat up straighter. "How dare she!"

"I do not understand, mother. Why should she not be Sullen?"

"She understands well enough. Do you not see? I have been persuaded by Edmund to take the role of Lady Bountiful, though I am in principle against play-acting. But he was so insistent.... And Lady Bountiful is Mrs. Sullen's *mother-in-law*! She is at least ten years older than I, and I am persuaded looks even older than that. And Edmund allowed this?"

"No, dearest, he had nothing to say to it. Certainly you are right, she did it on purpose. But there are many roles left. I am Dorinda, Gussie is Cherry, the best part, you know. I have an idea of how you may put Caroline in her place, however...."

Lady Abingdon smoothed her fair hair nervously. "I wish no revenge, dear. I am simply appalled that a woman of her station ... could behave in such a manner...."

Diana ignored this. She knew her mother's real feelings.

"Mamma, you must see that Caroline is determined to marry Edmund. And you know she is quite wrong for him, no matter how interested they are in flowers! Marriage is more than wandering through greenhouses together. And it seems clear that he has no suspicion of her intentions. If you will put a little effort into your relations with him, all will be well."

Lady Abingdon did not quite like to think of herself as a conniving female, but she agreed in general with what her daughter had to say.

"But, my dear, will she not be your sister-in-law? Should we not be nice to her?"

Diana shook her dark curls. "No, my dearest mother, the woman is a viper and we all know it. Such a sweet creature—until you are scratched by her claws. Her brother knows nothing of her true character, and I am certainly not about to inform him of it. But I shall beat her at her own game, you may be sure of it. She talks constantly of how we shall all live together, and I have no plans to do such a thing. But I shall manage it, you will see."

Lady Abingdon looked at her daughter, mystified. She had

never seen this side of Mariotta, and was not sure that she liked it.

"Dear, I do not like to hear you talk in such a hard way. But what is your idea?"

"First, you must not mope. It just gives her more time alone with Edmund. Second, you must dress more youthfully, emphasizing the difference in ages, and I will fix your hair in a new style."

"This is really necessary?"

"Yes. And when you play Lady Bountiful, you must be sure to look like you are the daughter and she the mother-in-law. Forgive me for my frankness, but you must remember how to be a woman—use fascination, artifice. It is all very well when you are dealing with your Bath friends, but here when you are modest and quiet it makes you seem . . . well . . ."

"Dowdy. Quite. Well, I have never cared about external things, but you may have a point." The chin was raised; the eyes were distant.

Diana judged it best to let her mother think about it for a while, but she was sure she had won her point.

The next day Lady Abingdon arrived on time for the play rehearsals and threw herself into the preparations. She became Edmund's aide-de-camp, as he told everyone, helping him decide on costumes and props. Diana was pleased.

Gussie and Diana spent the day watching Richard and Jack practice their leading roles, the two gentlemen who were down on their luck. Jack's character pretended to be the other's servant so that they could seem well-to-do.

Gussie's eyes shone with admiration. "Jack makes a wonderful Archer, doesn't he? So handsome . . . Oh, Mariotta, if only I could marry someone like that!"

Jack certainly did show to advantage on the stage, with his fine physique and striking looks, not to mention his voice. Of course, Diana reminded herself, Jack had experience in acting, but Richard had never taken part in anything more taxing than a recital. Richard did look very gentlemanly, no matter how hard it was to hear him from the back. Edmund was not satisfied, however.

"Richard, you are supposed to be a dashing gay blade! Show some passion, man!"

Diana rather counted it an advantage that her fiancé was no actor. She remembered a man who had acted too well, both on stage and off.

She thought she was doing well in her role of Mariotta. To be sure, she'd had to make it clear that Richard was responsible for the changes in her behavior. Sometimes she felt that Jack was testing her, suspicious, but then the next moment he would say something that made it clear he believed her to be Mariotta.

The Storbridges came into the rehearsal of the scene between Jack and Gussie, as Archer and the landlord's daughter, Cherry. Considering the nature of the scene, Diana was a little worried. She hoped Gussie would not put too much feeling into it, in front of her parents.

"*I was a-considering in what manner I should make love to you*," said Jack as Archer.

"*Love to me, friend*! " exclaimed Gussie as Cherry, with none of the required shock on her face, Diana noticed. Her reading of the line was more in the nature of an invitation.

The scene continued and Gussie seemed to be controlling her feelings. But then came the kissing scene.

"*Ay, my dear, take it while 'tis warm*," read Jack, and here they were to pretend to kiss, but in front of her horrified parents,

Gussie actually pressed her lips to Jack's. He pulled away and continued the next line.

"*Death and fire! her lips are honeycombs,*" read Jack, trying bravely to pretend all was as it should be. But Gussie's face was indication enough that it was not, and her parents stonily removed her from the stage and dragged her out the door.

"Ah," sighed Jack, "there goes our Cherry, I fear. I'm afraid that you will have to take the role, Mariotta. It appears that our Gussie will be indisposed for a few weeks. . . ."

"Poor child! Could you not stop it?"

"I had no idea the minx would do that! Of course I saw her mooning at me all week, but really, I had no idea of the lengths she would go to. Rather like Nellie at the Sarsfields' party, remember her?"

"Yes," said Diana quickly, trying to conceal her alarm. "But this is different." She dearly hoped it was.

"Yes, true, Gussie was not brought up badly, as Nellie was. That what you mean?"

Blue eyes met gray, and Diana smiled calmly. "Of course. But Gussie really is a beautiful girl."

"Yes. Too high-spirited, but she'll settle down in a few years. As you have." He looked at her speculatively.

"I hope I was never *that* silly, Jack!" The dimples showed, and she looked so beautiful that Jack experienced a slight shock.

"No, not with me, anyway."

Edmund made an announcement the next day that he had found some additional actors for them, and that it was time to run through the entire play. Everyone cried that they were not ready, but promptly at three o'clock they assembled in the little theater.

Lady Abingdon reported to her daughter that one of the

players was Lady Quennel, Mrs. Storbridge's sister, and one of Caroline Trelawny's closest friends.

"Depend upon it, she will help Caroline any way she can!"

Diana was not disturbed. "Mamma, you have been looking so well that ten Bath cats couldn't stop you."

It was true. Lady Abingdon had started wearing her new dresses instead of her old ones, pastel creations which were vastly more flattering to her than her favorite grays and browns. Diana did her hair in a less severe style, allowing it to curl a little around her face. The entire effect made Lady Abingdon look much younger, and much prettier, contrasting greatly with Caroline's colorlessness.

Jack had understood immediately.

"You are responsible for your mother's transformation?" he asked with a strange look as they were waiting for the run-through to begin.

"No, I was merely the helper. The prime cause lies elsewhere."

Jack laughed, showing his very white teeth, or perhaps, Diana idly considered, it was just his dark complexion which made them seem so.

"Edmund Huntington for a stepfather. Well, very well indeed. But I think that Caroline creature won't like it one bit—no, you needn't go through the formality of protesting that she is lovely, wonderful, and your future sister-in-law. I know you far too well, dear Mariotta. You cannot, and do not, like her. Yes, I imagine that Caroline will do something to impede progress. . . . What does your *fiancé* think of this?"

Diana gave him a cool stare. She thought he was rag-mannered and impertinent, even if he and Mariotta were very close friends. She had no intention of letting him get away with his mocking tone.

"Richard does not waste time on things which he considers *none of his business.*"

Jack looked very innocently surprised, as if she had simply misunderstood him. Really, he was most annoying.

They were sitting in the back of the theater, serving as testers for the sound of those on the stage, and Jack had stretched his long legs out in front of him, quite as if he were in his own parlor.

"But," he said after a few minutes of discussing acoustics with Edmund by means of shouting, "isn't his business his sister's happiness? Or doesn't he know she has plans. . . ? That's it, isn't it? The poor fish doesn't even suspect."

"He is not a poor fish," snapped Diana, an angry flush starting over her face.

"Now, Mariotta, don't tell me you are taking my teasing seriously? Where is your sense of humor? Of course he is a perfectly nice fellow, I wish you happy and so on, but really, if he hasn't noticed . . . I see, he notices only what you wish him to, and does only what you wish him to?"

"One way of putting it, I suppose." Diana was trying very hard to calm herself. She was furious with herself as well as with Jack: how had she let him irritate her to such a degree?

To make matters worse, Richard chose this moment to arrive in the theater room, and quickly came over to Diana. He was obviously upset about something.

"Mariotta . . . I wanted to speak to you." Richard glanced meaningfully at Jack, who turned away. Pretending to watch the stage, but certainly listening to every word, Diana thought bitterly.

"I really think that you should not play Cherry. Miss Coates has agreed to do it if you decide against it—"

"Miss Coates is twenty years too old for the part, Richard."

Diana was amazed at his self-confidence. "And I have learned my lines."

"I simply do not think it suitable that my fiancée should play opposite—"

"A very old friend? Jack, come, join the conversation, you have heard every word anyway, haven't you? Richard has the most absurd notion that you and I should not be playing opposite each other! Jack is just like a girlfriend to me Richard—is that not so, Jack?"

Jack stretched himself out further and said that it was certainly true that they had known each other forever, and that there had never been anything but friendship between them.

"I wonder that you worry at all, Trelawny. Even had I wished to express my passion for Mariotta, I would hardly do it in front of countless thousands at a house party." Jack gave a provoking smile, which palpably irritated Richard.

"If you like such a role, Mariotta, I suppose that your mother understands the implications . . . but I should much prefer you not to."

A devil rose up in Diana. She would play Cherry, and she would ask no one's permission to do so.

"I understand that implications, as you put it, may be involved, but I should like to think that I am respectable enough that no one would have such a low imagination as to think I am anything like the girl I play."

Richard rose, bowed stiffly, and walked over to his sister and Lady Quennel, who had just come in.

Diana was sure that Jack would make some comment on this scene—which must have given him great gratification. But he merely suggested that they go and practice now, since the others had finished.

Diana enjoyed being on the stage, and Jack was certainly

a pleasure to act with, unlike Richard, who always made her nervous. This was simply due to Jack's greater experience with acting, Diana had to remind herself. And she would certainly not make acting a requirement in a husband.

They ran through the scene, the one which had proved so disastrous to poor Gussie, who even now was observing them sadly from the audience, flanked by a parent on each side. All went smoothly until the last part, when it seemed to Diana that Jack was trying to throw her off balance in some undefined way.

"*You may depend upon't,*" said Diana as Cherry.

"*Upon what?*" Jack was looking intently into her eyes, as Archer was supposed to, but Diana was somehow confused by this look.

"*That you're very impudent.*"

"*That you're very handsome.*" Jack smiled as he said this, but it was too personal a smile, Diana thought.

"*That you're a footman,*" answered Diana-Cherry haughtily, very out of character for Cherry.

"*That you're an angel.*" Here Jack caught her hand and, bringing it to his lips, brushed it very lightly, but Diana could still feel that warm imprint after he'd put it up to his cheek.

"*I shall be rude,*" warned Cherry, turning away.

"*So shall I,*" shot back Archer.

"*Let go my hand.*"

"*Give me a kiss,*" said Jack-Archer, leaning close to Diana, his lips only an inch away from hers, his eyes gazing intently into hers.

They were waiting for Edmund to enter the scene, and in those few seconds Jack murmured that she should think of him as one of her girlfriends. Diana spoke her last lines and left the stage, very disturbed.

Her mother and Richard had been watching the rehearsal together, she saw with slight annoyance.

"There, you see," Lady Abingdon turned to Richard. "You were quite wrong to worry. They were exceedingly careful and proper."

"You have been worrying my mother with this, Richard?"

"I knew that if Lady Abingdon felt it was correct, it would be. You are so young; you are still in need of a mother's opinion, but I confess I need not have worried. I saw nothing on the stage to upset me."

Diana seethed, but her years of training with her father kept her from showing it. She smiled and said nothing.

Richard felt he had won a victory of some sort. He had been right; a little firmness was required with Mariotta, but sometimes one must defer to the mother, who, of course, knew best.

Lady Abingdon made no mention of Richard's "consultation" that evening before bed, for her mind was all on Caroline Trelawny. Caroline had countered Lady Abingdon's new dresses with some of her own, obviously made in great haste in Bath. They, too, were youthful, but on Caroline they looked merely ridiculous. But Lady Quennel was proving an important ally to Caroline, exclaiming to Edmund that she had never seen such a woman for botany, that she had a really miraculous feeling for orchids.

"What ever shall I do? It is really too much," said Lady Abingdon to her daughter. "I know nothing of these things."

Diana's mind was on other things, but she directed her attention to this question.

"Well . . . you must make your ignorance into an asset. Tell him you wish to learn all about his beastly flowers. You know you are as uninterested in them as I am—but you must realize that this is a good position to be in, that of the student. Men do like to teach, you know; and maybe Caroline will start trying to teach Edmund. We can hope for that. He wouldn't like it at all. Maybe she'll start correcting him. She is very proud of her knowledge. Let us see what vanity will lead her into."

Although she was a little upset by the cool cynicism implicit in what she recognized to be a very intelligent appraisal of the situation, Lady Abingdon thanked her daughter and said she would do precisely what she had recommended.

"But it will have to be done when Lady Quennel is not with Caroline. She is perfectly capable of ruining everything."

"Yes, she is quite sharp-eyed," said Diana. "Jack refers to her as the ambulatory sofa, you know, claiming an upholsterer must be her modiste." Diana giggled, thinking of what Richard would say if he had heard this.

Lady Abingdon started to giggle herself, thinking about Jack's name for Lady Quennel, even as she protested to Diana that it was most uncharitable to talk that way about anyone.

Diana thought there was hope for her mother yet, if she would but giggle three times daily.

The day of the dress rehearsal dawned, bright and fair, adjectives which were certainly inapplicable to the mood of the actors themselves.

Caroline Trelawny had arrayed herself in a particularly unsuitable gold-colored gown, which was cut quite low over her thin chest. She swept into the rehearsal, a proud smile on her face, and stopped dead when she caught sight of Lady Abingdon, resplendent in a remarkably flattering green muslin, which made her look absurdly young.

"But Lady Bountiful is supposed to be quite old!" said Caroline loudly to Edmund, who was happily pacing the stage in his tavernkeeper's clothes.

"But my shawl—what could be more appropriate than my shawl?" asked Lady Abingdon sweetly.

Edmund looked in alarm at the two ladies, who were glaring at each other.

"Yes, yes. I see. Cecily really does look much too young to be your mother-in-law."

"There. You see, you must dress in something gray and shapeless, and you should powder your hair as well," advised the happy Caroline.

"Oh, no," said Jack confidently. "There is a far better solution, which would occur to any director. They should simply exchange roles. Much better all round. Look at Lady Abingdon! Even hair powder could not conceal the difference in ages."

Lady Abingdon protested that she wouldn't dream of it, that Caroline would do the role perfectly well.

Caroline did not appreciate this christian attitude in the least, and turned on her rival in fury.

"You deliberately dressed in that childish gown so that I should look older!"

Lady Abingdon forgot about charity. "But you are older," she pointed out. "Therefore it would not matter what dress I wore. I thought only of how pretty the dress would look on the stage, not how old it would make *you* look. Of course I shall try to find some rags to set you off better—"

Edmund had dimly understood that matters were getting out of hand. "Now, Caroline, she can't help being younger; you are being unreasonable. It does not really matter anyway. A mother may be quite young, a daughter-in-law quite old, really, and the audience, composed of our friends and neighbors after all, will not care either way. . . ." He thought he had mollified everyone with this ill-conceived speech, and was therefore quite at a loss to understand why Caroline stalked off the stage. Lady

Abingdon comforted him by saying that all actors had attacks of nerves the day before the performance. . . . Lady Quennel was sent to bring back the missing actress.

Jack and Diana, backstage, were witnesses to this remarkable bit of stage business and were hard put not to laugh out loud.

"Your mother was wonderful! So noble! Forgiving!"

"And Caroline hated it! That was what did it. She'll never forgive her patronizing! I can't wait to see them acting tomorrow."

"Nor I. Far funnier than anything the play provides."

Diana had no inhibitions about discussing this with Jack, but when Richard took her aside after a very silent dinner, to ask for her account of the quarrel, she was unwilling to go into it at any length.

"Really, they were both at fault," was all she could find to say.

His brown eyes glowed with approval. "Yes, I told Caroline you would not fall into the vulgar practice of being prejudiced in your mother's favor, merely because she is your mother. You are just by nature. . . . Caroline has never been guilty of such behavior, and I told her that Lady Abingdon was very likely having an attack of nerves—"

Diana's determined chin went up, and her eyes were angry.

"Really, Richard, I did not say that at all! I said they were *both* at fault! Your sister as well. And if you have never seen her behave badly, I wonder at your powers of observation."

Richard was flushed and on his high horse.

"I suppose there may be differing opinions about what is correct. But I know my sister meant well, and certainly she has never behaved badly to me."

Diana wanted to say something about people who were nice only to their relations, but she saw that he was very offended. She apologetically said that perhaps she was mistaken, that the play-acting had worn everyone's nerves down.

"Yes, I am sure that is it," said Richard, easily won back. "Later you will come to understand Caroline, and her truly fine nature. When we are all together at Werton it will be a different matter."

Diana tried to concentrate on the fact that he was a nice, attractive man, with security engraved in every lineament, and desperately willed herself to forget about Caroline. She swore to herself that Caroline would never live at Werton, but would stay at the family estate. But she knew it would not be easily managed.

She told Richard that she felt a headache coming on, and that she would not be down for dinner.

He tenderly drew her to him and kissed her gently. She thought again of what a good man he was and vowed to be more diplomatic—really, she was turning into Mariotta!

The day of the first performance the skies were overcast, and by late afternoon a steady drizzle was coming down. But Edmund refused to be disturbed by the weather. His play was going to go on in his theater, and that was all that mattered. It was the dream of his life, made possible by a sudden inheritance, and what could bad weather matter? His guests would be enjoying a lovely, perfectly equipped theater.

The actors watched from behind the curtain as the audience took their places. Poor Gussie Storbridge was in the first row with her parents, Lady Quennel beside them. A number of neighbors and friends from Bath arrived, some fifty persons in all, some no doubt drawn by the promise of refreshments afterward.

The pianist struck up a country air, and after a slight tussle with the curtain, the performance began.

All went well, although Richard still seemed a trifle stiff—but Jack was vivacious and dashing enough for two. The end of the act came and Diana thought they were doing very well. The last scene of the act was the one with Jack alone. When he entered and began his pretty speeches to Cherry, Diana had the feeling again that something was a little off, but she forgot about it as they proceeded.

"*Give me a kiss*," said Archer.

He maneuvered her into a turn, which left her facing away from the audience, and before she was aware of his intention, he had actually kissed her, although the audience could not see it.

Jack's eyes burned into hers as Edmund came in with the next line, and like her character, Diana could not catch her breath for a moment.

"*You plaguey devil, how durst you stop my breath so? Offer to follow me one step, if you dare.*"

With that Diana ran off the stage, and hid in the ladies' dressing room, which was mercifully empty. She thanked her stars that she was not in the first scene of the next act, or else she certainly would have forgotten lines. She sat in the corner, trying to scan her next scenes, but she could not concentrate. She went up to the mirror and looked at herself. The color in her cheeks was as bright as the rouge. And her eyes were sparkling, full of excitement. A brief kiss from Jack Campbell, in front of fifty people, plus her fiancé backstage, although she didn't think he'd seen anything—this was what made her look like this. Her mind kept returning automatically to the kiss. No doubt this was how her mother had come to marry Black Walter. Rakes were very accomplished kissers. She shook herself, determined to regain her composure. And if he dared do anything in the next scene!

She was back on the stage then, as Archer asked Cherry what the signs of love were. Diana made her reading of the lines very mocking:

"A *stealing look, a stammering tongue, words improbable, designs impossible, and actions impracticable.*"

Jack smiled down. "*That's my good child, kiss me.*"

But here the kiss was addressed to the air between them.

The rest of the play went smoothly until Act IV, which provided the first scene between Caroline and Lady Abingdon.

Caroline, as Mrs. Sullen, was already on stage when Lady Abingdon, playing the medically talented Lady Bountiful, entered.

Caroline could not stop a sharp intake of breath, audible to the fifth row, when she saw Cecily Abingdon. Diana had carefully made up her mother to look even younger, using subtle rouging and a blue dot under each eye, tricks advised by Jack, who knew a great deal about theatrical makeup.

The total effect was quite remarkable, and Lady Abingdon made the most of her lines to her "daughter-in-law," lines which were in any case insulting.

"*I have been a-tampering here a little with one of your patients,*" said simpering Caroline–Mrs. Sullen.

Lady Abingdon looked regally down at the patient, who was a poor Maria Coates, very nervous about this onstage feud.

"*Come, good woman, don't mind this mad creature*; (a nod in the direction of Caroline) *I am the person that you want, I suppose. What would you have, woman?*"

Caroline had a good many witty lines, but she could not recover from the tone of Lady Bountiful's comments, and Caroline could be heard muttering darkly under her breath at various points of the last act.

But it was soon over, the candles on the stage were extinguished, the guests fed, and everyone congratulated. Edmund was happy beyond words, although the few he did say were all directed to Lady Abingdon, who still wore her stage makeup, much to Caroline's loud disgust.

After the guests had left, the company sat companionably in the drawing room, discussing their performances at great length. Edmund announced that they would have one more performance, a charity performance, open to as many of the public as could fit, the proceeds of which were to go to the local orphanage. This announcement electrified everyone, and no one was the least inclined to go to bed.

Jack was sitting by Gussie, Diana noticed, obviously flirting with the poor girl; but since her parents were there as well, there was nothing to fear. Diana was trying to think of a way to demonstrate to Jack that she had not in the least been disturbed by his kiss, which, thank heaven, had not been noticed by anyone, although Lady Quennel seemed a little cold. . . . But she would say nothing; no one could be sure that their lips had actually touched. Diana was surprised at how unworried she was about this aspect, what people might say.

Jack drifted over as soon as Richard moved on to Edmund's group, and made a handsome apology for his behavior.

"Oh, it was nothing, after all, Jack. No need to apologize." She was the picture of sophisticated unconcern.

"Ah, it was nothing at all to such a hardened temptress! In that case, I take back my apology."

"You may take back anything belonging to you."

But he did not want to fence.

"Ah, Mariotta, how can you marry the noble Trelawny? I suppose that he is a sort of replacement for the father you never knew . . ."

Diana was taken aback by his seriousness of face, and was unable to summon up the anger necessary to tell him he was interfering where he had no right to. Of course Trelawny was not at all like her father—that was his charm.

She tried to distract him with Gussie.

"Why are you flirting with that poor child? You will break her heart!"

He looked very smug.

"Oh, I only did it to annoy you."

As Diana was leaving to go to her room, Gussie, who had stayed behind, stopped her in the hall, looking very flushed.

"Diana, I had not thought it of you! Or of him!"

"Whatever do you mean?"

"You needn't pretend! When I saw the way you looked at each other—that was not acting! When I think of poor Richard!"

With a sinking heart, Diana realized that at least one member of the audience had seen the kiss.

It took twenty minutes of protestations to calm Gussie and convince her that it had indeed been acting. Strangely, Gussie never brought up the kiss . . . but she was finally persuaded.

The next day Gussie was back flirting with Jack, who seemed almost to encourage it.

"A very high-spirited young lady," sniffed Lady Quennel to Caroline.

"Yes. I think she is shockingly common for all that the family's well-bred."

Diana could not help smiling at that.

CHAPTER TWELVE

Mariotta was in the salon deeply engrossed in a book. Black Walter had gone to visit a friend, saying it was too nice a day to do any work. What work he had in mind was a mystery to Mariotta, but she was glad to have the house to herself. The windows were all open, so they heard a carriage draw up quite clearly.

The upstairs window revealed a carriage of the most lavish description, cream and maroon, drawn by a team of the best horseflesh, every bridle with gold fittings glinting in the sun. The owner had already entered the house, it seemed.

Someone very wealthy, Mariotta guessed. Then she had the most awful presentiment that it was Loulou!

Mariotta swept regally down the main stairs ready to do battle. The visitor had already been shown into the saloon. Caldwell gave her a speaking glance and informed her that Lady Green had come to visit. Mariotta could not tell whether this was a welcome visitor or not. Perhaps one of Black Walter's local flirts?

A vision in pale blue was sitting on the sofa in the saloon.

"My lord, how very much like your father! I had no idea! And so very beautiful. But why are you looking at me as if I were some rare species of plant life, my dear?" Cama's seductive voice broke off as she began to laugh.

Mariotta found herself smiling along.

"I am so sorry, didn't mean to stare, really. But, you do not seem like someone who . . . well, my father . . ."

Cama gave her a freezing stare, and Mariotta turned red, realizing in that moment who was in front of her. Camilla, Lady Green. Visiting the country for her health. A very famous hostess . . .

But Cama decided to forgive her, and smiled warmly.

"I gather you were expecting someone else. No, I am an old acquaintance of your father's, that is all. I suppose, with your childhood, you may be forgiven for assuming that every woman who arrives alone is . . . somehow connected to your charming parent."

Mariotta looked a bit dazed, and was clearly at a loss for words. Cama read her easily, however.

"Dear Miss Abingdon, I can read your face like a novel. You must really learn to dissemble, you know. I was friends with your father when we were twenty, and very stupid indeed."

"But how is that possible? Surely he is your senior by ten or fifteen years? Or are you mistaken as to his age?"

Lady Green put her chin on her hand and gazed happily at Mariotta.

"That settles it. I shall make you my protégée. I quite regret having no daughters if they compliment one so! I own the women in my family age well, but I am precisely your father's age. We once had one of those childish conversations about ages, months, astrological signs, and so on. Oh, yes, don't look surprised. Walter was quite silly once, like everyone young. Although I am not sure that he is not still silly, from what I've heard. When Drew told me about you, I resolved to make the acquaintance—I am quite bored here in the country, you know. When is your father expected back? I am not sure that I am up to seeing him today. You are quite enough, I think."

Mariotta had quickly become used to Cama's rapid style of conversation, and she thought her wonderful. So alive, so young in a way. It was unbelievable that she was the same age as Black Walter—or as her mother.

Camilla had taken a quick look at the house, and had a fairly good idea of how things stood. The girl, of course, was lovely, and at least dressed well, but she clearly needed a bit of polish— a little of the innocent miss about her, charming, but only if she were wise underneath. A dinner, perhaps, yes, that would do, invite the father, see how he had changed, although she never doubted that it was for the worse.

She mentioned these plans to Mariotta over a glass of ratafia, which the butler had had the presence of mind to bring in unrequested.

"Oh," said Mariotta doubtfully, "I don't think father wants to go out in society. He has a good heart . . . but lately . . ."

"You don't need to warn me, I remember him in his moods."

They chatted amiably for a while longer until Lady Green was ready to leave.

They said goodbye, but they agreed they would see each other very soon.

The invitation to come to dinner arrived the next day, and Mariotta began almost daily visits to Langley, usually in Cama's carriage, which was sent to get her. More often than not, Drew was to be found lounging in the library, his nose in financial papers; but Cama always persuaded him to join them for a drive, or a card game, or charades. Gradually Mariotta began to realize that this must be what life in London was like, with this light banter of good friends, careful manners, and casual discussions of ideas and politics, always politics. In the presence of Cama she was aware that she was learning more than she ever had in her years of schooling.

Cama consciously wove a net around her new friend, and encouraged her confidences. This proved useful to Drew, and pleasant for herself.

"My dear, you must stay a while after she leaves," whispered Cama to Drew one day after they had been to Tunbridge Wells. "I have news."

After Mariotta had been safely delivered to Chalford, they settled down for a talk in the carriage which Drew had been driving.

"It is really despicable! I cannot credit it!" Here Cama fell into a reverie, it seemed.

"Cama! Wake up! What is despicable?"

"The letter. From Gerald."

Drew almost overturned them, so stunned was he.

"How dare he! What does he say to her?"

"The impression is one of great passion. Everything a young girl could wish in a love letter. Plus the idea of running off to Gretna to get married if there is no other way to do it."

Drew's lips tightened. Gerald must be lonely; who knew, perhaps Leila was also receiving letters like that. Gretna! How could one begin a marriage in a more shabby way?

He did not talk the rest of the drive, he was too angry. Cama saw it and wondered at it. Really, things were turning out very unexpectedly.

Drew could barely keep from riding off to London to tell Gerald what he thought of him. He had thought that he had made progress. Diana had begun to talk of Gerald as if he would never return, obviously preparing herself for that eventuality, painful though it might be. Now Gerald had made it clear, apparently, that the game was not over yet. It was all beginning again . . .

They drove up to Langley Manor, each wrapped in his own thoughts, until they caught sight of the black horse being taken to the stables.

"*Mon dieu!* I do believe Black Walter has finally come to see me. Quick, I must go in another way, I can't bear for him to see me so dusty from the ride!"

Drew smiled, but quickly turned the carriage to the side and let Cama off at the servants' entrance. He went in the front door and waved to Black Walter, who seemed surprised to see him there.

"Drew! My boy! No idea you were here today. Just thought I'd pay my respects to the old lady. Knew her way back when, you know. Very beautiful once, you know."

Black Walter seemed quite nervous, so Drew ordered some brandy and soda, which seemed to help a great deal.

"Cama is just changing—we were out driving. She'll be down shortly."

Black Walter asked questions about where Cama lived in London, and whether her health had improved. Drew began to sense that Black Walter imagined Cama to be some bedridden, gray-haired old lady, who walked with a cane and wore dowager turbans. . . . But he did nothing to dispel this impression.

They were enjoying the brandy and soda when there was a discreet knock at the door to the drawing room.

"Here I am! So wonderful to see you again, Walter."

A vision in sapphire-blue gauze floated across the parquet, and Black Walter looked stunned. In twenty minutes she had managed to arrange her hair and face to perfection, Drew saw.

And the gown was very girlish in a way, although only the most sophisticated Parisian dressmaker could have cut it. The total effect was of youth, or rather, of a youthful middle-age, quite a different and more pleasant thing, having nothing in common with the old, who merely tried to ape the young.

Black Walter, who had indeed been expecting something different, had to admit that she had aged far better than he. Time had only made the regality of her looks more marked, and the fine profile was even better on a lady of over forty than it had been on one of twenty, when the nose had somewhat over-powered the girlish face. Now she had come into her own. She looked thirty-five, not a day more.

Drew was amused enough to forget Gerald's letter as he watched the subtle looks exchanged by his companions, each very obviously trying to examine thoroughly the other without seeming to. After twenty minutes Black Walter changed his approach from that of the old friend, to one more suitable to a would-be suitor. Drew was very interested to see how he began to charm Cama, little comments, smiles, pats on the hand . . . and it brought results, Cama was smiling back, this time genuinely.

Drew told them that he had business to attend to, and took his leave. He did not think that they regretted his departure overly much.

"A fine fellow," said Black Walter when Drew had gone. "As good a friend as I have had. Think he's going to marry Diana."

"How very odd," said Cama. "Neither of them has said anything to me about it. Is this perhaps your desire rather than theirs?"

He gave her a frank look and a smile. "No putting varnish on it, my girl, I need money, and soon. About to lose Chalford."

This was news to Cama, but she did not react. "Oh, really? How very sad for you. And Diana." With this she seemed to dismiss the subject. Black Walter understood: Cama had money, and she knew very well why he no longer did himself. He could not really blame her, but he could make her remember what they had been to each other once.

He had come out of gratitude—he knew that Diana was spending almost every other day here with Cama—and out of curiosity of course. Even though Cama had always been a beauty, he had expected her to be a mere wreck of her younger self; but here she was, still attractive, her charm completely intact. Would he have been different if she had accepted him? He could not help wondering.

"Walter, whatever are you daydreaming about?" Her shrewd eyes bored into him.

"Just thinking about the past. You do look remarkably well . . . I was thinking, if only I had married you . . ."

Cama assumed a look of mock horror. "But my dear! I should never have married you! I knew what you were even then, even in my innocence! You would have seduced my maid the day after the wedding, and spent all of my money on her. No, I thought you quite fascinating and evil, there was a great attraction, but I never would have agreed to marry you. I was very happy with Herbert, you know. He made me happy, he was reliable, he loved me—"

"And he was as rich as Golden Ball. Yes, I know. A very suitable match."

Cama, now clearly Lady Green, set her teacup down with a bang.

"You really have a rather common mind, Walter. I did not realize it before. There is such a thing as love and affection, in marriage. And I had it. Sadly, you seem never to have experienced it. I can only pity you."

Black Walter did not like any woman speaking to him in

this manner, never mind a strikingly handsome rich widow. Here he was completely at a disadvantage. For one moment he saw how he must look to her—the aging, poverty-ridden rake, with nothing to recommend him. He became very uncomfortable and decided to leave. She had nothing but contempt for him.

But she surprised him.

"So, you wish to marry your daughter to Drew. Perhaps I may be of some help. . . ."

She had his interest; nothing could have made him leave at this point, and she knew it.

"You know," she said vaguely, "he is not inclined to fall in love. I have known him since he was a child. He appears to have no need of a wife—his parents are dead, his position is secure. Although his relations wish him to marry and have children, he himself does not regard that as necessary. He will not shackle himself, he tells me, to any woman just for the sake of having a brat to bear his name."

"But my daughter is beautiful, is she not? And her birth is unexceptionable, despite my reputation. And she has been brought up well, despite what you may have heard. Why can he not fall in love with Diana as well as anyone else?"

"That is just the problem. He falls in love with no one. He is your opposite in that. He sees no reason to get into such an illogical state, you see."

Black Walter's rakish smile surfaced. "If he only knew the joy that a woman in love can give. . . . Ah, I cannot regret a single woman. I loved them all, even you, young Camilla Courtland, those eyes, that *élan, vital* . . ."

The gray eyes were gazing at her with such intensity that Cama shook herself. Really, certain things had not changed at all in the man! The harsh lines seemed to disappear for a moment and once again he was the young rakehell. But Cama reminded herself that one could be a fool at forty as well as at twenty.

She turned the conversation back to Drew. They began to build castles in the air: Drew and Diana would marry; they would have children; Walter and Cama would be the grandparents, in a manner of speaking.

When she later told Drew about this absurd conversation Cama left out all references to herself. There was no need to go into that, or into the way Walter had kissed her hand and bowed when leaving. He had not forgotten how to do that either.

Two days after this news of Gerald's letter to Diana, Drew received one from his nephew himself, requesting him to "explain" to Diana why he had not yet been able to tell Leila the truth.

"But Drew," wrote Gerald, "I swear it is as good as done. As soon as Leila comes back to London!"

Drew threw the letter into his fire, wishing that he could wring Gerald's neck. He did not like what he was going to do, but now there was really no choice. The plan must go into effect.

The next day Mariotta and Drew went riding in the morning, as they usually did, finding a new route each time to the top of a nearby hill. They would always sit in their favorite spot, looking over the valley. But this day Mariotta could not stay—she had to go shopping at the Pantiles in Tunbridge Wells, with Millie and Cama.

They were sitting on the hill, Mariotta leaning against a tree, the wind ruffling her hair, and Drew stretched out on the grass beside her.

"Another day we will bring up a picnic," said Drew. "It is really too bad that we can't stay today. I have to get back as well—I leave tomorrow to go and see the mills up at New Lanark."

They reluctantly got up and went to where the horses were waiting.

Drew was standing by Mariotta's horse, ready to help her up, but when she looked up to signal that she was ready he made no move.

"What is it?" Mariotta could not read his expression.

For answer he bent down and kissed her, softly but thoroughly.

It was a moment before she could manage to speak.

"Why did you do that?"

"Impulse, sweet Cherry. An uncle's kiss. And because you are looking so beautiful today. Put it out of your mind, it will not happen again."

Then, as if nothing unusual had occurred, he helped her into the saddle and rode back with her. He confined himself to very ordinary subjects on the way back, for which Mariotta was very grateful. Her head was whirling, and all she knew was that, shamefully, she wanted him to do it again. It was not that it was exciting, as it had been with Gerald. It was just that it felt so entirely right.

She said goodbye without looking him in the face and rushed into her room before her father could see her. She was sure it was written all over her. She really must talk to Cama. Something was very wrong with her. How could Drew make her feel like this, so strange inside, but so happy? But she could not be in love with both him and Gerald. It was impossible. It was all her imagination.

But as she thought about the weeks of friendship with Drew she knew that she was comfortable with him as she never would be with Gerald. And deep in her heart she admitted it. She loved him. But now Gerald had written her that letter! And poor Leila Grayson! No, she could not do it, Gerald had already given up too much. She would have to forget Drew. It would be base to do anything else. And, after all, Drew had acted as if it were nothing: Maybe to him it *was* nothing.

This horrible idea began to dominate her thoughts, and she spent the night crying instead of sleeping. Oh, how could she have thought she loved Gerald? It had been mere infatuation, now she knew it. Drew had tried to make her see that he was not the one for her. . . .

And then the full force of it hit her. Drew did not even know who she was, and when he did he would think her unworthy of his love—living a lie, just as Gerald was with Leila.

She cried herself to sleep as the birds were beginning to awake.

CHAPTER THIRTEEN

Jack thought the house party at Ardwell was better than a Sheridan comedy. There was, for example, the reaction of his fellow players to the little write-up of their play in the Bath *Gazette*. Everyone pretended to dislike publicity, indeed to be quite shocked at what everyone would think of such frivolity; but it was easy to see that they were all thrilled beyond reason. Everyone seemed to have obtained his or her own copy of that particular issue—supposedly for absent friends—and they were reading them to shreds, savoring every comment. Jack and Mariotta had received good notices, of course, as had Edmund. But Richard had not even been mentioned, and the reviewer had commented that the lady playing Lady Bountiful had clearly been too young for the role. Caroline was left out. The notice ended with the comment that there was to be a public performance in four days, and that the public should certainly take advantage of it—to enjoy themselves and help the Bath orphans as well.

This was all very amusing: Caroline fuming about the upstart who had posed as a friend and then had written such a thing— under an assumed name; Edmund glowing with his good notices; Richard being haughty. But even more entertaining were the developments on the Cecily-Caroline front.

Lady Abingdon had taken her daughter's advice, and was deep in botany, with Edmund as a very attentive teacher. She now prattled on about Portuguese laurel, camellias and rhodo-dendrons, ignoring Caroline's acid comments about her rival's "shallow understanding" of things botanical.

The truly satisfying event was the arrival of the dwarf trees from China. Edmund was so excited that he couldn't sleep the night after their delivery, but stayed up, gazing at them in wonder until dawn, when the servants were dragged in to admire them as well.

He was constantly debating with everyone about how it had been managed. They were elm trees, at least a hundred years old, but no more than two feet high. Cecily was just as fasci-nated as he was, which inspired Caroline to tell Lady Quennel, in Jack's hearing, that if Cecily Abingdon knew an elm from a yew, *she* was the Queen of England.

Poor Caroline's shrewdness had been overcome by her belief in her own taste when Edmund had first shown her the trees. She had never seen such stunted things, and of course had no idea they were considered rare and wonderful. She said that they seemed quite ugly, but perhaps they would grow. Although it might be an oriental trick of some sort, and they would just die.

Lady Abingdon caught the tragic expression on Edmund's face at this remark, and immediately swept up to the trees, crying that they were magnificent, and would they be kept in the greenhouse or planted?

Jack saw that Caroline had quickly realized her mistake, but there was nothing to be done. She retired from the battle for a while. Lady Abingdon would make a mistake sooner or later, and then . . .

Both Jack and Diana watched all of this with enjoyment, but Richard was quite annoyed. Now he had to hear his sister saying spiteful things about his future mother-in-law.

Diana was in a state of turmoil. She had diagnosed her illness, and had faced the fact that it was Jack, nothing more or less than that. She thought about him without thinking anything specific; she just seemed to think of him in an amorphous, emotional way. This was madness, she knew it; yet she could not stop— all of her will was not sufficient for this. Sometimes she caught herself staring at him. She waited for him when he was not there. It was clear: all the worst aspects of obsession. She looked in the mirror and saw faint blue lines under her eyes, and she knew what had put them there. Well, she wasn't going to fall in love with a man like her father, and she would not allow her emotions to lead her into an unsteady existence with a woman-izing do-nothing, no matter how much he attracted her. But her convictions could not overcome her emotions, and when those intense blue eyes smiled at her, she smiled back, whether she wanted to or not. It was very annoying.

Her mood was not helped by what she saw from her window as she paced in her room one afternoon. Jack and Gussie were walking up from the lake, and he was bent toward her in a most intimate way. Surely he could not enjoy that ninny's company! She was beautiful, certainly, but she had not an ounce of sense. They were all invited to a ball that evening at Lord Clifden's castle, and Diana was tempted to plead illness. But somehow the sight of Gussie and Jack made her change her mind.

She summoned Jenny and had her do her hair in a new style, and prepared her best gown. She was determined to shine at the ball, and it had nothing to do with impressing Richard Trelawny, she had to admit to herself.

Lord and Lady Clifden were the social leaders of the area,

and an invitation to their castle was much prized. Edmund had managed to have them include all of his house guests in their ball plans and was quite proud of the fact. He talked a great deal of the beauty of Clifden in advance, but the party was not prepared for the thrilling sight of the huge castle, rising up from the River Avon in the dusk.

They passed through a magnificent baronial hall containing every possible accouterment of the knight's trade. The ball was already in full flower when the Ardwell party arrived, and they quickly entered into the flow of people on the dance floor.

Diana danced the first two dances with Richard, and was then claimed by various unknown young men. One of them gave her an especially warm greeting, and asked if her mother were here.

"Yes, over there, with Mr. Trelawny." Diana smiled but she was terror-stricken. This person obviously knew Mariotta. Who was he? What should she say? She made a few remarks about the ball and then, much to her relief, Jack came up to ask for a dance.

"Who was that?" He looked at her closely.

"Oh, it is the silliest thing. I can't remember his name, but I'm too embarrassed to ask it. Now where did I meet him? . . ."

"You should not let a thing like that upset you so," said Jack, noticing her disturbed look.

They had their dance, and then Diana was taken away by their host. She was constantly aware throughout the rest of the evening of Jack dancing by with Gussie, and then various other ladies, but always returning again to Gussie. Gussie was incredibly beautiful in a white tulle gown embroidered with roses. Diana herself was in pale blue satin, trimmed with lace, and knew she was looking her best; but Gussie, she admitted, was the star of the ball.

Jack came to claim Diana for the last waltz, and she noticed that he held her more firmly than her other partners did. Trust Jack to be impudent even on the dance floor! They danced very well together. Dancing with him required no conscious thought.

He looked down at her and smiled, and she noticed again how white his teeth were against his dark mustache.

"You are a very good dancer, Mariotta. You have greatly improved, I must say."

Diana's dimples appeared. "Not very gallant. You should never imply that a lady has ever danced anything but well." Her eyes narrowed. "How does dear Gussie like your manners?"

He whirled her faster and brought her very close to him on the turn. "She is a charming child, and does not take offense. Why are you upset by her? Or is there some other problem?" His eyes seemed both mocking and concerned.

She looked away from him and did not answer. She could not very well tell him that *he* was the problem, with his silly kiss which set her on fire and made her future seem more arid than secure.

The ball ended, they went home, and Diana could remember nothing of the evening but Jack's face, and how it felt to be in his embrace. She wondered what it would be like to kiss him again.

She felt incredibly exhausted and fell into a deep sleep with unusual speed. But at four in the morning she woke from a terrifying dream, screaming herself awake. The noise brought her mother rushing in from the room next to hers.

"What is it? A nightmare?"

"Yes . . . I'll have something warm to drink, it will be all right."

Her mother insisted on bringing the warm milk herself, and tucked her back in bed. Diana pretended to sleep and then got up as soon as her mother had gone.

The dream had been horrifying. The girl fell slowly from a horse, hitting her head on a rock, and then there was a sense of great pain, followed by a feeling of nothingness. She heard the words "Diana! Come now!"

She knew it was Mariotta, that she had had an accident, just likethe one when they were children. Only now Diana knew that it was not just a nightmare happening to someone who looked like her. It was real, real!

There seemed to be a pain in her head, as if a burning needle were lodged in the back of her skull. She must do something!

She quickly dressed and thought of a thousand plans, but none of them were suitable. She would have to go herself, risking exposure; there was nothing to be done. What if Mariotta were lost? What if no one knew that anything had happened? When she got there, she knew she would be able to find her sister. She was certain of it. But she would need help.

The maid Jenny came running at the third bell-pull. She looked half asleep.

"I have something to tell you, Jenny, but I think you know it already. I am not Mariotta. I am her twin, Diana."

Diana quickly told the story and then related the dream.

"Well, if that don't beat all!" Jenny was amazed. "I had my suspicions once or twice, but . . . well, what do you want me to do? I'll help, miss, you know I will. I love Miss Mariotta. You'll be going there, I suppose?"

Diana was thankful for Jenny's quick understanding, even at this hour of the morning.

Diana would take the coachman Risdon, and go into Bath, as soon as the coachman was up. Her ostensible reason would be to see Mrs. Oakes about household matters, and to have a new dress fitted. Diana had planned to do all of that, and her mother would think it true. But Mrs. Oakes would be told the real truth.

"I know she will keep the secret, Jenny. Then I will go on to Chalford. Of course Risdon will have to know, but I think I can pay him into silence. But you must protect me here, Jenny. They will probably wonder, but do what you can."

Jenny thought this was the most exciting thing she'd ever been involved in, despite her worry about Mariotta. With great enthusiasm she swore an oath of silence about the entire affair.

At seven that morning Diana was on the road south.

At Chalford the entire household was in an uproar. Miss Diana had gone out riding alone at two in the afternoon; it was now seven in the evening, and there was no sign, no word from her. Sir Walter was not due home for another hour, and a search party sent out at five had come home with nothing to report.

Marmaduke, the coachman, seemed to be the only person who kept his head. After interrogating the search party he sent a boy over to Drew Hall.

"Seeing as they went out riding all the time," he explained to the butler laconically, "I thought Lord Drew might have an idea about where she rode."

Drew was deep in a discussion with Cama, who had come for dinner, when the messenger from Chalford rode up, obviously in a great hurry. Seeing him from the window, Drew immediately went out.

"Miss Diana! Gone, sir. Marmaduke said to ask if you know where she might ride, have an accident or some such."

"I'll go to Windover Hill. That's the place she liked the best."

Drew quickly saddled up his horse and rode off, giving the boy orders to return to Chalford and have a party sent to the Hill, in case Miss Diana was hurt in some way.

Drew was apprehensive, but he did not think it could be anything more than a turned ankle. Diana was a fine rider, after all.

He made his way through the darkening hills, finally arriving at their favorite spot. There was no sign of Diana or her horse, however, and he began to feel alarmed. He was about to ride off in a new direction when he caught sight of something white down in the ravine below. He made his way down and saw that it was Diana, lying on a rock, as still as death.

He was almost afraid to go nearer, to find out. His heart beat painfully, and he felt that he had stopped breathing. He got up his courage and approached the still figure. He saw the congealed blood at the back of her head, a red path in the middle of the dark curls. Gently he lifted her slightly, so he could listen to her heart.

"Jack, what are you doing?" came a very faint voice suddenly. Her eyes were barely open, and she looked dazed, but Drew had never been so glad to hear human speech in his life. He could not speak for a moment.

"It is Drew, Diana. Not Jack."

She smiled weakly. "Of course, Jack is Bath, you are Chalford. Silly of me. But my head hurts so much, you know."

He made her stop talking, and began to carry her very slowly up out of the ravine. It was the longest walk in the world, and every time she collapsed against him he was afraid she would not wake again. Finally he got them to the top, and sat down with her in his arms to wait for the Chalford party.

The efficient Marmaduke had brought the doctor with him in the old coach.

"Knew *you* would find her," said Marmaduke with a smile that looked very close to tears. "Here let us put her in the carriage. I've made a little bed there."

As soon as she was out of his arms, Drew began to shake. The doctor made the patient as comfortable as he could, giving her a little brandy to sip. He said he would not give any laudanum until they knew more of what had happened.

Drew rode behind the coach all the way back, unable to think or feel, simply numb, so worried he could not allow himself even to admit it.

Black Walter was waiting at Chalford, but he seemed ready to faint himself when he saw his daughter carried into her bedroom. But Cama, who had immediately gone over to Chalford after Drew rode off, calmed him with a drink, and poured one for Drew as well.

His face told her that it was a serious fall; she did not even need to ask. The three of them waited for the doctor to finish his examination, and no one could find anything to say. They sat in tense silence until the doctor came down.

"It is a bad cut," he began, "and she is in a state of shock. But there are no further symptoms, and I am able to say that I think she will heal completely, with no serious problems."

Drew felt the tension drain from his body, and silently gave thanks to God. He resolved to tell the girl the truth about himself and Gerald as soon as she was well enough. No more of this particular game.

Cama ordered everyone to bed, refusing to let Drew ride home.

"You are in no condition for it. I see your face. No, you will sleep here. I've already had a room readied."

Realizing that he would be able to find out the latest news of the patient if he stayed the night, Drew finally agreed and went off to an exhausted sleep, from which cannons could not have waked him.

But Black Walter was in no state to sleep. All of his guilt came pouring out, and Cama saw that he needed to talk more than he needed to sleep. She sat down with him in the library and gave him her most sympathetic manner.

After an hour of breast-beating he realized that she, too, was tired.

"I don't know, Camilla," he ended. "I've been a shockingly bad father. I should have married again. Perhaps I shall. . . . There is a charming young woman, Loulou Freneau . . . perhaps a mother . . ."

Camilla had been quite a good listener until this point, but now she abruptly announced that she was going to bed. A mother named Loulou! She could well imagine just what *this* was. Enough, the man needed a lesson badly, but this was not the time for it.

After twelve hours of traveling, Diana reached the town of Lewes, completely exhausted, as was her coachman. She sent Risdon to bed at the inn, and had a message taken to Marmaduke.

A half hour later Marmaduke arrived, to confirm her worst fears. Mariotta had been badly hurt. But, Marmaduke insisted, there was nothing to worry about, Mariotta would be all right.

Marmaduke, it turned out, had realized from the beginning that a different girl had returned from Bath with him. He knew nothing of the twins, but had deduced that this was the only explanation.

"Well, you always were the smart one," said Diana with a smile. "I'm afraid I shall have to switch back, if Mariotta can manage to do it. I could stay somewhere, I suppose; but I don't have much money. I'll ask her how strong she feels." Thinking of Jack, Diana really did feel she couldn't go back to Ardwell. She had to escape him before she ruined her life. . . .

"You must help me, Marmaduke. Leave the library window unlocked, and I'll come in at midnight. Leave one of my night-gowns in the window seat."

Marmaduke didn't think much of all this, but he knew Diana. It was useless to argue.

Risdon dropped Diana off at the gate at midnight, and then went to wait in the little grove down the road. His orders were to leave if no one had come by two. Lacking Marmaduke's intelligence, he questioned nothing. The money he would be paid was enough.

Diana, vaguely enjoying herself, slipped into the library at midnight. She found the nightgown and quickly threw it on over her clothes. That way if anyone saw her, they would assume it was just Mariotta, wandering about in her sickness.

She crept to her own door, and slowly pushed it open.

Mariotta was asleep. Her cheeks were flushed, and she looked like she had a fever. Diana began to think the change back would have to be put off. She sat down in the chair opposite the bed and looked at her sister, moved by some very deep emotion she could not name.

Mariotta's eyes opened. At first she thought the figure in the chair was a dream, and then she realized it was her sister.

"Diana! I knew you would come! But so quickly!"

"Yes, it was quite a feat. How are you feeling?"

Mariotta sat up, a happy smile on her face.

"Fine, really. A bit tired is all. But it doesn't hurt any more. Shh! That sounds like father coming! Get behind the door. Sometimes he comes in to check!"

A few seconds later Black Walter knocked and softly called Diana's name. When there was no answer, he walked away.

Mariotta began to giggle.

"If he only knew! It is so funny!"

"All right, stop laughing, I'm sure it isn't good for you right now. I am here to change back, what do you think? It seems a logical time. I came because I had a dream . . . you know. Of your accident. Like the one when we were children. But I had a lot of difficulties, and one of us has to go right back, or everything will be discovered. So, do you want to, are you in condition to?"

Mariotta thought quickly. Really, it was the perfect solution. If she went back to Ardwell, she would have time to think about whether she loved Gerald or Drew. Maybe she'd forget Drew's kiss; maybe everything would go back to the way it had been in the beginning.

"Yes. But what about London, and our inheritance, and our grandmother?"

"I assume that we will still do it. We shall have to tell Gerald and Richard sometime soon. Let us agree to meet at our grandmother's in London the day before our birthday. Then we can reveal everything to them, we'll have them come meet us there."

Mariotta thought this would do. They began to tell each other all the recent events, but certain things were left out on both sides. Diana did not talk about Jack in any but the most casual way, and Mariotta did not mention that Drew, her good, trusted friend, the uncle of her beloved Gerald, had kissed her and completely changed her view of everything.

Richard and Gerald dominated their conversation, if not their thoughts. Lady Green came up several times, and Mariotta made sure to convey the degree of her kindness as well as her fascination.

"You will have to play Cherry in the play, Mariotta. Do you think you can learn it that quickly?"

"I don't see how I can," said Mariotta. "Can I be sick, and then say I've forgotten a lot of things?"

"Actually, that might be better in general. Yes. You'll have caught a terrible cold while in Bath. Mrs. Oakes will back you up, I'm sure. She was very sympathetic when I told her everything. I also warned her that there might be further developments."

Diana saw that Mariotta was far weaker than she would admit

to being, but she was determined to leave that very morning. They both felt very upset as Mariotta was dressing to leave, but they could not say anything, until it was time to go, and Diana was helping her sister through the French doors and walking with her down to the gate.

They kissed each other goodbye and Diana felt tears come to her eyes.

"Silly," said Mariotta, whose own eyes were wet, "we spend all our time saying farewell. We haven't even had time to know each other."

"But we've lived in each other's lives for a while. Surely that counts as knowing," said Diana.

Diana watched as the coach left. Risdon was completely amazed by the sight of two Mariottas, and kept exclaiming over it. Diana was very much afraid that the coachman would not be able to keep silent about such amazing events, but she paid him well and hoped for the best. It was the last money she had left, and she dearly hoped she would not need it in the future.

Diana went back to her own room in a depressed state. This was her home, but her thoughts were all of Ardwell, and Jack.

CHAPTER FOURTEEN

When at last she reached Ardwell, Mariotta was in a state of complete exhaustion. While she slept, the household buzzed with the news that Miss Mariotta was sick—and it might be serious.

Caroline did not give this information the attention it deserved. Lady Abingdon was still winning the battle for Edmund, and Caroline was deep in plans to expose her rival's ignorance of botany. So the matter of the sudden cold was filed away for the moment.

The next morning Mariotta felt much better, and Jenny pronounced her well enough to pass for a girl almost over a cold.

Her curiosity about the company gathered at Ardwell put Mariotta in a good mood. It would be so interesting to meet Richard Trelawny—what if he kissed her! Diana had not said what she might expect along those lines . . . and, this made her realize, Drew might kiss Diana, although that seemed less likely. This was all very enjoyable, a true adventure.

The company proved to be just what Diana had said they were—with the exception of Richard. After the naturalness of Drew and Gerald, Mariotta was unpleasantly struck by Trelawny's style, all punctiliousness, and it was a great strain to deal with him as a fiancé. She could not fathom what Diana had seen in him. Nothing could make up for such pomposity. Diana had described him as gentlemanly, but Carlton Drew, with his easy manners, was a gentleman; Trelawny was merely a fussy man too proud of his background.

Jack was a great relief, and even her mother seemed a welcome companion. Diana had certainly worked wonders there.

In the afternoon, reminding herself that she must act more like Diana, Mariotta settled down for a comfortable chat with Jack. They discussed his sister Mary, who was due to arrive back in England in a few weeks. She would go directly to London, where her husband's family lived. This news was so exciting that Mariotta almost told him that she would be in London then as well. It was very hard not to tell him, but she refrained, thinking that it would only be ten days or so before she could confess everything.

She was having a very enjoyable time with Jack when Richard came up, and with a proprietary air, asked her to come for a walk in the garden with him.

"Mariotta," he said when they were out of Jack's hearing, "I really cannot approve such a free and easy manner with Campbell."

Cool gray eyes surveyed him contemptuously.

"He is not *Campbell*, he is *Jack*, and he is one of my oldest friends."

Richard did not care for this answer, and proceeded to give her a lecture on what society, as opposed to her little Bath circle, would think of such easy familiarity. She was, after all, an engaged woman now. Mariotta realized, as she listened to Richard drone on, that it was going to be much more difficult than she had imagined to keep pretending to be Diana. The weeks stretched ahead like years.

On the day of the final performance of *The Beaux Stratagem*

Mariotta was very excited—it would be her first performance on a stage. Jack seemed amused by her visible agitation.

"Why are you so excited?"

"Because it is the last time I shall ever be on a stage, probably. My final performance. Somehow, it's exhilarating. Are you quite ready? I had a little trouble remembering everything, probably because I was sick. I think I shall read the lines a little differently tonight. For variety."

She played her role with enjoyment, and every time someone called her Cherry, she thought of Drew.

The play went well, and when it was over, Gussie Storbridge came up to Mariotta, her eyes shining with happiness.

"Oh, Mariotta, forgive me! I did not believe you when you said there was nothing between you and Jack, but now I do, I see it is true. You are not in love, after all."

Mariotta simply smiled uncomprehendingly, and wondered what Diana had been up to. This was very unexpected. She must have had a flirtation with Jack—understandable when one had seen Richard. . . . Well, there was something to find out . . .

At the supper after the performance Jack was especially gay, and whirled her around the room in a waltz—despite the fact that there was no music—just as he used to do when he and his sister came to visit. But Mariotta was busy thinking about what Gussie's remark might mean, and everything Jack said and did was analyzed in that light. She came to the conclusion that Diana did not love Richard, and might, just might, have fallen in love with Jack. It would be so wonderful . . . but no, she mustn't think about it. Diana would do what she thought was best, and she, Mariotta, must not interfere. But she could not stop building castles, and in bed that night she imagined a wonderful world in which she and Drew were married, and

Jack and Diana. And tedious Trelawny would go off to his disgusting cottage with Maria Coates, who obviously adored him.

It was noticed in passing by the others that her illness had produced some changes in Mariotta. Lady Abingdon found she no longer got such good advice about the war against Caroline, and Trelawny thought her much improved. The others detected greater vivacity and a willingness to be amused.

Lady Abingdon announced to her daughter that they would be leaving Ardwell very soon.

"But won't that leave the field to Caroline?"

"I wish her joy. I hope she spends every waking moment with Edmund. If he does not see my virtues then, I wash my hands of him."

Mariotta was admiring. "Spoken like a tartar, mother. Well said and true, as Jonathan Cabe would say."

The party gradually broke up. When Lady Abingdon left first, Edmund was tactless enough to say in Caroline's presence that the heart had gone out of the house party for him. Caroline took offense, and left the very next day, and her friend Lady Quennel followed quickly. After that it was a very short time before Edmund was alone with his plants, and he found himself missing Lady Abingdon.

Lady Quennel and Caroline made a point of meeting for an exchange of information as soon as was feasible. This took place at Lady Quennel's elegant house, which was one of the best residences on Lansdown Crescent. They had spent a great deal of time listening to servant's gossip and Lady Quennel had become suspicious of Marriota's illness.

"There is a mystery," she said. "A definite mystery. About Mariotta."

Caroline jerked to attention. "All I remember is that the coachman seemed to be lying. What else is there?"

"I have done some work since then, made inquiries," sniffed Lady Quennel, rubbing one of her enormous rings against her sleeve. "I do so hate to pry, but I would greatly dislike it if my friends, the Trelawnys, were *taken in*."

Information gathered by Lady Quennel, or rather, by her maid, had revealed that Mariotta had not stayed in Bath those two days, had not had influenza but something quite different, a cut of some kind on her head. And it was rumored that she had traveled all the way to Tunbridge Wells and back when she was supposedly in the house on Laura Place.

"Tunbridge Wells! They don't know anyone there, I'm sure of it. There is something havey-cavey here, and I mean to find it." Caroline's eyes shone. She did not like Mariotta, and did not want her as a sister-in-law. She felt it her duty to discover whether her brother knew of this affair, or, indeed, whether Lady Abingdon did.

She visited Laura Place the next afternoon, looking, as Jenny later said, like a rake with a dress on. The butler. Booth, gazed down at her with what seemed to Caroline a smirk on his face. She wished they had someone less tall, less forbidding.

Caroline was led to the drawing room, past Jenny. Jenny was busy, but something in Caroline's face, recalling a cat who had trapped the canary, made her find a reason to go into the drawing room, where she interrupted a scene of high drama.

"I have never heard such nonsense in my life! What can you mean? Ridiculous, and why would you come carrying such a tale about your own brother's fiancée?" Lady Abingdon was sputtering.

Jenny quickly closed the door, and ran upstairs to Mariotta's room.

"You'd best be prepared, miss! Caroline Trelawny is here and by the sound of it, she knows a lot. That one will find out the truth. I've no doubt that Risdon will tell her everything! He isn't so very intelligent, you know. She'll run rings around him."

Mariotta ran to consult with the housekeeper, Mrs. Oakes, who had been so helpful before.

"I don't know, miss, I'm afraid it will all come out. You'd best leave Bath, if you can. That's the only way to avoid a major inquisition."

Mariotta thought quickly. Leaving seemed by far the best idea, and she had just received a warm letter from Jack's sister Mary, who was already in London. It was early to go and meet Diana, but she could stay with Mary . . .

She took the letter with her to the dinner table. Her mother had not come to ask her about whatever Caroline had said, and Mariotta thought it was possible that her mother might not mention it.

Soon after they sat down, Mariotta mentioned that Mary had written, inviting her to come and visit. Mariotta saw the relief in her mother's face, and quickly pressed her advantage. Mary was a married woman, an appropriate chaperone; she had never been to London, that is, as far as her mother knew; she was supposed to see about the inheritance in a few weeks anyway. So why not go now?

Lady Abingdon felt conflicting emotions. If Mariotta were not here, no one could ask her anything, and nothing would be said to Edmund about it, in all probability. But her conscience would not let the real issue disappear so quickly.

She went to her daughter's room that evening at bedtime, and was visibly ill at ease.

"There is something I wish to ask, and you know that I can usually tell if you are lying, not that you would at your age, but . . . Did you make a journey to Tunbridge Wells when you were supposed to be in Bath? While I was at Ardwell?"

In all good conscience, Mariotta was able to say that she had most certainly not, since, in fact, Diana had made that particular trip.

Her mother almost laughed, so great was her relief.

"I knew it! It is that wretched Caroline! I do wish she were not going to be your sister-in-law. I am quite certain she does not wish you well, believing such stories!"

Mariotta got herself ready to go to London in less than two days, and was grateful that Richard was away on business, so no farewells were required *there*. Mariotta had found Bath terribly uninteresting after Chalford, and she prayed that London would take her mind off her problems.

Gerald would be in London, she told herself when she was traveling in the coach. But instead of Gerald, she kept seeing Drew, smiling, pushing back that one unruly brown lock . . . and kissing her. "Put it out of your mind, it will not happen again," he had said . . . but she wanted it to happen again. What was wrong with her?

Diana was sick of lying in bed, and if she had to drink any more herbal teas or oxtail soup she would certainly die. She was starving to death. This did nothing for her mood, and when the formerly much feared Carlton Drew was announced in her sick room, she was very annoyed. She could not imagine what the uncle of Mariotta's true love wanted. She supposed he had come to offer sympathy.

She was amazed to see a well-dressed, very attractive man of no more than thirty-five. He came up to her, bringing the last roses from his garden, as he said, and kissed her on the cheek. He called her Cherry. She was thankful that Mariotta had at least seen fit to tell her that he was called Drew and not Carlton, and that he had never wished to marry her, Diana. But she had certainly not prepared her for this man.

He paced restlessly, making a few conventional comments.

"I imagine," said Diana watching his nervousness, "that there is something unpleasant you wish to tell me."

He shot her a startled look, and gave a mirthless smile.

"You seem old to me today. I seem young. . . . What I have to tell you reflects no credit on me, I fear . . . but I hope you will listen, with all the compassion and understanding you can summon."

Diana's mood lifted. So, something interesting was about to happen.

"When I understood the depth of Gerald's feelings for you, but knew that he was still engaged to Miss Grayson, I determined to end his affectionate relationship with you any way I could. I decided to make you fall in love with me. I do not know whether I succeeded, but when I kissed you I realized what a scoundrel I had become. Then, when I saw you almost lifeless, lying there, I . . . knew I had to confess everything. I want you to know that I had very real affection for you, and only my fears for Gerald's future made me do this base thing. I will understand if you no longer wish to regard me as a friend, or even receive me, but I should regret the loss of such a friend as you. There, that is everything. I shall throw no further obstacles in Gerald's path. . . ."

Diana cursed Mariotta for having left all of this out. She had no idea of how to behave. She chose a neutral tone.

"Well, it is certainly unfair of you to have done such a thing, but I think . . . no harm has been done. Gerald still holds his place in my affections, but I am sure that you and I should remain friends as before. I suppose I can understand your fears. . . . I am hardly what one would call a good match, I see that. But love can make up for many things." Diana did not believe this last, but she knew that was how Mariotta would have felt. She was amazed that Gerald was already engaged. This certainly changed her picture of her sister's romance.

Drew looked at her for a moment, and then he quickly thanked her for her mercy, and said that yes, they would be friends. He was stiff, however, and left very quickly.

Diana's head was filled with conjecture. She thought he had seemed a little surprised that she felt nothing for him, that is, that Mariotta felt nothing. What had been the nature of that kiss? If it bore any relation to Jack's, she would be very worried about her sister.

It was a peculiarity of Diana's makeup that although she herself was determined to marry for position and a certain kind of compatibility, she wanted her sister Mariotta to marry for love. She told herself that this was because Mariotta was not mature enough to deal with a marriage based on anything else.

The next afternoon, Gerald appeared out of nowhere. He burst in upon her and pulled her to him with passion, raining kisses on her face.

"Just as beautiful as ever! How have we borne this separation!"

He continued on in this dramatic style, and Diana felt an acute sort of embarrassment. This, of course, could only be the famed Gerald, and he was certainly handsome enough, blond and manly looking; but she thought he was the most spoiled, conceited creature she'd ever seen. He did appear to have a certain amount of charm, but she thought him vastly inferior to his uncle. Cora was right. Mariotta had simply become infatu-ated. Surely she could not love this silly Romeo. . . .

Diana was glad to learn that he had to post back to London

immediately. She was very worried about her sister's future, and did not at all think that the problems were even on their way to being solved. Gerald told her, quite artlessly, that he had to get back to London to help Leila pick out the wallpapers for the house her parents had chosen to give them as a wedding present. She wanted to shake him and ask him what he was doing! This was certainly not an engagement that seemed to be over. Of course Mariotta might see it all through the haze of love, as one more romantic obstacle to be overcome.

The next day Diana came home from a ride to find Black Walter in one of his glass-smashing moods.

"Drunk as a lord and wild as a boar," whispered the butler in warning.

But Diana's stay with her mother had made her better able to handle this. She walked up to her father and took the glass out of his hand before it could follow the others in the fireplace.

"Now, father, sit down, and tell me what has happened. Perhaps I can help."

Bemused, Black Walter allowed himself to be led firmly to the sofa.

"I have troubles . . . no one helps . . . the house has been sold out from under me. . . ."

Diana knew all about that from Mariotta, and she also knew it was not the trouble now.

"And what else?"

He muttered and mumbled and it finally came out that he'd had a letter from Miss Loulou Freneau, a beautiful creature, much admired, who demanded that he come to see her in London or else she'd find someone else to love.

"And she is important to you?"

"I have asked her to be my wife."

Diana stifled the urge to laugh. She could not believe it.

But she knew she must control her impulse, and she did, as always.

"Let us go up to the city, then. You can stay with Bob Clare, I am sure he will be glad to see you, and I shall go to my grandmother. It is time for me to see about the inheritance, you know."

He seemed to sober up at this idea.

"Yes, I could go to Bob. But my mother . . . I don't know how she'll deal with you. . . . Might work, depends on her mood. But in any case, I heard that Cama went back yesterday, she'd certainly take you in, she's invited you to stay many times."

It was settled, but Diana wondered if she had done the right thing. Who knew what this Freneau person was? What if Black Walter really did intend to marry her, hard though it was to believe? But she knew she could not stand staying at Chalford. All she did was brood on all the moments she had spent with Jack. And then there was Trelawny, who' would be coming to see her in London, after her birthday, if Mariotta arranged matters as she was supposed to. . . . It was too awful to think about. What if she never saw Jack again. . . ?

Drew had returned from his visit to Diana in a confused frame of mind. On the one hand he had been greatly relieved to tell her the truth. On the other, he was stunned, and a little offended, to see how Diana had taken it. She seemed so remote, as if it were a matter of happy indifference to her. He thought back on their kiss, how she had curved into him; she *had* felt something, he knew it. But what had happened since? Had she thought of Gerald? Had the fall affected her more than was supposed?

He went to Cama with his tale, and she too was puzzled.

"In general it does not at all sound like her. Normally she would have wanted to talk about it all at length, find out everything, especially about Gerald, and so on. I am quite surprised.

I would help you, by speaking to her myself, but I must leave for London tomorrow—Cousin Jane is having a ball, and it is to be my official return to society. I shall be leaving here completely in another week, I think."

Drew was very sad to see her go, and decided to leave himself, to go north to see about a new shipping concern. Perhaps the journey would help him to come to a decision about Diana. As for Gerald, there was no doubt in his mind that he was going to marry Leila—while claiming to love Diana up to the last moment.

But on his trip he saw it clearly: Gerald must be forced to marry Diana. That would be the only way to make up to her for what they had done. He would have to determine, of course, that the boy really did love her, and not Leila. But if he could bring it about, he would. He was halfway to Scotland when he turned his coach around and headed back to London, wondering if he were mad, but feeling much better. At least he was taking action. But the cost to himself would be high, of that he had no doubt.

CHAPTER FIFTEEN

There may have been a more selfish woman in London than Althea, Lady Chalford, but no one of her acquaintance could think of one. Now sixty-seven, she refused to give up her dinners for the powerful, her flirtations, or her diamonds. Age mattered only for others, especially her enemy, Jane Courtland. Lady Chalford liked to point out that Jane was actually a year older than she claimed, and that they had been to school together, though, as she said, no one could believe it, so old did Jane look now.

Lady Chalford no longer rose before noon, her one concession to age, and so it was that Mariotta was cooling her heels in the blue salon of the Cavendish Square mansion known as Chalford House. Mariotta did not mind waiting in the least, but used the time to examine all the furnishings and handle all the curios in the cabinets. The splendor, the luxury, was overwhelming. The paintings looked to be genuine, and all were recognizable works of very famous artists, most of them Italian. The furniture was entirely French, and the rugs Persian. All in all, an incredible house, fit for royalty, really. And so enormous, from what Mariotta could see. Unlike the other houses in the area, there was quite a bit of land around Chalford House, and Mariotta imagined that in price, it must be comparable to the Prince Regent's home. She could not say why she was thinking in terms of value, something she never did generally, but Mariotta felt that everything in this house had been chosen for its price: *Only the most expensive need apply* could have been engraved over Lady Chalford's door.

Mariotta had gone straight to Jack's sister Mary upon arrival, but her friend was not sure that approaching Lady Chalford would be either easy or pleasant.

"She is not precisely the usual sort of grandmother," said Mary hesitantly. "She was a great beauty, and she has still got a number of elderly admirers. But that is not the main thing. She is a powerful, haughty woman, and she may very well not wish to have grandchildren hanging about. . . . I don't really know, but those who know her say that she can be very . . . temperamental. I would not like you to be treated badly."

Mariotta just laughed. "Oh, now don't worry, Mary! She is my grandmother, it will be different with me."

But now, watching how the servants bustled about, obviously afraid of being caught doing nothing, she began to think that Mary might not have been so wide of the mark.

After what seemed a very long time, the butler returned and announced that Lady Chalford would see her now.

The bedroom was decorated in shades of gold, and, like the rest of the house, seemed stuffed with objects. It took a while to locate her grandmother in all this welter of side tables and plants and sculpture, but she finally heard the voice from a corner, where a large mirror was set up.

"So, you have finally come to see me. Come here, let me look at you."

An imperious face could be seen from under a preposterous

lace cap. She was sitting in a gold silk dressing gown, having some strange-looking little man make up her face. He did not seem to exist, at least as far as her grandmother was concerned.

"Yes. The image of your father, who was the image of my late husband, Chalford. A real Chalford, that's what you are. . . . And when may I expect her, your sister, that is?"

"I don't know, exactly. But within the week, certainly. We are going to receive our inheritance on our birthday."

The sharp black eyes stopped their constant movement for a second and bored into Mariotta.

"Do you have any idea of how much it will be?"

Mariotta sensed that the question was not casual.

"No, I have no idea. It has always been secret—why, I don't know. But you must have an idea. Why would my grandfather make a secret bequest, not to be opened until we were of age?"

Lady Chalford patted her bleached hair. "Well, he was a *most eccentric man*. He left the bulk of the estate to me, of course, but he left this house to his attorney! Of course the attorney is a very old friend, and there has never been any question of anyone but me living here, but you see! Remarkably eccentric! I have no idea what he was thinking of. I expect he has left you some of his mother's jewelry, or some such thing. I seem to remember that not everything came to me. . . . Well, I'm sure I wish you something wonderful. I imagine your mother is still pinching pennies?"

Mariotta very much disliked the tone of this last, and she bristled.

"I don't think it is really anything I should like to discuss. You can have little interest in her, since you have seen her only once in your life."

The rouge had been applied, and now an imperious cough indicated that Lady Chalford's dresser should come and help her. She gave Mariotta a look, however, which promised that anyone who dared be impudent did not last long around her. Mariotta stiffened. She would not be treated in such a way.

"I am sorry, grandmamma, but I am not used to people speaking to me as if I were ten years old!"

This was too much for Lady Chalford. She did not brook such behavior.

"Martins, come and take this ill-bred creature away!" she screamed to her butler, who was just outside the door.

Mariotta did not wait for him, but stormed downstairs. She was waiting for her cloak when the door opened and Diana was shown in.

"Oh, Diana, I am so glad to see you!"

They kissed each other warmly, and quickly exchanged explanations of their early arrivals in London.

"But Diana, our grandmother is not . . . what I had expected! I do not think that we can deal with her."

Diana heard briefly about her sister's reception, and advised that they go to Lady Green, as their father had suggested.

They were about to leave when Lady Chalford swept to the head of the stairs and gazed down like a blond eagle, no doubt about to scream some final imprecation at her grandchild. But the words died on her lips as she saw not one, but two, dark curly heads.

"But . . . you are identical!"

She had moved halfway down the staircase.

Diana looked up at her coolly. "Did you not even know that we are twins, ma'am?"

"Of course, you ninny. But I did not realize that you were completely identical; often twins are not."

"Farewell, *grandmother*, we will take our leave now, if you have no objection."

"But I do. You must stay. Martins, take them to the breakfast room; give them what they want. I shall be down shortly. And mind the ham this time."

Mariotta was amazed by this development and lost no time in telling her sister that their grandmother was vicious and completely untrustworthy, and that they should leave. This, much to the enjoyment of the servants, was said in a perfectly audible voice.

"But really, we have no choice. Let us see what she has to offer us. We really should not be throwing ourselves on Cama's doorstep, not unless it is very necessary."

When Lady Chalford finally appeared in the breakfast room, where the sisters had finished an enormous meal, she was in a very different mood.

"I must beg your forgiveness, children, but I am always in a terrible mood in the morning. And noon is my morning. And I was not prepared for your arrival, I had no idea."

She began to talk about the dinners she would give, the balls they would attend, vouchers for Almack's and so on, leaving no doubt in the minds of the twins that she planned to do them proud and introduce them to the ton.

Before they could even discuss it, they were swept off to Mme. Dulaine, a very expensive dressmaker in Bruton Street, where they were fitted out with entire wardrobes. The only problem was that everything was identical.

"What is she intending?" whispered Mariotta. "Why are the clothes the same?"

"It's some kind of trick," whispered Diana as she put on a green velvet pelisse. "She's got something in mind, no doubt about it. Wants us to look exactly alike—to impress some one, perhaps? But we can always wear the clothes at different times. At any rate, I am not going to turn down clothes like these, I assure you. We'll see what she wants when the time comes, is my feeling."

But Mariotta could not be so sanguine. When Lady Chalford smiled, it never reached her eyes. This was a woman with an eternal hidden motive. But Diana seemed sure they would manage her, and after all, she knew more of the world. . . .

Before the twins could do anything, their grandmother had sent letters to their parents, informing them in the most arrogant phrases, that their daughters had come to her for protection, and "that which you seem unable to provide, namely, an atmosphere of elegance and refinement." She declared that she expected no interference from these parents, and that the girls, in any case, had no wish to see the people who separated them so brutally, and then lied to them.

When Diana read a copy of the letter she was horrified.

"What will they think of us!"

"Nothing, Diana. They know the Empress. They'll assume it's all her doing, that we had nothing to say to it."

"I hope so, but I'm afraid that mother might think it true."

"No, she won't. Besides, she's so busy with Edmund that I doubt she'll pay it much attention. I expect that they will announce their impending marriage any time now."

Very gradually, over the course of the next week, they began to see what their grandmother needed them for. She had a social rival, Jane, Lady Courtland, a legendary hostess who had never been beautiful but had broken a score of hearts just the same. The rival had a niece newly come to town, and the niece was supposed to be very lovely, indeed. It was expected that she would outshine everyone at the next major event, the Tarrants' ball. But Lady Chalford, accompanied by her stunning granddaughters, would take care of that dream!

They got their first look at their grandmother's rival at the

Italian Opera. In a box opposite sat Lady Courtland and her niece, a lovely blond girl. They took turns looking through the opera glasses at the very surprising Lady Courtland, who turned out to be a rotund little person with a very merry expression. But the niece was really quite lovely.

"Yes," said their grandmother, fanning herself languidly, "that is the chit. Leila Grayson is her name. They say she's already engaged to some well-bred pauper, but I don't credit it. Why would they allow it, when she has only just been introduced to society?"

Mariotta sat turned to ice. The girl opposite looked very angelic. . . . She dearly wished Drew were in London. He would find some way to advise her. . . . She could tell Diana, but Diana wouldn't be able to help the way Drew could. And what of her own attitude? Did she want Gerald to marry the girl opposite? Was that her real desire?

That night as they got ready for bed Mariotta told Diana who the girl at the opera was.

"And you feel guilty, is that it? But it is surely up to Gerald, isn't it? If he loves you, you can't expect him to really want to marry her. I think it's quite clear."

But Mariotta did not think it clear in the least.

"But I don't know myself. . . . Maybe I don't want him to . . ."

Diana looked at her sister, but said nothing. She longed to tell her that Gerald was completely wrong for her, and that she would be well rid of him, but she felt that it would be interfering. She had not yet told her sister that Carlton Drew had tried to make her fall in love with him. From what she saw, it did not matter; Gerald was on her sister's mind, not Drew. She pretended to fall asleep, feeling that was the only way she would keep herself from being too frank.

But it was Mariotta who really fell asleep, and Diana who lay awake for hours. At the opera she had seen the back of a tall man with dark curly hair, and had been sure it was Jack. But he turned, and it was not. In that moment she realized just how much she missed seeing him every day.

But Richard was due in town any day now. The idea of seeing him made her panic. If only she could have a little more time to think. . . . What would happen when he heard the scandalous tale of the trip to Tunbridge Wells, and the exchange? His sister would certainly make sure he knew. . . . Would he cry off? she wondered. And discovered that she really did not care very much whether he did.

When she fell asleep she dreamed of a mustached officer who swept her up on his horse and rode off with her, laughing as she protested.

Lady Chalford revealed her plans to them the next morning, that is to say, noon. She would give a very select dinner party for her granddaughters, and invite her enemy, Lady Courtland, to underscore, as it were, her assurance that the Abingdon twins could outshine anyone. She did not consult them about the guest list or the seating arrangements, but she did warn the twins that Leila would certainly be looking her best, and so would they if she had anything to say to it.

Mariotta was in a state of nerves, and nothing Diana could do seemed to help. She could not be calm about actually meeting and talking to Gerald's fiancée, the girl she would supplant.

But Lady Courtland, quite a strategist herself, arrived ahead of the other guests, and sent Leila up to talk to the twins. She shyly introduced herself and said that she thought they were the most beautiful girls in London. This quite broke the ice.

"I wish Cama were here tonight," said Leila almost to herself.

Mariotta looked up. "Do you mean Lady Green?"

"Yes, do you know her?"

"Very well! Is she a friend of yours, then?"

"No, that is, now she is, but she is really Aunt Jane's friend—they are very distant relations and call each other cousin. She is quite wonderful, I think."

And so began a long and very interesting conversation about Cama, including all the rumors each had heard. Before the dinner began Leila and Mariotta had become extremely friendly, making Diana wonder if she were going mad. Mariotta was really incredible! She was somewhat worried about Cama's relationship with Lady Courtland: would Cama be less inclined to give them help if they needed it, if she knew that Mariotta was Leila's secret rival? For her external calm masked Diana's very real conviction that their grandmother tired very quickly of people, especially unimportant people. They would not be able to stay long with her before she began to pick fights with them.

Mariotta and Diana entered the drawing room together, five minutes after Leila made her entrance. They were dressed in simple white dresses, with pearls of the highest quality setting off their pink and white coloring. For a moment all conversation ceased. Alone they would each have been striking, but together they were simply dazzling. Lady Chalford smiled complacently as she watched Lady Courtland's face.

The Empress had placed the young ladies next to men she considered suitable. Observing the happy smiles these two gentlemen were giving their partners, she felt satisfied.

Lady Chalford kept close watch on her guests. Her grand-daughters were a credit to her. Diana was quite visibly at ease, taking part in various discussions with tact and elegance. Mariotta was in a different style, charming by her directness and high spirits.

But the most glorious victory had to be the look on Jane

Courtland's face when the full horror of it dawned on her: two rivals, and identical! All of London would stare only at the Abingdon twins, and Leila Grayson would be cast into the shade wherever they appeared together. And Lady Chalford intended to see that they went everywhere. The season did not begin until April, but that time would be used wisely, she'd make sure of that. Poor Jane Courtland!

Mariotta and Diana were fascinated by Lady Courtland, a small round woman, almost buried by her jewelry. She might be short physically, but she was large in spirit. Her black eyes missed nothing, and her wit was as sharp as her person was soft. She was good-natured and captivating in a way that Lady Chalford would never comprehend. But she had no intention of letting Lady Chalford get away with anything, as her witticisms at the end of the dinner showed.

"Nice, unpretentious dinner, Althea, just the way I like it. So glad you didn't exert yourself too much for us. I don't like my friends to exhaust their resources."

This was a pointed comment on the smallness of the portions, which Lady Chalford preferred to the large ones prevailing at other dinners. The Empress was vain of her slender figure, and was determined that no one should overeat at her table.

"I thought," answered Lady Chalford in her loud clear voice, "that you were on the vinegar and biscuit diet, Jane. I didn't dream that you would require two servings of duck as well as all those jellies and creams. Do forgive me. I should have known that you would need more."

But Jane could be teased about her size, and merely bubbled over with infectious laughter, of the kind which had won her an earl despite her looks.

Diana and Mariotta shot each other looks which conveyed the information that they were both on Lady Courtland's side.

When the ladies and gentlemen separated after dinner, the twins quickly sat down in a corner together.

"Oh, Diana! Leila is so nice. It makes me feel like such a villainess!"

"Now, stop, calm yourself. She is very nice, but perhaps she would be unhappy with Gerald, did you ever think of that? And obviously she will have no trouble finding someone else even better, if she wishes."

This was very comforting to Mariotta. "What do you suppose grandmother is up to? I can't believe that it is all just for Jane's benefit. It does not seem enough."

"I agree. But we do not have enough information to guess what it is."

Lady Chalford went to bed happy. She was beginning to see a way out of her difficulties. Wretched Gordon would not win in the end! Lady Chalford once again cursed the memory of her dead husband. How could he have done it, the fool!

CHAPTER SIXTEEN

Jack Campbell was very exasperated to hear the news that the Abingdons had left Chalford and gone to London. He had made a trip for nothing, and the fact that he was making a fool of himself as well did not help his mood.

The housekeeper made him sit down and have some cheese and ham while the boys took care of his hard-driven horse.

So it was that when Carlton Drew rode over to see Diana some time later he found an unknown gentleman lounging in the dining room with a plate of food in front of him.

The butler had suggested that Drew have a talk with "Mr. Campbell," since they both were going to have to go to London to see Miss Diana. This information made Drew a little stiff in his manner when they were introduced.

"It is the damnedest business," said Jack. "I rode all that way, with one thing on my mind, and now I am cheated of it. It simply did not occur to me that dearest Diana would be gone."

There was a sarcastic intonation here that Drew disliked.

"I had come to see her myself, you see. Had something serious to discuss."

"She seems to have many friends here," said Jack warily. "Are you an *old* friend?"

"You keep yourself informed as to the degree of her various friendships?" A well-bred eyebrow was raised. Drew was beginning to be more than a little annoyed with this large fellow who was lounging about in someone else's house.

Jack looked at Drew closely, and then made a decision.

"Tell me, did *your* Diana change lately, in small ways?"

At first Drew wasn't going to answer, but he changed his mind. Something in Jack's eyes made him think he could trust him.

"Well, yes . . . after the accident, she was very different."

"Accident? Now that would be interesting to hear about. Please tell me what you can."

When Drew finished his recital of the facts, leaving out his visit to the patient, but remarking that her attitude to him was different, Jack stretched his legs out and smiled.

"Well, I have some news for you, Lord Drew. We are dealing with identical twins. I suspected that they changed places, and now I think they changed back. I was pretty sure, but until now I had no explanation. *Your* Diana is really Mariotta. Mine is the real Diana."

Drew was too stunned to believe it at first, but then Jack told him about his first visit to Chalford, and the girl who looked like Mariotta, Mariotta's impulsiveness, and Diana's desire to live in Bath. All together it was very convincing, and it explained the sudden change that Drew had seen.

They both left Chalford and rode over to Drew Hall, full of plans.

The next morning they were on the road to London, and managed to reach it in record time. They quickly made their way to the unfashionable district where Black Walter was living.

Black Walter was in his cups, and in a mood which matched his name. He did not even ask why they had come, but began immediately railing against women.

"Vile! Devil's spawn! Better to be a monk!"

The idea of Black Walter as a monk was funny enough, but his tragic poses made it difficult to maintain a serious demeanor. He managed to knock over a glass and send a plate flying to the floor, all in the course of telling them about what a betrayer one Loulou Freneau was.

"What did she do?" asked Jack, who did not really care to know.

"She demands that I marry her. Introduce her to my friends and family. Now. You understand, I always intended to marry her, but just not at the moment. And you two no doubt know about my daughters—yes, I discovered how they deceived, lied to me! They have gone to live with my mother. She wrote me a letter, poisonous as only she can compose them. Viper! Here, read it yourselves!"

Drew read the letter, but found it difficult to concentrate. He knew what Mariotta would say if she knew her father was planning to marry Loulou. It was but the latest in a long line of insults to the polite world provided by Black Walter. But Loulou! A stepmother to the twins! He did not know her, but he knew enough about her from what Walter had told him over a drink to know that she was supremely unsuitable.

Jack read the letter and understood that Lady Chalford would be very difficult to deal with. He was certain that neither girl had seen the letter before it was sent, and he told Black Walter so.

"Oh, I know it my boy! I know how the harpy does her work!"

"Well, Walter, we are going to see Lady Green. She may be able to give us some information about the twins. I don't think we want to brave the icy weather in Cavendish Square until we know how the land lies."

Black Walter looked very much as if he would like to be invited to go along to see Cama, but they did not react to his remarks to the effect that he hadn't had a good meal since he came to the city, and that he'd heard that Cama had a good cook. Drew firmly led Jack out.

"Lord, man, did you hear! Loulou Freneau!"

"What is she like? Her name?"

"Precisely. An opera dancer, no better than she should be. Incredibly stupid, and incredibly beautiful."

"Not so stupid," said Jack. "She's got Black Walter actually considering marriage. That's something no one else has done in a long time, from what I've heard."

They arrived at Cama's house in Jermyn Street just as she was sitting down to dinner.

"Cook," she called out as soon as she caught sight of them in the hall, "we are going to have two more for dinner. We will need enough for two young savages—look to be starving they do."

Like Mariotta, Jack was very struck by Cama's youthful appearance. She was dressed in regal purple and glittered with diamonds—she was going out after dinner to a private gambling house with friends. Cama's dark eyes surveyed this new player in the drama of the twins.

"Well," she began with a smile, "I already know there are twins—my cousin Jane has seen them. Was there a switch?"

Amazed by her intuition, the gentlemen said that there indeed had been, and they briefly sketched the complications for her. She was not told that Jack was in love with Diana, and that Drew had a special interest in Mariotta, but she deduced as much from their conversation.

"*Very* interesting. A problem to be solved, I see. You know, I was quite surprised to find out that the very same Leila Grayson who is engaged to Gerald is my cousin's niece. Quite a complication for Mariotta, I should imagine. And Leila took a great liking to Mariotta at a dinner Lady Chalford gave. . . . But there are, I must report, *complications*."

"Of what sort?" Drew knew this word was always very bad when used by Cama.

"Their grandmother is not precisely a *benevolent* despot, but you get the idea. I wonder if Walter is somewhere in London . . . he might be able to give us some ideas of how to approach Lady Chalford."

Drew and Jack began to laugh.

"No, no, he has no ideas at all! He's staying near Billingsgate, with a friend. Very bitter about everything." Drew then told Cama about Black Walter's plans to marry Loulou Freneau.

Cama became still. "Very fine of him, I must say! The man has absolutely no sense! She is . . . well, I shall just have to help him, then. Perhaps I might give a small dinner, and introduce her to some of his friends and relations."

"Really! Cama, what are you thinking of? Not at all the thing. She's straight from the stage, with no genius to recommend her!"

But Jack only smiled lazily and said that anything Lady Green proposed to do would meet with his approval.

Cama rewarded Jack with a smile and some more Madeira. Such a charming fellow, and so awake on all suits. . . . It was really quite unfortunate that he was so young and she was so old. . . .

She wrote down Walter's address and shooed them out, saying that they must come back the next day, when she would have things thought through.

They walked down the street together, enjoying the London dusk and the autumn bite in the air.

"Let's go to White's, they have a good dinner," Drew suggested.

"I belong to Boodles, but as you wish."

"And how did you like Cama?"

"A wonderful creature. She'll help us, of that I'm certain. That is, if we can be helped. And to put herself out for Black Walter . . . But she has something else in mind, doesn't she?"

"Oh, yes, nothing is ever simple with her. But you know, she has undoubtedly decided that I want to marry Mariotta, and nothing could be further from my thoughts. I merely do not want to see her throw herself away on Gerald, unless she truly loves him. I am here only in the capacity of a friend, you know. I do hope Cama has not got the wrong bee in her bonnet."

Jack looked at Drew as if he very much doubted these words, but all he said was that he hoped they would be invited to Black Walter's engagement dinner.

They spent the evening together, having a very good time, gambling and talking about whatever interested them. It was clear to each that they had a great deal in common, and could become friends quite easily.

Around midnight they each went to their quarters, Jack to his house on Half Moon Street, and Drew to his rooms in the Albany.

Drew was just sitting down to have a cigar and think over the evening's events when his man told him that his nephew was waiting to see him.

Gerald seemed to be in an exalted state, and a flash of anxiety went through Drew. This was justified by what Gerald had to say, standing before him in the attitude of Kean playing Hamlet.

"I have decided to do what is right, uncle. I must give up Leila and marry Diana, who is, it is true, poor and without advantages, but she is beautiful and good. I must do the correct thing. I have sent a letter to Leila, telling her that we can no longer consider ourselves engaged, since I have committed myself to another."

Drew tried to point out that, if anything, he owed Leila more than he did Diana. He also told him that Diana's real name was Mariotta, and that there had been some very mysterious events at Chalford. But when he was finished explaining, Gerald merely thought Mariotta even more wonderful, to have managed to pull it off.

"A resourceful girl! That's what a diplomat needs in a wife."

Drew wanted to shake him until all that blond hair fell out, but he gave up. Gerald now saw himself as a hero. Nothing and no one but Mariotta would change his views.

With this in mind, Drew decided to brave the cold waters of Cavendish Square the next day, before Gerald could do so. After all, he still owed Mariotta an explanation. No doubt Diana had told her about his visit to the sick room, but he should do it himself anyway. And if she wanted Gerald still, she should have him, but she must be told of the dangers.

He was deposited by a hack in front of the massive Chalford House. The butler who answered his knock seemed haughtily surprised. He did not know this fellow, therefore he could not be worth knowing, no matter how fine his clothes.

"Lord Drew for Miss Mariotta Abingdon? I shall see if she is at home."

Drew was forced to sit in the hall, like a boy selling apples, while the butler, no doubt, consulted with Lady Chalford.

"Who? Lord Drew? Lord Drew! I knew his father, and his grandfather! How very interesting. But he does not know her, he cannot be permitted to see her. Send him to me."

Drew was ushered into Lady Chalford's boudoir, where he was subjected to an exhaustive interrogation, to which he gave nothing but false answers. He had a message from her father, at Chalford. He was an old family friend. He had known her as a child. Yes, she was a bit impulsive. No, he could not give the message to Lady Chalford, he must give it to her personally.

Lady Chalford had called up all of her known information about the Drews, and realized that the young man before her, so well-mannered and well turned out, had a vast fortune and managed those of his relatives. His contacts in the economic center of London, the City, were many. He would be a good man to cultivate. With all of this in mind she graciously gave her permission and allowed him to see Mariotta alone, but with her lady's companion, Miss Forbes, at the other end of the large drawing room. Drew did not think this qualified as alone, but it was better than he had expected.

Mariotta and Diana were in the small back sitting room, the only room they felt comfortable in, since it had none of the magnificent furniture found everywhere else in the house, but was simply comfortable and cozy. They were trying to write letters, but unsuccessfully. They were happy to hear someone come to the door.

"A Lord Drew, for Miss Mariotta."

Mariotta's pen fell to the carpet. She gave Diana a look of fear combined with delight.

"How do I look? What shall I do? What can he want? . . . Oh, I don't know how to be! He has asked for me by my real name!"

Diana said thatone visit to Chalford would have been enough to make everyone realize that there had been an exchange.

Mariotta took a deep breath and left, leaving her sister to meditate on Drew's confession and the possible interpretations of her sister's distraught behavior.

The hallway seemed very long, Mariotta noticed. She wanted

to run to him, she was so happy to think she would see him again.

He smiled at her in greeting and gestured in the direction of Miss Forbes, sitting like a mountain at the end of the room.

He was pale, she saw, paler than she remembered. And the lock of brown hair was down on his forehead, and the most understanding, warm hazel eyes were smiling at her.

Mariotta was dressed in a simple pale yellow muslin, but Drew thought she had never been so dazzlingly beautiful. He looked into that warm little face and began to smile.

"Lady Chalford likes understated elegance, I see," he said, looking around at the incredibly overdone room, a sea of marble-topped mahogany and brocade.

"Diana calls this Museum Hall . . . but, what brings you to London? Business?"

"No, not really . . . I have come to tell you that Gerald has finally sent a letter to Leila . . . and I hope I may wish you a happy engagement any time now. You have not . . . changed in your feelings for him?"

He managed a smile of congratulation, but he could not have said another word if his life depended on it.

Mariotta was silent. She was happy—disturbed—it was wonderful—it was frightening. She did not know what to think, but she knew she was supposed to be happy, so she gave a weak smile.

But Drew's mind was now on something else. He stood up and began pacing nervously about the room, visibly disturbing their chaperone.

"Whatever is the matter, Drew? Why are you pacing?"

He stopped, and sat down beside her. "I have something to confess. Your sister may have already told you. . . . I thought she was you, after the accident. Those weeks at Chalford, when we were together . . . I was deliberately trying to fascinate you, make you fall in love with me . . . so that you would not marry Gerald. I wished him to marry Leila, so that he would have some money and a girl who would suit him. I thought what he felt for you was merely infatuation. You are so beautiful that I thought that was all there was to it. . . . So, you see, I did a reprehensible thing . . ."

Mariotta's eyes were very bright. "Do not feel bad, Drew. No harm was done, was it?"

He wanted to say that the harm had been done to himself, but he did not.

"I suppose not, but my intentions were anything but noble."

She was looking up at him, the intense gray eyes were questioning. But all he could do was look, when he really wanted to take her in his arms.

"And was your friendship pretend as well?"

He took her hands in his and laughed involuntarily.

"No, Cherry, never that. We are closer friends than I even dreamed we would be. At least I hope we still are."

"Oh, yes, forever, Drew."

He managed to assume his customary light manner.

"Now we are done, all confessed, all absolved. I know you will want to make plans with Gerald. He said he would see you tomorrow at the Tarrant's ball. I'm quite sure that your grandmother would never let him see you here, she's a high stickler, I'll say that for her. I am going now, but I want you to remember—if there is anything you need, come to me."

This last was said with an emphasis which appeared strange to Mariotta. A moment later he was gone, after a brief kiss on her hand.

She sat in the salon for some twenty minutes, but she could make no sense out of what she felt. It was, of course, wonderful that Gerald and she would at last be officially engaged, but her thoughts kept shifting to Drew, how sad he had looked, how worried he had been about deceiving her. She felt sorry for him. She did not wish him to feel so guilty.

The impatient Diana came to find her and demanded to know why she had not come back with the news.

"I don't know. . . . I have been sitting here, trying to understand what it is I think. Gerald has finally written Leila, and Drew made his confession, which, apparently, he had already made to you." Mariotta looked a trifle hurt.

"Dear sister! I did not feel I could tell you. It wasn't my business, and since you were still in love with Gerald, I didn't think it could matter. . . . Why are you crying, you silly goose? Or are you pretending, you are so good at that."

"No, it's real, and I don't *know* why I'm crying. I suppose it's the idea that finally, I'll get married . . ."

Diana was not so sure of that, but she didn't know what to do. She did not believe in prying into other people's private feelings, but she had her own opinion about all of this just the same. Why could her sister not see that Gerald was wrong, and that she didn't even really want him? She was obviously still very blind to Drew, and what Drew felt for her. . . .

The next morning Mariotta stayed in bed, and Diana went off to ride in Rotten Row.

She was resting her horse and looking at the dark clouds that threatened rain when she heard that familiar caressing voice.

"'Her lips are honeycombs' . . . do you recall that line?"

"And the one that follows as well: 'I wish there had been bees too, to have stung you for your impudence.' And where do you come from, Jack, on this gloomy London day?"

"From my house on Half Moon Street. And I am in London to see how Mr. Trelawny fares."

His white teeth flashed in a mocking smile. He was so infuriating!

"I am expecting Mr. Trelawny any time now. Is that what you wished to know? He has finished the plans for our house, and plans to announce the marriage to his relatives here."

Diana was very collected, annoyed by his impudence, but her pulse was racing, and she could not stop thinking of his mouth, and the kiss he had no right to take.

But Jack was not taking their banter as he usually did. His face turned cold, his voice dripped disdain.

"I see. I was wrong to think that the calculating Diana had a heart, or perhaps discovered one at Ardwell. You are a bad bargain for anyone, my girl. I was fool enough to fall in love with you! Yes! You may laugh if you like. I knew I was dealing with Diana, not Mariotta, if that is what worries you. You are not at all alike. Mariotta knows how to love. I pity poor Trelawny, pompous though he is. Even he does not deserve a china doll with a mercenary streak where her heart should be!"

Diana flushed angrily and without thinking drew back her arm and slapped him as hard as she could, maddened beyond speech.

His eyes were cold blue ice. "So, she is not even well-bred. Poor, poor Trelawny."

He rode away, leaving a Diana who was horrified at what she had done. She had never done anything remotely resembling this before. What had possessed her? She began to cry tears of anger as she rode home, hoping no one would see her like this.

Mariotta took one look at her sister's face, and followed her to her room.

It was some time before Diana was coherent, but she managed to get out enough for Mariotta to piece together the general scene.

"I cannot credit it! Jack insulted you? But why?"

"Oh, he did not like the fact that I am still going to marry Richard. But do not pay attention to me! It is simply an attack of nerves. Jack was just Jack, that's all. He called me heartless and mercenary . . . and I slapped him."

Mariotta stopped twisting her handkerchief. Mariotta knew her sister well enough now to know that Diana did not cry or engage in public gestures, such as slapping someone like Jack in Hyde Park. This was astonishing, and worthy of some prolonged cogitation.

"Well," sniffed Mariotta, "you will tell me the whole when you are ready, but it was decidedly *not* a case of nerves! I am your sister, Diana. I feel what you feel, but I shall ask you nothing further. But don't tell such fibs! You have never had an 'attack of nerves!'"

There was something strangely comforting in Mariotta's sternness, Diana thought. If only they had grown up together, perhaps everything would be different, and she would not feel this lead weight in her heart when she thought of the look on Jack's face as he said those hateful words.

CHAPTER SEVENTEEN

The Tarrants' ball was a sad crush. Everyone noted with satisfaction that they formed part of the huge crowd.

The Abingdon twins, against their will dressed alike, took all eyes. In silvery gauze with dark blue ribbons, set off by the exquisite sapphire earrings which were a present from their grandmother, they were stunning. But they were uncomfortable seeing each other on the dance floor, feeling that a mirror was constantly present, weaving in and out of the crowd.

It was certainly going to be a difficult night: Mariotta caught sight of Gerald, and her happiness at seeing him was tainted by the realization that Leila would arrive at any moment—now, in all likelihood, fully aware of who her rival was.

"Diana, what shall I do?" she hissed to her sister as Gerald approached on one side and Leila and her aunt, along with Cama, came in the main door.

"Nothing. Let him deal with it." If he can, was Diana's unspoken thought.

Gerald was upon them then, kissing their hands, talking all sorts of delightful nonsense about their dazzling effect on the company.

Diana's eyes were onthe Courtland party, however, which had just taken in a new member: Jack Campbell, who beckoned Lord Drew to join them as well.

Diana had been trying to prepare herself to behave calmly if she met Jack soon; but now the color rose in her cheeks, she could feel the warmth, and she had to turn away. She could not bear to meet his eyes, even accidentally.

Mariotta pulled at her sister's arm. Diana looked and saw that Drew and Leila were coming toward them. And Leila was smiling.

Gerald looked ready to bolt from the spot, but Mariotta held his arm. Diana shot him a contemptuous look which left him in no doubt as to how one of the twins felt about him.

"Gerald! Such a wonderful surprise! And you have met the dear twins, simply wonderful, aren't they. Had you met before?"

It burst upon all of them then that Leila must not have received the letter from Gerald. Mariotta took her hand away, Gerald relaxed visibly, and Drew smiled mysteriously.

Gerald was virtually forced to ask his official fiancée for a dance then and there, and Drew had a word with Mariotta.

"I don't think we wish to spoil the child's evening. Let us say nothing."

"Of course, Drew! Did you imagine I would say something? It is really up to Gerald."

"And we know what he will do," said Drew dryly.

"Yes, darling, he doesn't exactly impress one as brave, does he," interrupted Diana, who could not bear to let this chance go by without a reminder of how spineless Gerald was.

"It is just that Leila is so sweet that he does not wish to wound her." This, from Mariotta, made Drew and Diana both feel it was hopeless. She was blind and would not see.

Mariotta tapped her fan mechanically.

"You must dance with Drew, Diana. I'm sure he dances well."

Diana thought she would love to dance, love anything which would take her away from the sight of Jack, talking gaily to a pretty little redhead.

While they danced, Mariotta went up to Jack and took him away from his companion, claiming an emergency.

"Jack, what has happened! Diana is in the most despondent frame of mind. What did you say?"

Jack looked down at her and sighed. "I told her the truth. That I loved her. That she is heartless. She told me that she is going ahead with the marriage to Trelawny. What can be her reason? I am convinced that she feels far more for me than for him. I have seen enough women to be able to tell that!"

"T'is no compliment!" Mariotta dimpled. "Virtually anyone would be more lovable than Richard!"

This conversation was a revelation to Mariotta. Diana had not mentioned Jack's confession of love. . . .

Diana and Drew found a good subject of conversation in Gerald. Drew asked what she thought of him.

Diana tilted her head to one side and looked at him through the thick dark lashes. "Are you laying a trap, sir? I cannot insult him, he is your nephew. . . ."

"I have my answer, then, Diana—may I call you Diana? I agree, he is unworthy of your sister. But what is to be done? She must love him."

"Oh, no, I do not think so! It was infatuation, but now it is chiefly a moral question."

"You have my complete attention, Diana. What do you mean?"

"Surely it is obvious to a man as sensitive as you: Leila. She will be guilty of terrible frivolity if she takes him away from the lovely, sweet, kind Leila and then does not marry him! It will all have been for nothing. She does not say this, but I am reasonably sure that I am correct. And have you not thought of how unhappy she will be as a diplomat's wife? This is not at all what she wants. It is merely what she imagines she wants. Really, she is a country girl, and always will be."

Drew was utterly fascinated, and tried to keep his joy masked.

"But you think she will go ahead anyway?"

Diana looked up at him, suddenly daring. "That will depend on you, I should think. We have to make her understand all of this without saying it. . . . Between us, we can at least try."

Drew smiled and whirled her around in the waltz, feeling happier than he had forweeks. Of course he was too old for her, but he might hope . . . especially if Gerald were no longer a rival.

But looking at his nephew dancing by with Leila, Drew realized again that his relative had everything he did not: youth, a handsome person, high spirits. It was useless to hope. Just because she might be kept from marrying Gerald did not mean she would marry him. . . .

"Do you think, Diana, that they really did love each other, perhaps? In the beginning?"

"It seems to me that it was a romantic setting, they had only each other to fancy, and so they very conveniently came together, two handsome children. But I do not call that *love*; I call that *circumstance*."

"I am very afraid," said Drew, leading her to seats near Lady Chalford, "that circumstance itself is often the basis for love. . . . One does not really pick and choose. . . . It simply happens."

The two of them fell silent, then. Diana respected Drew just as much as she despised his nephew, and she was struck by the similarity of his views to Jack's. Jack also thought love was something that could not be planned. That was obvious. But suppose one were incapable of love? Surely then one must be forgiven for planning. . . .

Lady Courtland and Lady Chalford, watching from different corners, came to different conclusions about what was going on. Lady Chalford, with her imperial self-assurance, was certain that the twins were the stars of the gathering. But Lady Courtland was quite puzzled. It was unclear—who was with whom? She was happy to see Gerald and Leila, obviously enjoying themselves, dance set after set together. But when she looked at the twins she felt something was wrong. They looked anything but gay, and their partners also seemed to have their minds elsewhere. They obviously weren't at all like their grandmamma, Leila was right about that, and Cama was certain of it too.

Camilla had a different view from either of the two other chaperones. She was completely satisfied with their present partners, and regarded their downcast looks as perfectly acceptable. It meant that matters were taking shape.

She was a little sad to see that Black Walter was not there—of course their host did not know he was in town. It would have been nice if he had been here to help in her schemes. . . .

Diana was restless and full of mixed emotions, and when Sir Reginald, a suitor favored by her grandmother, approached her, mischief took hold.

"Mariotta, we shall switch places, agreed?"

"Yes, it will be great fun!"

The man came up, looked from one to the other, and then asked which was Diana.

"I am," said Mariotta, looking haughty.

Mariotta was almost laughing out loud as he led her off for the mazurka.

Diana was satisfied; content to be alone for a while. But her satisfaction was short-lived. Jack came up, assuming of course that she was Mariotta.

"I hate to see her dancing with that fop. Why such a beauty rewards such mediocre men, I cannot imagine."

"And lets one like you alone?" mocked Diana.

"Yes, I suppose I am absurd to think it, but really, Mariotta, what is my flaw? Why am I unsuitable?"

"Perhaps she thinks you are *a* rake, a wastrel."

"Ridiculous. Why should she think that?"

Diana shrugged her shoulders, and asked what he thought of Gerald Drew. Jack was made uncomfortable by the question.

"I don't really know the fellow. Seems nice enough."

They did not continue on this theme, because Cama joined them and began to ask Jack what his plans for the coming year were. Diana was very surprised to hear them. He was going to live in town and do a great deal of entertaining for his political patron, a highly placed Whig. He was also to take part in various meetings devoted to diplomatic problems. She had had no idea of his serious interest in these things. She wondered who was going to pay for the house in town.

Her question was answered after he left, when Cama chided her for having fallen in love with Gerald instead of Jack.

"There he was on your doorstep, Mariotta, the only heir of Lord Amancross, and a rich fellow in his own right, a bright, talented fellow—but no, a childhood friend is never the one we see, until it's too late. Still, I suppose Gerald has his attractions, those blond looks and so on. Although the uncle is vastly more charming."

She had one more conversation with Jack, after supper, when he again took her to be Mariotta. He talked of his plans again, but then broke off.

"But I am boring you, dear Mariotta. I know you have little

interest in such things. But it is always a pleasure to share your plans with close friends."

He looked at her with such warm affection that she became self-conscious.

"Why do you look so? Have I said something?"

"No, it is the way in which Gerald looks at Leila that bothers me," said Diana quickly. Indeed, Gerald was gazing at Leila as if the wedding were to be tomorrow.

"You must not imagine things," said Jack, comforting her. "He is merely playing a part. She can be nothing to him after he has known you."

She saw his sincere desire to make her feel better.

"You are kind, Jack."

"No, I am just Jack, your old friend who knows what a very good heart you have. But here, Diana is coming back from supper. I think it better that I go."

A thousand emotions rose at once in Diana. Regret, dismay, embarrassment. That she should be the cause of his leaving! At once she saw her own behavior in the harshest of lights, that of self-knowledge. He was nothing like the rakes who visited her father—empty, vain fellows. What could have made her think them alike? And now she knew that she had been wrong in assuming, from a chance remark, that Jack was a wastrel like her father. Cama would know, and Cama thought Jack marvelous. And she had done everything to make him loathe and despise her, all for Trelawny and sure security.

She began to drink more champagne than was good for her, and threw herself into the dancing as if her life depended upon it.

Drew watched the twins, and guessed their switch. No matter how much she tried to act like Diana, Mariotta simply did not dance as well. And now Mariotta was dancing with Sir William

Candelford, fifty if he was a day. The man was a good dancer, and Mariotta seemed to be enjoying the conversation with him as well.

"Yes, Candelford is quite a fellow," said Camilla in a reflective tone. "Althea will manage to get the girl married to him before the year is out, if I know her. A good match."

"You are not serious! He is far too old. Mariotta will not think of him that way."

"My dear boy, fifty is nothing. As you see, he is in quite acceptable condition. And a perfect gentleman who knows how to charm a lady. She could do far worse."

Drew could not take it seriously, but this conversation put him into a bad mood anyway. What if Gerald cried off, only to be replaced by Candelford! No, Candelford would never be considered; he could only be a friend. . . .

Drew's mood made him less tolerant of Gerald, who complained that it was getting very hard to go anywhere in London without meeting Leila and Mariotta together.

"Get it over with, then! Tell Leila, if she hasn't gotten the letter—tell her!"

Gerald was offended. "I will, *uncle*, but in my own way."

"Yes, sixty years old, and he finally breaks the news." Gerald walked off haughtily, saying he did not think it in the least comical.

Camilla saw all of this, and decided to talk to the two young men who were obviously in need of advice.

"Jack, go and get Drew away from Lady Chalford. I wish to talk to both of you, or rather, *at* both of you."

Jack smiled, and did as he was told. Resplendent in gold net and amethysts, Cama reminded him, he told Drew, of a very intelligent butterfly.

"No, something much more extravagant, a peacock, only

with brains. Something else. We'll think of it eventually. Now I wonder what she wants . . ."

Cama had found herself a regal setting in the conservatory, on a chair resembling a throne.

"Now, please sit down, and listen to a meddling old woman. No, don't protest. I am not ancient like Althea, but I am old. Nevertheless, or perhaps because of it, I know a few things about love. And you are both going about it all wrong. Do not dance with the twins, do not even look in their direction for the rest of the evening, unless you have been promised a dance. You both of you look like storm clouds in frock coats. Not an attractive state. Whatever you wish to happen will not when you are in a weak position, which you are tonight. Now, you may play cards, you may dance with others, but on no account are you even to *glance* at the Chalford party again."

Unexpectedly, the two gentlemen did not even question her wisdom, but meekly agreed to everything. This made Cama even more sure that things had been going badly. But really, it was very hard to manage things when you didn't have all the information you needed. Well, it just made it more of a challenge, and she was fairly certain that Drew did indeed love Mariotta.

When Cama got home that evening she had a great deal to think about. She was feeling the slightest bit put upon. She had been plunged immediately into the war of those two titans, Jane and Althea. Meanwhile, her own plans had to wait, and now she had taken on the job of stopping those two handsome young fellows from ruining their lives. And this dinner for Black Walter must really be gotten under way. And what was he up to, anyway, announcing this very unsuitable connection as his future wife? Well, perhaps she would be able to do something about *that*.

The Chalford party stayed for the last round of champagne. The twins seemed, if anything, to be even gayer after the departure of Jack and Drew.

Gerald was especially relieved after Leila left, and did his best to smooth things over with Mariotta, making her laugh with his usual nonsense. Though she laughed, she was not convinced. She was too aware of how Leila had looked at Gerald, and felt very ashamed of her own role in the concealing of their relationship.

She could not find that same sense of pleasure she had once felt in Gerald's company, that meeting of two minds in unspoken agreement. But she put it down to the influence of London manners. He was still strong and handsome, his vivacity matched hers as they danced through the early hours of the morning, and she saw how all of the other girls envied her.

Diana was also determined to be gay and forget the painful impression produced by the conversation with Jack. Sir Reginald, the man she danced with earlier, was happy to help her do so. He was trying deliberately to fascinate her with every weapon at his command, and this was, in its way, both flattering and humorous. He would say virtually anything to get her interest. He finally hit upon something in their last dance.

"I know a secret," he whispered in her ear. "What will you promise me in exchange for a secret, concerning Lady Chalford?"

"A ride in the park. Alone. At eight this morning."

"Done. Although how you will do it, I don't know. It is already three."

They sat down, and with a portentous look he began. Last Monday he had run into Lady Chalford as she was coming out of the law offices of Weybright and Hull, the firm he himself used. She had been visibly upset and had demanded that he give his word that he would tell no one. It had to do with an important surprise, and he would ruin it, et cetera. She had been in such a state that he had understood that it was really a very great surprise.

"And so you broke your word."

"For you, Diana. Worth it, I think."

"What if I break my word to you?"

He looked very dismayed. This had not occurred to him as a possibility. Diana smiled sweetly and left the ballroom.

Mariotta and Diana were tired, but they met in Diana's room to talk anyway. Mariotta was very interested in the secret.

"There is something behind it."

"Yes, and not a pleasant surprise for us, I should think."

"I think that Jack should help us. He knows about such things. Perhaps he and I should visit these attorneys tomorrow."

Diana nodded agreement. Jack's name set off a little shock, although nothing was more natural than his name on Mariotta's lips.

At Chalford House the post had just been delivered, and Diana found two letters waiting for her, one from her fiancé, the other from her mother.

My dearest Diana,

I hope to see you on the 4th when I come to town with my sister and Lady Quennel. There is much to discuss, as I am sure you understand. Looking forward to seeing you.

I remain, yr obt svt, Richard

Her mother's letter was much longer, and in it she took the blame for the separation of the twins, saying that it had seemed the fair thing to do at the time, but now she saw how wrong it had been.

There is much I regret, but there is little enough to be done now. I am glad you have met, though I cannot approve of the deception practiced on so many. I am staying in Bath a little longer—Edmund wants my advice on some new things he is doing at Ardwell—but as soon as I can, I shall come to London and rescue you from Althea. She is a very suitable sponsor in London society, and will take good care of you, but I cannot like her or her lack of spiritual depth. You both have all my love and affection.

Your mother

These two letters gave Diana a great deal to think about. Especially Richard's. . . . Obviously those two harpies, Caroline and Lady Q., had told him what they suspected. She needed to discuss it all with Mariotta. They would have to devise an explanation. . . .

She awaited Mariotta's return with impatience, but two hours went by and there was no Mariotta. What could have happened to keep them so long? As Jack was along, Diana was less worried than she would have been otherwise. But she began to think that something very interesting must have occurred at the offices of Weybright and Hull, and she began to imagine all sorts of possibilities, none of which was half as interesting as the truth proved to be.

CHAPTER EIGHTEEN

The late morning drizzle had become a steady shower as Mariotta and Jack rode in a hack to the offices of Weybright and Hull, in the heart of the City, not far from St. Paul's. They had decided that Mariotta should simply request that the reading of the will be arranged for the day after the twins' birthday, while Jack tried to find out something from the clerks.

Mr. Weybright met them himself, smiling and bowing.

"Miss Abingdon, I have long anticipated the pleasure . . . Do come in. And Mr. Campbell, believe one of your relations is Lord Dee? Many years a client of ours, sad about his death last year, but at eighty—what would you?"

After a little discussion of the weather and the change, Mr. Weybright finally asked how he might be of service.

Mariotta, with a becoming show of shyness, said that she wished to arrange the reading of the will, since she had no idea of what her grandfather had left her and Diana.

"Do you mean to say that your mother has never told you what it was?"

"No, she did not know herself. I believe that my grandmother is the only one who might know . . . and she has not said."

"Most peculiar . . . I had nothing to do with the original document, that was Mr. Hull, since retired. Well, we certainly can make the arrangements; the day after your birthday, that is, next Tuesday, will suit us perfectly."

After a few more bows and smiles, they left.

Jack and Mariotta went to a coffee house across the street, not a very suitable place for a well-bred girl, but Mariotta was fascinated by the crowd there.

"You don't want to go back home yet?" She looked at Jack, who seemed pensive.

"No, I have a feeling our Mr. Weybright was lying about something. . . . Let's stay here until he leaves for his luncheon."

They only had to wait a half-hour and they saw the portly figure of Weybright come out and go around the corner. Once again they went up into his offices.

"You must be shy, but appealing," instructed Jack. "And you have quite mislaid Mr. Hull's address, and could they possibly find it for you, if it would not be too much trouble."

The clerk, who was much taken with Miss Abingdon's looks, was only too happy to do anything she wished.

"Please," she implored him when she had the address in her hand, "do not let Mr. Weybright know how shatterbrained I am! It would sink me in his estimation forever. I know *you* would understand, but *he* . . ."

"Oh, Miss Abingdon, do not worry on that score! Not a word!"

Jack decided to take a chance, and ask the clerk what he knew.

"Do you happen to know . . . whether the inheritance is money or jewels, or something quite different?"

"Oh, yes, I would so love to know just the general category! That way I can pretend to guess, and win a bet from my sister."

The clerk was young and bored and did not like his superior. This girl appealed to him greatly, and he found it difficult to say no to such a face. And after all, the will would be read in four days anyway. . . .

"All right, I'll take a quick look."

He went to some drawers and looked for a packet, which he found in a few minutes. He opened it and pulled out a thin sheet of parchment.

"Here it is. Jewels. That's what it is, the Chalford garnets, rubies, and sapphires. Pretty nice, I should say."

The couple thanked him profusely and went on their way.

"Well," said Jack as they were on their way to Mr. Hull's address in Knightsbridge, "I don't think he left you jewels. I think that's what Althea wants you to have."

"Yes, it makes sense. She never wears any of those things, and if the jewels were the inheritance, why not the diamonds as well? She wears them all the time, though. But how could he know, fifteen years ago, what she would be wearing now? Wouldn't he have just left them all to us, with the exception, perhaps, of things he'd bought her? But the diamonds are from his mother. . . ."

"I'd say there is a good chance that Weybright is up to something. On Althea's orders, of course."

"But it doesn't make sense. Grandmamma has plenty of money. Even if he left us a great deal, it wouldn't hurt her; she still has her own fortune, plus what he left her outright. What could our grandfather have left us that she wants so badly? Perhaps you are wrong, Jack, perhaps it is just the jewels. . . ."

"What did Sir Reginald want in return for the secret about Lady Chalford?"

Mariotta, happily back in the role of Jack's old friend, did not even think before answering.

"Oh, Diana had to promise to meet him in the Park this morning."

Jack tensed, angry with Diana, angry with himself. What did it matter if she did things like meet a man in the Park? What was she to him? At least he would be better than Trelawny. . . .

They arrived at their destination, a neat little house on Marlborough Street. They were expecting an invalid, since Mr. Weybright had emphasized Mr. Hull's great age, well beyond seventy, and had said that he did not think Mr. Hull's memory was any too good any more. But a housekeeper showed them into a little study where a perfectly hale and hearty gentleman was reading the newspaper.

Mr. Hull was extremely thin, and somewhat bent over; but he had a ruddy complexion and a shock of white hair, and seemed very alert and intelligent. He was delighted to have such young and handsome visitors, he said, and invited them to have a little tea, or something stronger—this said after a sharp look at Jack.

After a conversation which covered the weather, politics, and the current corn crop, Mr. Hull pushed his cup decisively out of the way and asked what he could do for Miss Abingdon, for he knew it was she who was the chief party.

Mariotta hesitantly told him the story of her relations with her grandmother and the visit to Mr. Weybright. He did not interrupt with questions until she was done.

"So, you think something is amiss. . . . Well, you are right, of course. It was Weybright himself who dealt with the will, not I. He has been under Lady Chalford's thumb any time these last forty years or more. She was quite a stunning woman, and Weybright would have paid *her* to come and see him on business. Wonderful to look at, she was, so blond, and those violet eyes. She looked like an angel. But she wasn't, not by half. . . ."

Mr. Hull seemed to be in a reverie and Jack had to prompt him.

"Do you happen to know what the terms of the will were?"

"Not supposed to, but I do. Always liked Gordon Chalford. This young lady is his image, by the way—same dark hair, same gray eyes. Anyway, to cut the story short a bit, I wondered how he'd settled accounts with his wife, the proud beauty—all of whose money came from him until her uncle died and left her his heiress. Wills are curious things, you know. Sometimes husbands and wives find out more about each other then than theyever knew during their life together. He left her the *money* all right, and the jewels, with a bit going to his son the wastrel. Excuse me, young lady, but that is how he referred to him."

"So he did not leave me the jewels? But that is what it says in Mr. Weybright's copy of the will!"

"And how did you find that out, miss?"

Mariotta blushed, and Jack explained.

"Very resourceful, I must say. Well, the point is, he left you and your sister something much more important, in a symbolic manner of speaking. He left you virtually all the property."

"You can't be serious!" Jack exclaimed. He immediately understood what this meant. The property, bought some fifty years before, was now worth a great deal, but the main thing was that Chalford House itself, with its magnificent architecture and location, not to mention the frescoes, marble staircases and so on, was the only place Lady Chalford would ever want to live. And it did not belong to her. And she had no intention of giving it up; that was what the visit to Weybright had meant. They were in it together.

Mariotta did not immediately grasp the full import of this bequest.

"But why would my grandfather do that? He surely knew that

she loved Chalford House above all, and even if he had wanted to repay her—but what was he angry about?"

"Why, I don't quite know how to say it, but you're old enough. . . . It was that she had many lovers, and she did not do it discreetly. She thought she could do anything she wanted with Gordon, and generally she was right. But after he died he left it to the will to punish her."

Mariotta felt inadequate in the face of all this information. She looked at the clock. They had been gone three hours, Diana would be worried.

"But," said Jack, frowning, "what of the fact that Lady Chalford has already had the will doctored in some way? How will the girls receive what is due them?"

"Oh, it is not a problem. I have the second copy of the will, you see. Gordon Chalford gave me one copy, just in case. He knew his wife. He even told me to keep it at home, in case of a fire at the office, but I think he knew already that Weybright was a victim of Lady Chalford's beauty."

"And why did he decide to trust you, Mr. Hull?" Jack was curious.

Mr. Hull laughed, very amused. "Why, I never liked yellow hair. I like them dark, like the young lady here. I never said a word about Lady Chalford, but he knew well enough what I thought of her. A hard, grasping woman underneath that angelic exterior. Why did she need more when she had every-thing already?"

They finally said that they must get back to Cavendish Square, and Mr. Hull told them that he had enjoyed the visit greatly.

"But I'll tell you one thing, young people. Be careful. Althea is not going to take this lying down. She'll strike back somehow."

Jack was certain he was right about that, but he did not

want Mariotta worried, so he told her on the way home that he thought it would all come out all right in the end.

Mariotta was thrilled by her prospects. "You realize he said that we get Chalford House and the estate in Devonshire as well! That must be worth a great deal in itself! Oh, Jack, now Diana won't have to marry Trelawny!" Mariotta regretted the words as soon as they were out. She really should not be discussing her sister with Jack; she knew Diana would not like it if she knew.

But Jack did not pursue this theme. "Yes, perhaps she will look elsewhere," was all he said.

She was so excited when they got to Chalford House that Jack told her to calm down. It would not be good if Lady Chalford sensed that she knew anything.

"You should get your sister out of the house before you start telling her about this. The walls there definitely have ears. You do not want to give your grandmother warning, or she will do something dramatic before the will is read."

Mariotta did her best to restrain her emotions, and went up to her sister's room.

"I want you to come to the Pantheon with me, Diana. I need some new ribbons for the silk dress, and I need your advice."

"But we were just there. Have you changed your mind already?"

"Yes," hissed Mariotta. "Now come, this instant."

Her sister's face was very eloquent, and Diana hurriedly put on her pelisse. She took the two letters with her and followed Mariotta out the door.

Not bothering to inform their maids, they quickly made their way to Camilla's house on Jermyn Street, sure that she would have a private corner in which they could discuss things.

Cama was delighted to see them, and told them that they were free to use her little rose sitting room as long as they wished.

Mariotta poured them a small glass of sherry and then took a place at one end of the elegant striped sofa, and was overtaken by a fit of the giggles.

Diana stared and then began to laugh herself, so contagious were Mariotta's little gurgles and chokes.

"Do you like this sofa?" asked Mariotta when she finally had control of herself.

"Of course, though I don't like gilt trim. Why in the world do you ask?"

"I thought we might buy one like it for our house."

"What house?"

"Chalford House. I think we might redecorate a bit, don't you? All that Louis this and that is so boring."

Light dawned in Diana's mind.

"No! You mean! Chalford?"

"Yes, yes, and the estate in Devonshire as well. We are the owners of all of it, as of next Tuesday, and grandmother will not be able to do anything about it."

Diana, by virtue of exhaustive questioning, managed to get the entire story out of her sister, and only then did she begin to really believe it.

"I think we are going to have to leave Chalford House before Tuesday," said Diana thoughtfully. "In her anger at being frustrated in this plan she will want to throw us out in some theatrical manner. Best to be gone Monday. We'll say we are going to stay with Cama a bit before going back to Bath. But you know we won't ask her to leave Chalford. It is her home, after all. Even if she has been repellently devious, we cannot really make her go."

"No," sighed Mariotta, "it is really too bad, but we cannot. And there are other properties too, I believe, less valuable than the Devonshire estate, but little houses in Kent and Surrey, and they come to us as well. We should be able to sell them for a good profit. That's what Mr. Hull said anyway."

Diana smiled a wide, happy smile. "Yes, it will do very well, Mariotta. We shall be women of property! And no longer have to put up with grandmamma's ways. We shall buy a little house in this area. It will be famous!"

"But," said Mariotta morosely, "you'll be married, and so will I, and we won't really be able to enjoy it."

Diana looked suddenly grim. She had quite forgotten all of that in her dream of having a little house of her own in the city.

"Well, yes . . . but we will be able to use it when we come to town . . . with our families. We'll take turns. . . ."

There was a knock at the door and then Cama came in, followed by Jack and Drew.

"Jack has told us everything," said Cama smugly, "and now I thought you might wish to discuss it with all of us."

Ignoring Diana's look of annoyance, Mariotta said that they were all very welcome, and that in any case, their advice was needed.

The discussion that followed was long and essentially enjoyable as they all pondered what it meant that the twins had inherited all the Chalford properties, and what Lady Chalford would do when she found out that she had been checkmated.

Cama had her guests served food and drink and contented herself with charting the various tensions present in the little sitting-room. Drew and Diana seemed to talk chiefly to each other, as did Mariotta and Jack. There had obviously been trouble, and she was very sad to see it continuing.

She invited them all to Black Walter's engagement dinner, which had finally been arranged. She did not tell the present company how grateful Black Walter had been. It had been quite difficult to arrange the guest list. One needed guests who were suitable but who would not be disturbed by the presence and possible misbehavior of that common Freneau person. But she had managed it, and Walter knew very well what trouble it had been.

The twins said goodbye to Cama and left, accompanied by Jack and Drew, who were walking them back to Cavendish Square.

Mariotta took Drew's arm, and told him she wished to have a word with him on the way, much to Diana's discomfort, since she would now have to walk with Jack.

Drew had felt a kind of dread at the news of the inheritance. Now Mariotta would have enough money to make Gerald's lack of fortune unimportant. When Gerald heard of it, he would certainly never think of Leila again. . . .

Mariotta was shining with happiness. "Now I can buy back the deed to Chalford, Drew, and give it to my father. Is it a difficult legal process?"

"No, since I never did take it out of his name in the first place. I shall simply hand it over to him."

Mariotta stopped walking and looked at him. "You amaze me, dear Drew! You have been shockingly taken advantage of by our family! I do not know what to say . . . but thank you, thank you, Drew."

Well, these were not the words he most longed to hear from her, but they were sincere and affectionate, Drew reflected.

It seemed a very long walk for Diana and Jack. They talked about the inheritance for a while, and when that was exhausted there seemed to be nothing else to say. Diana kept thinking of Richard, who was due in a day, and she wondered how he would find her at Cama's. . . . Perhaps she would leave him a note at his hotel. . . .

Jack was as ambivalent about the inheritance as Drew. Now

Trelawny would be doubly glad he was engaged to Diana. Jack felt the anger rise every time he looked at Diana's profile, but he could say nothing. He had lost the right to speak freely to her.

When they reached Chalford House Mariotta said her farewells with her customary warmth, but Diana was noticeably restrained.

Drew and Jack walked back to Cama's in silence for a while.

"Shall we stay with Cama a bit?" asked Drew. "I don't feel like going back to the Albany with my thoughts. . . ."

"Nor I. Cama will have some ideas, and lord knows I need some."

Cama seemed to be expecting them to stay, and they all settled down to talk a bit about sensitive subjects. They stayed for a late supper, and Cama did her best to soothe them.

"The problems are different," she said between bites of veal in wine sauce. "We must be frank with one another, it is the only way. You, Drew, can only hope that either Gerald or Mariotta discover they are not suited. You must simply be friendly and warm. Nothing else can be done as things now stand.

"But Jack, you have an entirely different problem. Much of this mess is of your own making. You chose to quarrel instead of winning by devious, but certain, means. So now I must tell you: Diana certainly does not care for Trelawny, and it is possible, from all that you have said—and not said—that she may like you a great deal. So you must stoop to a terribly worn, but terribly powerful, ruse: a rival. It is the only thing likely to show her just what she feels. And nature will have to do the rest. Diana, unlike Mariotta, does not give in to her emotions, unless they are very strongly affected. Jealousy is such a thing. . . ."

Drew and Jack objected, and then agreed to take this advice. But where would Jack find someone to get up a flirtation with, someone who would understand, and not take it seriously.

Drew's eyes lit up. "I can help you there, old man. My cousin is none other than Amanda Tentrees."

His companions looked at him with new respect. Amanda Tentrees was the most famous flirt in London. She had the record for most engagements—and hearts—broken in a single season. And all of the castoff lovers had been respectable young men whose families no longer spoke to her. The young men themselves, unaccountably, still spoke to her, however. It was said that she had no heart, but with her beauty she did not need one.

It occurred to Cama when she retired (she often had her best ideas when she was supposed to be sleeping) that Amanda would be a perfect guest at the dinner party for Walter and Loulou Freneau. It would be quite an evening.

CHAPTER NINETEEN

The reading of the will was brief. The twins were left the jewelry which had belonged to their grandfather's mother. Lady Chalford congratulated them warmly, unaware that they had already had their possessions (with the exception of her gifts to them) transferred to Cama's house on Jermyn Street. Their grandmother stressed the great value of the emerald necklace and the ruby ring; the others, she said, were worth far less. She did not wish them to be cheated.

It was at this point that Mr. Hull opened the door of his office and came out.

"Well, Althea Chalford! Lady Chalford, I should say. But we are such old friends, are we not. Now I have here a very different will, no doubt you will give me the one Mr. Weybright read, so I may examine it."

Lady Chalford turned to stone, and her face began to match her white hair. Weybright seemed hypnotized by this resurrected partner. Since the clerks were present, he had no choice but to hand it over.

Mr. Hull gently said that this will appeared to be a forgery, but that he would not pursue those responsible as long as the terms of the real will were carried out.

"Fool!" shouted Lady Chalford at Weybright. "I won't stay for this mockery! I won't hear my house taken out from under me!"

And before the twins could explain that they had no intention of taking Chalford House away from her, she was gone, after telling them they need not come back to her house, for she would give orders to the servants not to admit them.

As luck would have it, Lady Chalford returned home in a rage to find that there were two visitors waiting to see the twins.

"Lady Quennel! It has been a very long time. How have you been?"

Lady Quennel, flattered that her ladyship remembered her, introduced her dear friend Caroline Trelawny, and the three ladies sat down to have a social visit.

"So you have come to see my granddaughters. . . . I fear they will be out for the rest of the afternoon. Sad gadabouts, I am afraid."

By this she meant nothing but an explanation of her granddaughters' absence, but her listeners immediately sensed that she was dissatisfied with the twins.

"They are so very *high spirited*," said Lady Quennel, trying to make herself comfortable on a small gilt chair which was unable to expand enough to hold her. "Not that one believes all that one is told. After all, with a preceptress such as *you*, dear Althea—"

"Dear Sally, whatever do you mean, by that phrase? Have they been naughty? Do tell me. Really it is my duty to know all that is said of members of my family."

Caroline said nothing, but the expression on her face would have told Diana just how much she was enjoying the contemplation of the destruction of her brother's fiancée.

Lady Quennel gave an admirably brief and to the point

narration of what had been learned about the mysterious trip to Tunbridge Wells and the equally mysterious return.

"And the point is," put in Caroline, afraid that it would be overlooked, "is that they were gone an entire night. Now perhaps they spent the entire time traveling; obviously they exchanged places. But we have no way of knowing when they left either place. So there is an interesting question. Where did they spend the night?"

Lady Chalford thought that Caroline was a despicable little worm, but she was obviously going to be a useful little worm, so she decided to immediately make use of her.

"Tragic. It is the blood, you know. My son Walter . . . well, you have no doubt heard of his exploits. And the twins have managed to get themselves into little troubles even while staying with me. I'm afraid that your poor brother is going to have his hands full. . . ."

Caroline understood. "Would you be very upset, Lady Chalford, if I told Richard some of what you said here today?"

"Oh, no, of course not. I should feel remiss had I let him think all was well. No, the girls are sadly unsteady."

Her listeners could barely keep from jumping up to leave and tell everyone they could. But they restrained themselves and actually sat there another fifteen minutes.

Lady Chalford smiled as she watched them leave. Their heads were bobbing up and down with excitement, and they made a comical sight, one so large and fat, the other so little and thin. They would do all of her work for her; she knew she could count on it. But to be sure, she would do a little crying on a few select shoulders. The girls might put her out of her house, but they wouldn't find a house in London to receive them afterward.

The twins, blissfully unaware, returned to a celebration dinner at Cama's with Drew and Jack, and Jack's sister Mary and her husband Evan Leigh. It was a gay company, and no one said anything to mar the occasion, though Cama noticed that Jack and Drew were having a deal of trouble keeping away from their favorite twins.

Another letter had arrived, one announcing that Edmund had finally proposed to Lady Abingdon. This, too, was the source of many toasts. Mr. Huntington would be coming up to London on business soon, and would stop by to see the twins.

Diana thought about it, and told her sister later that they had best confess the entire Tunbridge Wells incident to Edmund, before Caroline told him her version.

"I don't know. Won't he think we are terrible?"

"Oh, I know how to handle Edmund. Leave him to me," said Diana. "He has a terribly good heart, after all, and I don't think he really cares too much any more for Caroline. She was awful about the stunted trees, and she was rotten in the play. We shall meet him somewhere for tea, and confess, charming blushes, lowered eyes, and he will declare himself vastly amused by it all. Depend upon it."

"But what about Richard? How are you going to manage him?"

"Oh, I shall pull it off." Diana felt far less enthusiasm about that task, however.

Mariotta was not so sure, but she said nothing. Up till now, Diana had handled things very well, but she had a feeling that Richard would be difficult.

This feeling was turned into a certainty when Richard Trelawny presented himself at Jermyn Street a few days later, looking as stiff as a palace guard.

Mariotta took one look and ran up to find Diana.

"Richard is downstairs with Cama, and he doesn't look happy. I'd say that Caroline has already done her worst."

But Diana refused to be worried. "Oh, just give me a few minutes to fix my hair, then I'll go and take care of him."

Diana wondered why she was so calm about it. It was almost as if she didn't care. But if she didn't marry Richard, Jack would crow that she hadn't done what she'd said she'd do. No, she would show him, she would persuade Richard.

But Richard surprised her. He looked like a thundercloud, but he was not interested in the exchange.

"I don't really care about all of that, Diana. I presume that a woman of your breeding and intelligence did nothing to be ashamed of, no matter what Caroline and Lady Quennel say. I accept your regret, and your explanations. But I am far more troubled by your quarrel with Lady Chalford."

He said "Lady Chalford" as if he were trumpeting it, Diana noticed. And she didn't care for that glancing reference to his sister and Lady Quennel, as if she should simply understand their natural desire to poison him against her.

"It is not a quarrel, Richard. We have said nothing. And she will not be thrown out of her house. But she has conspired against us, after all, and we can hardly be friendly with such a devious person."

"No, Diana dearest, I understand, but you must reconcile, I insist." He spoke paternally, as if utterly convinced of his point of view. "Your grandmother is extremely powerful. She can and will do you great harm if this is not settled."

He spoke as if he were addressing a child, and Diana's hackles rose.

"I care nothing for what she may say. My reputation does not worry me."

He looked nonplussed.

"Surely you must see that she could do a great deal for us, in the way of introductions to important persons and so on."

Diana turned away so that he should not see her anger and contempt. She stared at one of Cama's favorite collage portraits, a peasant girl carrying a basket which held real straw. Most amusing.

"I am very sorry, Richard, but I am terribly tired, and have a headache. Please excuse me."

He saw through this, of course, but he had no choice but to make his farewells, since Diana immediately went out into the hall and called to Cama and Mariotta to come and say goodbye to their guest.

In her annoyance, she told Mariotta what had been said. Her sister's reaction was vehement.

"He is no gentleman! Drew would never say such a thing, nor would Jack! They would not even think it! Such commonness of mind." Mariotta realized the tactlessness of this only after the fateful words had been spoken.

Diana's eyes were very bright. "That may be, but at least he didn't try to make me fall in love with him under false pretences so that I should not marry his nephew!"

Mariotta gave her a piercing look of reproach, and left the room in tears.

Diana sat down, shaken. She had reacted so violently, she realized, because what Mariotta had said was true. Jack would never have thought it, nor would Drew. . . .

Neither sister slept well, and in the morning Cama told them that she was going off to see her friends the Fanes for a few days. Being alone in the house together, on such bad terms, was hardly a pleasing prospect. At dinner they hardly spoke, and when Mariotta left the table there were again tears in her eyes. Diana could not endure any more.

"No, Mariotta, come back! I want to tell you something."

Mariotta walked back in, pale and unhappy.

"Oh, Diana, I was wrong to say what I did!"

"And I was wrong to say that about Drew, but I was so unhappy that I wanted to hurt someone, anyone. So I hurt you, the person I love." Diana took her sister's hand and kissed it. They made peace, but they each resolved never to bring up the painful subjects of Drew and Richard again.

That night at Lady Courtland's rout, the first blows were delivered in the campaign to ruin the twins.

Diana noticed that two or three people whispered to each other whenever she or Mariotta passed by, and she wondered. When the evening was half over Lady Courtland summoned Mariotta to her.

"Well, gel, what's the true story about that trip to Tunbridge Wells? And are you throwing your 'poor' grandmother out into the street?"

Mariotta was shocked, but she managed to say that Lady Chalford would still have the house, and that the trip was much exaggerated by those who knew nothing about it.

Lady Courtland looked at her shrewdly.

"Well, I can tell there's more to it than that, but I can also tell that Althea is up to mischief. Half the room thinks you're throwing the woman out of Chalford House. I have a feeling that Althea doesn't know you are letting her have it. You'd best look to it that you don't get caught in any more situations, or mine might be the only house open to you."

Mariotta was horrified, and went to tell Diana.

"Lord, what are we going to do! We are ruined, Mariotta, if this keeps up."

There was not a friendly face to be seen by the end of the rout; everyone seemed merely curious to see these shocking twins. Only Leila and Lady Courtland continued as before.

Mariotta and Diana had never wished for Cama so much as now, but she was gone from the city for a few days.

Lady Courtland tried to make up for their dwindling invitations. She invited them to her house almost every day for something—cards, supper, or simply tea. These occasions were a kind of torture for Mariotta, who seemed to be doomed to spend *a great deal of time* with Leila, who was nicer than ever to her. Gerald was busy with briefings about Russia, the country to which he was slated to be sent as a secretary to the ambassador. He had used his work as an excuse for the delay in telling poor Leila that the engagement was over, and every day she spent with that charming young lady made it harder for Mariotta to even consider it. The position she was in was horribly dishonorable, but she saw no way out.

At one of these evening parties, during which everyone played charades with great enthusiasm, Diana was very surprised to see Jack, in the company of an extremely beautiful blonde.

"That is Amanda Tentrees," said Lady Courtland happily. "She is said to actually be serious about Mr. Campbell . . . I wonder if it is possible that the butterfly will settle down."

"I doubt it," said Diana acidly. "I doubt if she is capable of being serious about anything. Something like six engagements, is it not?"

"Oh, but you know, even these shocking flirts settle down when the time comes. I can remember Alicia Fane when she was Alicia Tierney. No one thought that that one would calm down either, but she did, and now she's happy as you please. With two fine children."

They switched to the pleasant subject of a friend in common, namely Lady Fane, but Diana did not take her eyes off Jack, who was helping Amanda Tentrees with her charade, which ironically was that of a "bride left waiting at the church."

When Cama returned from her visit, Diana asked her casually what she thought of Amanda Tentrees.

Cama looked at her closely. "Well, she's a beauty, a heartbreaker, but when she finds the right man, she'll make an excellent wife and a lovely mother. It's a question of suitability. She's not just your ordinary society flower, she's got a bit of steel to her. Hard to find her match, you know."

This answer left a sense of unease in Diana. It really began to seem that Amanda and Jack were something more than a casual flirtation. Despite her will, this left her feeling very empty. Why, oh, why could she not get over him? She must try harder.

Cama watched with satisfaction. Things were going nicely. Now if only she could take care of this horrid gossip that was spreading like poison. Perhaps it was time to make use of her highest connections. . . .

CHAPTER TWENTY

It did not take Gerald Drew very long to discover that he had made a terrible mistake. He sat in his rooms at the Albany, idly playing with the presse-papiers Leila had given him in happier times. . . .

He was happy to see his uncle. Any interruption was welcome.

"What is this, Gerald? Inside on such a day—won't be very many more of them, you know." Drew was very cheerful.

"Women are the very devil," pronounced Gerald morosely. "I can't see my way out of this coil, Drew. I don't know what to do."

Drew pretended not to understand. "What is the problem, my dear fellow? Some gambling debts, perhaps?"

Gerald began to speak at some length, and with an exclusively selfish point of view, about his mistake in choosing Mariotta over Leila. Mariotta, to be sure, was beautiful and exciting, but Leila was what he really wanted in a wife.

"I'm not sure that Mariotta would know how to be tactful," said Gerald pensively. "Leila is better at that sort of thing."

"But hasn't Leila received that letter by now? Isn't it too late?" Drew was determined not to prejudice the case, but he already felt a buoyancy swelling through him.

"I don't understand it. She should have received it—perhaps it went astray. At any rate, she does not act any differently, she has said nothing about it. What can it mean, other than that she never received it?"

"So, you are certain, Gerald, Leila is the one?"

For one moment there seemed to be some consciousness of his own behavior in Gerald.

"I know, uncle. I've been an awful fool, a cad, if you will. But now I see my mistake. It is just that these women are so attractive, and you think you're in love. . . . Really, they should be more slow to enchant a fellow!"

"Gerald, I am asking you, because I intend to help you. But once I do, it is all quite irreversible. Leila is the one?"

Gerald looked up at his uncle with a smile of intense joy and hope. "Oh, will you! I shall be so grateful! I knew you'd find a way to get me out of this!"

That was the problem, reflected Drew as he drove his curricle over to Lady Courtland's. Someone always had to get Gerald "out of it." Well, soon that would no longer be his problem, but Leila's; and, if he was any judge, Leila's mother would not put up with any mistreatment of her daughter. Since she was accompanying them to St. Petersburg, Drew thought she would manage to make Gerald a little less self-absorbed. . . .

One remark of Gerald's had interested him greatly: he said that Mariotta needed to marry a fortune. Obviously he was the only man in London who did not know about the Chalford inheritance . . . which meant that Mariotta had not bothered to inform him . . . which in turn meant that she did not really want to marry him! Drew hoped his reasoning was correct, because he was about to put an end to any troubles in the Grayson-Drew engagement.

Leila was pleased to see him sitting in Lady Courtland's drawing room, which was already filled with visitors.

"I should like to take you off to a quiet corner, Leila. I have some serious things to discuss."

Leila looked a little alarmed at this, but being a biddable girl, she quickly led him to the conservatory, which was relatively thin of company.

"Now, Leila, I'm going to speak frankly, but I do not want you to feel upset, or embarrassed. Did you receive a letter from Gerald, telling you that he had become engaged to Mariotta? The truth, now."

He spoke sternly, and Leila's large green eyes looked so stricken that he had his answer before she spoke.

"Yes." It was a whisper. Drew smiled encouragingly, and asked her why she had pretended not to have seen it. "I thought that if I pretended not to have seen it, he might change his mind . . . and like me again. Mariotta is so wonderful, so exciting, what he likes, so I suppose now—"

"No, she is not what he really likes. He likes you, and he is searching for a way to make a break with her, which, I suspect, would suit her admirably as well. You must leave everything to me, and above all, never tell Gerald you did receive the letter! I will wish you happy within three months."

An amazed Leila, beginning to smile hopefully, watched Drew leave the room quickly, as if he had an urgent mission.

He made his way to Cama's, where he found several quite unpleasant visitors.

He was met at the door and conspiratorially summoned into the little sitting room by a distraught twin.

"Just in time to meet Lady Quennel and Caroline!"

"Diana, I—"

"No, it is Mariotta! I am pretending to be Diana. She is out, and I thought to get it over with. She will thank me, you know. She had been quite loathing their visit. Come in, and help me, pray do. Cama is out shopping, she would know how to put them in their place. They are here to sniff and snoop about the quarrel with grandmamma, and Diana's ride in the Park with Sir Reginald. They know a great deal, and I think grandmamma must have deliberately told them things to use against us."

An amused Drew was introduced with great ceremony to the ladies, who were impressed that Diana knew such a well-placed gentleman as Lord Drew. His presence served to somewhat mute their interrogations.

Drew was torn: on the one hand, the fat Quennel and the scrawny Caroline were loathsome; on the other hand, they were there to do a good deed, namely to end the engagement between Diana and Trelawny. Mariotta seemed to be suffering from the same mixed feelings. But she was rattling on about all sorts of improper meetings, friendships, and visits to places which were not precisely the thing. She even expressed regret that she had not been able to attend the Cyprians' Ball.

Drew took her aside, when Cama returned, and told her that she was making a mistake in this approach.

"Oh, I don't agree! I know that she will not be able to bear their insinuations. I wish only to make them report everything to Richard. Perhaps then he will end the engagement, which is the best thing for Diana. If you could only see how she mopes. It is Jack she cares for, though they quarrel. She will thank me for it, I am persuaded."

Drew was certain that Diana would want to decide all of this for herself, but he was unable to persuade Mariotta; they had to rejoin Cama and the two harpies. He knew how stubborn and wrong-headed Mariotta could be when she was so sure of herself. This was bound to end badly.

But there were wonderful comic moments for Cama and

Drew as they watched the two bloodhounds sniff, unknowingly, at the wrong fox.

"And you will live in the country happily, you think?" Caroline was trying to be friendly.

"Oh, no," Mariotta shook her head vigorously. "I couldn't bear it. Not to be in London! To be stuck away in the country! Never. I am sure I will be able to convince Richard that the house is best rented out to someone."

Caroline turned beet red, and Lady Quennel had to come to her aid.

"My dear, he worked so hard on the plans, surely you can reconcile yourself."

Here Mariotta permitted herself a melodic, cascading laugh, extremely artificial and extremely effective at stopping conversation.

"Oh, Lady Quennel, men have such *quaint* ideas before marriage; but afterward, I am told, a woman is often able to change their views."

This was followed by a look of deep significance, in the direction of Caroline, who correctly interpreted it to mean that Caroline would certainly not be invited to live with them after the marriage. Her thin, Chinese features seemed to narrow even more, and she abruptly announced that they were late for a promised visit. A few minutes later they were out the door.

Mariotta started to giggle as they were on the front stoop.

"Drew, have you ever! Such a goose! And that large pudding of a Lady Quennel!"

Cama told her to calm down, and was about to tell Mariotta that she was incorrigible when she caught sight of Trelawny lifting the knocker on the front door. Quickly she let the curtain drop and told Mariotta and Drew who had arrived.

"And I'll have to be Diana with him! What shall I do? Drew, help!"

"I can't. But you'd best behave yourself. I don't think Diana will like this one bit."

Feeling *de trop*, Drew made his exit almost as Trelawny entered. He would return later, he told Cama, to find out how it went. He had a momentary wish to be invisibly present during this scene, which promised to be amazingly unpredictable.

Trelawny was surprised at Diana's warm welcome. More often than not, lately, she had been cold and somehow distracted, as if she were not really listening to him when he talked of their future and his plans. He ignored his sister's insistent advice, and thought that with a little smoothing of the rough edges, Diana would make him a fine wife. But he was very glad to see that she had become easier to deal with now, despite their disagreement about Lady Chalford.

Mariotta had every intention of making up for her performance with Caroline, which now she realized had been too outrageous. But when Richard began asking about the will, and whether they had made any attempt to smooth Lady Chalford's feathers, her good resolves were all but forgotten.

"You must understand, Richard, my sister and I cannot see her as the injured party. She tried to do something very wrong, and she was caught. That is why she is setting about all of these rumors."

"Such as the one about you spending a night out. I suppose there is nothing to that? You must see that that was very improper behavior."

His smugness was insufferable.

"Yes, it was. I admit it. What else would you like, a public apology, perhaps? If you have such low, mean-spirited suspicions, I wonder you wish to marry me!"

This was said with some heat, as Mariotta had begun to slip into her role to the degree that she actually felt herself to be the offended fiancée.

Richard was stung by this charge, and told her not to be nonsensical. He decided to change course and see if he could not interest her in something else, something less touchy.

"You will be happy to know that I have found a housekeeper, a perfectly reliable person. My sister has checked into her references and interviewed her."

Mariotta raised her eyebrows. "Your sister? Is that not my concern, the hiring of the housekeeper? Do you think that I am unable to choose my servants? Next you will be choosing the children's nurse without me!"

"Children?"

"Yes, or has Caroline decreed there shall be no offspring?"

This was a sore point, although Mariotta, indeed Diana herself, had no way of knowing it. Richard Trelawny had no plans to start a nursery; he felt it ridiculous at his age. He had been too delicate to bring it up with Diana, preferring to wait that particular discussion until after the wedding. But now, here it was, the prickly question. And Diana had chosen this day to turn into a complete virago!

"Surely this is better decided after we are married. Then you will understand my reasoning."

"I do not think husbands are the only ones to have a say in such a matter. You are positively gothic in your notions, and I wonder what you can be thinking of! Do I understand that you wish no children?"

His face was answer enough; and Mariotta coldly told him that he should be going, she did not think there was anything else to discuss at this time, and in any case, she felt one of her headaches coming on. She left him standing in the drawing room alone, where Cama found him a moment later.

Richard thought her behavior unforgivable, but he explained mendaciously to Cama that Diana had suddenly fallen victim to a migraine. Trelawny managed to contain his anger at his fian-cée's remarks, and reminded himself that women were often at their most irrational before a marriage. He decided to go and seek comfort from his sister and Lady Quennel, women who never made him feel anything but right.

Mariotta was bursting with her contempt, and told Cama everything that had been said, but Cama was worried more by the charade.

"I do not think Diana would have handled it in just that way, you know. I am sure that you had better tell her everything and expect a good scolding."

Cama struck terror into Mariotta's heart. Suddenly the enor-mity of her sins overwhelmed her with their full force. How could she have done it? What if Diana still intended to marry Trelawny? How could she ever tell Diana!

But Diana had other things to think about. She had been to an exhibition at Sir John Soane's museum in the company of Lady Courtland and Leila. While wandering through the exhibit she had come upon a tender scene of affection, between none other than Amanda Tentrees and her escort, Jack Campbell. They had not seen her, she was sure of that, so she turned and fled in the opposite direction, virtually hiding until Lady Courtland was done with the collection.

It was burned in her memory like a scar: Jack, with the tenderest of warm looks, was bent over Amanda Tentrees, who was sitting on a little bench. She said something to him, and then he laughed, the delighted laugh of the happy lover. The scene ended as he raised her hand to his lips. Diana had not stayed to see more. It was all quite enough.

She felt sick as she waited for Leila and Lady Courtland to retrieve their cloaks. So that was what his love was worth! How right she had been to discount it from the beginning!

She came home to find Mariotta in tears. Gradually the story was told, and at first she was quite upset. But then the comic aspects of everything struck her.

"Oh, I would have given anything to see their faces!" Diana started to laugh, hysterically, or so it seemed to her twin. This was so peculiar that it stopped Mariotta's tears completely.

"Oh, it will be all right, I can twist him around my little finger if I try. I'll even manage this one. I'll tell him that you were playing a questionable joke on me. He is not as much of a stick as he seems to be."

Mariotta wanted to ask about his desire to reconcile them with Lady Chalford, a thing which was of greater importance at the moment, but she had learned her lesson. No more impulsive remarks or actions. If her sister wished to marry Trelawny, as she seemed to, that was her affair. But it was peculiar. A day earlier Mariotta would have sworn that her sister was ready to end the engagement to Trelawny. What had happened in between?

CHAPTER TWENTY-ONE

Cama had returned from her stay with the Fanes in a fine mood. Nothing seemed to disturb her; she heard all the various tales of disaster and destruction with a cheerful expression, as if sure that she could make everything right. This was due in part to various mysterious events which had taken place at the Fanes' country house: a chance meeting with the well known actor Corin West, and a number of serious conversations with Nick Fane himself.

The twins did not ask the source of this self assurance, they were happy enough to benefit from it. Cama's first concern was to neutralize Lady Chalford.

"Lady Courtland is giving you and Leila a ball," she announced suddenly one morning. "I think we had better go and see about ball dresses this afternoon"

The twins erupted with questions, but Cama would give them no satisfying answers. It was a ball. That was all. Really, it was silly to get so excited about seeing one's ordinary friends dressed in evening clothes.

Mariotta and Diana suspected something was behind all of this, but they gave up trying to get it out of Cama. The business of choosing the gowns was very entertaining and took much of their attention for days on end, as they went to drapers and had fittings at the dressmaker's.

Diana's dress was of white satin, with silver net, embroidered with lilies of the valley. Mariotta's was pale blue satin, with an overdress of cream net, trimmed with blond lace. They were both shockingly bare around the bosom.

"Don't you think it's too revealing, Cama?" asked Diana.

"Oh, no, darling. You know what full dress means: virtually no covering. Seriously, it is very flattering, and exactly what everyone else will be wearing. You will get used to the feeling. Your grandmother's jewels, after all, will provide some coverage."

The jewels had been considered in the choosing of the gowns. With the white, Diana would wear the emeralds. With the blue, Mariotta would wear the sapphires. They took a simple pleasure in all of this, which pleased Cama no end. They were such charming girls, if only they would manage their lives better. . . .

The ball came, and Lady Courtland had the house decorated with thousands of flowers, and millions of candles. It was like living in the middle of a diamond, as Black Walter, who was escorting Cama, said.

Cama was in fine form. Her striking rose-colored gown showed off her lovely figure, and her hair was adorned with sprays of diamond flowers. She was magnificent, and knew it quite well, as Walter told her.

All went as planned, the crowd was happy, the three girls were dancing every dance, and suddenly there was a hush in the ballroom and the word went round: the Prince Regent had arrived!

Since no one had suspected that he was invited, this was quite a stunning event to many of those present. Diana and Mariotta correctly assumed that this was Cama's doing somehow.

The Regent, who had lost his daughter and grandchild the year before, had grown monstrously fat. But he was still the Regent, and his presence at the ball gave it a stamp of importance. That alone would have been enough for Mariotta and Diana, but he actually came up and engaged them in conversation for some twenty minutes, a mark of favor not given often outside of the Regent's circle of close friends. This was in the nature of a miracle, and all they could think of was that Cama must be incredibly powerful to arrange it. The Regent, as everyone knew, was not easily persuaded to do anything which caused him the slightest amount of trouble.

He stayed an hour and Lady Courtland was in heaven. Everyone at this ball would tell their best friends the next morning, and all of London would know that her rather small ball had been graced by the royal presence.

"How did you do it, Camilla?" she asked in a manner which brooked no evasions.

"Oh, it was all Nick Fane. He knows him well. They are old drinking companions. He and Alicia talked Prinny into it, though. As you may imagine, it took a great deal of talking."

But that was all she would say, and Jane had to make do with that. But it was clear that Althea had been beaten.

The Regent's approval was worth more than a dozen Lady Chalfords' complaints, and people who had had their doubts about the twins managed to forget them, since they were obviously favorites of the Prince. And that Lady Courtland and Lady Green sponsored them also spoke eloquently of their qualities.

Cama basked in the glow of this triumph for several days. So much for Althea, and so much for her social rival, the odious Lady Quennel, who had not even been invited to the ball. But she must not linger over her great moments of satisfaction, she must press on with the next campaign: the dinner for Black Walter.

She was occupied with the task of the invitations when Black Walter himself came to pay a visit.

He looked around the magnificent library, remarkable chiefly for the fact that it contained so few books, and said that she had certainly done well by herself, and that not marrying him had no doubt contributed to all of this prosperity.

"Always bring the subject back to yourself—something Byron lives by as well, I believe. It is nice to see you looking so well, Walter. Here is the list for our little dinner."

He read it with growing amazement.

"Tentrees . . . Abingdon . . . West . . . Freneau . . . Sarton . . . Good lord, how did you get them all to accept? I had not expected this! I could not ask this of you, it is too much!"

Cama was sitting at the mahogany secretaire, writing a note with great concentration. She looked up from it in surprise.

"Why, Walter, I am not doing it merely for you! I am doing it for your daughters, who are quite charming, and need some attention paid them by you. Their fiancés will be here, and you have not yet met Richard Trelawny. Also, Lord Candelford will come. Drew said, quite rightly, that it was about time that your daughters met their stepmother-to-be. It will be good in many ways."

Black Walter was caught between emotions. He had certainly intended to take pleasure in forcing society to accept Loulou, but he had not really thought about the baseness of involving Cama and her no doubt very proper friends. He felt a slight twinge of conscience, but he allowed it to die. Cama was quite able to cope with anything, and he would make it up to her somehow if Loulou did anything too outrageous.

"Well, I don't want you to feel taken advantage of by the Abingdon family, Cama."

She heard the slight note of discomfort in his voice, and her eyes met the gray ones so like his daughters' at this moment, since the habitual ironic sneer was missing from them.

"I assure you, it will all be quite delightful. My first formal dinner since my illness. I have been quiet long enough."

But when he left she began to wonder if she were really doing quite the right thing. Suppose all of her plans were based on misconceptions. . . . But she regained her confidence quickly. After all, she would do nothing but present opportunities, and the actors in this play might choose their roles and reactions.

In the meantime, it was rather comic to have Black Walter actually expressing gratitude.

Mariotta and Diana came in to help with the invitations and the seating arrangements, since her secretary, Cleves, had chosen exactly this inopportune moment to come down with a beastly cold.

"Who is Corin West?" asked Mariotta. "I know all of the others, but I've never heard of him."

"Oh, a theater acquaintance," said Cama airily. "A good fellow to have present when the conversation flags. I think you will enjoy him."

They all worked for a few minutes in silence. Then Diana uttered a brittle little laugh.

"Whose envelope is that, dear?" asked Cama, who knew very well.

"Oh, Miss Tentrees. I had no idea you were such friends."

"Oh, tolerably close. Not to her, to her family. Wonderful people. Of course, she's the problem child, but you know, I believe that dashing Jack Campbell is in a fair way of taming her. She's already much less wild."

Diana put that envelope down with a resolute gesture, and took up the next.

"Isn't Gerald invited?" Mariotta did not see his name on the list.

"No, dear, he has a bachelor dinner that evening with a friend of his who is getting married. He told me that he can't get out of it." Cama neglected to add that this was one of the reasons she had chosen November 1 for her dinner.

"I see that Lord Candelford is coming," said Diana. "He is a lovely man. I wonder how grandmamma ever got him to her table. . . . Oh, it is really too bad that Leila and Lady Courtland will not be here. You would think that Lord Thorpe could have chosen a better time to fall ill!"

Lord Thorpe was Leila's grandfather, and very close to her; so she, her mother, and Lady Courtland had gone off to Cornwall to visit with him during his illness, which was feared to be very serious.

Cama, of course, was just as happy to know they would not be present. It would only help her plans to advance. . . . If she could have found a way to cut Trelawny from the list, she would have, but he expressed nothing but delight at the prospect of a dinner, even for Black Walter and his opera dancer. This was strange, and made Cama fear that the fellow was trying to ingratiate himself with his fiancée to make up for some quarrel. She would have to think about this . . . he really must not come to the dinner.

But this line of thought was broken off by a chance look in the mirror opposite her chair: Were those gray hairs showing through the chestnut? With horror she leaned closer. Yes. Well, she would have to make a purchase of the hair dye, and very soon at that.

Diana, too, was unhappy that Richard would be at this very

important dinner. He would not like her father; she knew it already. She had spent a long afternoon explaining to Richard that Mariotta was simply mischievous, and not evil, and that the masquerade during which she had said all of those shocking things to Richard had been undertaken out of misplaced high spirits. But Richard, for a long time, insisted on seeing it as a sign of some sort of dementia. This was very funny to Diana, as was his sputtering recapitulation of all the terrible things Mariotta had said, many of which struck her as quite true, if baldly put.

He had finally forgiven Mariotta, and implicitly her, saying that he knew *she* did not share her sister's views. So everything was as it had been. They were still engaged; he had even set the date, the first of December.

Diana did not ask herself why his absolution had been no cause for joy, or why she felt no anticipation, joyous or otherwise, about the wedding only a month away. She was aware, however, of a sort of leaden feeling in her heart. But she dismissed it; she would not listen to it. All it ever said to her was that she wanted Jack and no one else.

Jack, seen everywhere now with Amanda Tentrees, seemed very happy. He no longer came to call at Jermyn Street, but merely bowed from across crowded rooms. Mariotta talked to him occasionally, when they were at the same party, but he never approached Diana.

She would not regret her behavior. She had been right to suspect him of being a ne'er-do-well. And if he was not, well, she had been wrong about it, but anyone would have thought him utterly without ambition or money, who saw him at Ardwell, that is. Besides that, worst of all, he had told her he loved her, and had then fallen immediately under the spell of Amanda Tentrees. He might have money and ambition, but he was obviously inconstant. She would never have been able to endure that. So it was really just as well that he no longer came around to talk to her. Now she could spend all of her time with Richard, who was at least honorable and faithful.

Mariotta noticed her sister's depression and could guess the reasons, but she had resolved to interfere no more. The lesson was learned; Diana would have to choose her own future.

Not that Mariotta was glowing with happiness herself. She could not explain it to Cama, but it seemed to her that everything had become difficult, confused. Gerald and she were alone together more, and seemed to have less to say to each other. Every once in a while a tiny voice would say that she shouldn't marry him, but she had decided that being mature meant taking the responsibility for your own decisions. And she had decided.

Something kept her from telling Drew everything, which normally would have been her first idea. He was different with her now and seemed to have little time to stop by Jermyn Street. Cama still saw him everywhere, but Mariotta did not. So at this important moment of her life, she felt isolated. . . .

Cama, who lived with the sisters, saw their moods and was encouraged. There was hope yet, if everyone would play their parts correctly. . . .

"What have you decided?" she asked Drew in one of their hurried conversations in Meyler's bookstore.

"I have told Gerald that he must write Mariotta a letter of farewell and go down to Cornwall, after Leila. Mrs. Grayson will have them married down there, where they have many relations. She does not know the truth, but I told her that it was better that they wait no more. The fact that Lord Thorpe is sick means they must hurry. If he were to die, there could be no wedding for months while they were all in mourning. So Gerald leaves tomorrow morning."

"Wonderful! Very good! But I have done something even better. Trelawny will not come."

"But he has already said he will!"

"You will see. He will find a reason to be sick, or some such thing."

Drew was all admiration. This was really difficult, since Trelawny was now bent on marrying Diana, the heiress of London. . . .

"Everything will then be ready, but how do you know that it will work? Suppose they don't speak to us?"

"Don't be such a ninny, Drew! If they don't, you will speak to them until they answer. I shall do what I can, but it will depend on what has happened that day. In the meantime, I don't want to see you two about—go into hiding for a week if necessary, but no more public appearances, especially with other females."

"As you wish, Madame Machiavel."

Richard Trelawny sat down, his heart beating. The invitation was from the duchess of Tarborough! He would actually be at a dinner with the duke! How had they heard of him? The duchess claimed to have known his mother; it was possible, but still . . . but such a wonderful chance. Royalty was often to be found at Tarborough Castle; one met very powerful people there. . . .

He reread the invitation, and then it burst upon him: it was the same date as Lady Green's dinner party. At first he was simply miserable, but gradually he began to see his way.

He was honest with himself: It was wrong to lie to Lady Green. There was no use pretending it wasn't. But if he managed to make some friends among those who frequented Castle Tarborough, he might indeed buy a townhouse in London. Then there would be reason to; he would belong to the rarefied world of the very powerful and very wealthy. He daydreamed about it the rest of the day, and by the next morning had convinced himself that he was doing it all for Diana.

He dashed off a note to Lady Green, saying that a very close friend had become very ill, and that he would have to go out of town and see them.

Cama read the note with great pleasure: He was just exactly the sort of man she had estimated him to be. It was so rewarding to be right. She threw the note aside and went down to tell her guests that there would be one less person at the dinner.

Mariotta was visibly delighted that Richard would be gone. Diana frowned and wondered aloud why Richard hadn't driven over to tell her in person about it.

Cama's dark eyes, had Diana looked at them, would have told her a great deal. But she turned away so that they would not see her triumph in her face.

She was so caught up in the affairs of the twins that she almost managed to forget about Black Walter and Loulou Freneau. . . .

CHAPTER TWENTY-TWO

The evening of the dinner party found Black Walter in an uncertain frame of mind. He himself was dressed in a very fine black dress coat and breeches, mated with a subdued white marcella vest, white silk stockings, and black slippers. His neckcloth, after long contemplation, had been arranged in a "mathematical," and, all things considered, he looked superb. But Loulou! He had made her change her dress twice, and was still not satisfied.

"What in the world is the matter with the gold? You liked it at the Pearsons'!" Loulou could screech as well as she could murmur, and it was the former voice she was practicing now, on a very irritated fiancé.

"This is different. These are my family and friends."

The beautiful face clouded further. "You think I don't know how to dress, Walter? I know how! The rest of these dowdies will look like nothing next to me and you know it!"

Loulou was wrong there. The Abingdon twins were dressed in their presents from Cama, two matching silver gowns, with dark blue trimmings in satin. The only thing that set them apart was the shawl which went with each gown. Mariotta's was blue, Diana's was silver. They loved the gowns, which were very much the *dernier cri*, but they asked each other why Cama had dressed them basically alike—it was so unlike her to be insensitive to their desire to be perceived separately.

But in the preparations for the dinner, this question was lost sight of. And Cama lent them pearls to wear with their gowns, earrings for Diana, a necklace for Mariotta.

But when they came downstairs, they agreed that Cama quite put them in the shade. She swept down the staircase as they watched, wearing a gown of cream satin, with her hair dressed high in coils which were held with sprays of emeralds. The sticks of her fan were adorned with small emerald points as well, and the entire effect was magnificent and regal, from her shining chestnut hair to her cream satin slippers. Cama had lovely rounded shoulders, and the embonpoint of a much younger woman, and she had drawn attention to this by wearing an emerald necklace of stunning size. They were proud to be at dinner with her. They did not deserve it, they told her.

"Nonsense! You are the beauties, I am an old lady. Jewels do not make up for *that*. I assure you. I had my moment, now you will have yours. I ask nothing more."

The twins' faces showed that they doubted this last.

"Now, Mariotta—you are in the blue shawl?—yes, both of you, I wish you to be especially nice to Miss Freneau, no matter what she may turn out to be like. It is entirely possible that she is a well-bred actress. We shall have to see. But I wish her to feel at home, and relaxed."

They agreed, but they found this a little peculiar. Why should this unknown person be encouraged to feel at home? They were aware that Cama already did not like her. . . . This was being terribly noble, too noble for Cama. . . .

Diana thought very hard and began to see something, but there was no time to consult with Mariotta: guests were arriving.

Diana prepared herself for Jack's arrival. She would be calm, collected. But her stomach would not go along with this plan; the butterflies began as soon as she caught sight of his dark head, bent, naturally, over Amanda's blond one.

Mariotta was talking to Lord Candelford in the drawing room, and had not seen Drew arrive. The sound of his warm voice took her by surprise.

"Hello, Cherry. Looking quite ready to break hearts tonight. Is Gerald coming?"

She turned away from Lord Candelford and saw, suddenly, the dearest face in the world. In that instant, she knew what had been missing from Gerald: everything that was Carlton Drew. To her, Drew was handsomer than his blond Adonis of a nephew, and she realized just what that meant.

"No, he is not coming," she managed to answer. "He told me that he had to go to Cornwall."

Drew would have throttled his nephew if he'd been handy. The cowardly fool had not bothered to tell Mariotta that he would in all likelihood be married in two weeks!

"It is just as well," Mariotta continued. "Gerald likes all dinners to be useful in some way, and this won't be useful. Oh. My goodness!"

Drew turned in the direction of Mariotta's stunned stare.

Entering the room as if she were taking possession of a stage was a person who could only be the much-awaited Loulou Freneau. Her auburn-haired beauty was obvious, but what took the eye was her bottle-green satin gown, which was cut so low that virtually nothing was left to the imagination. Black Walter had provided her with a silk shawl to mask some of her charms, but she had deliberately let it slip off her shoulders, so that great expanses of that much-praised milk-white flesh were visible to the inhabitants of the drawing room.

"Black Walter certainly has an eye for women," said Drew.

"But not an ear," answered Diana, who had come over to join them. "You should have heard her voice when they arrived—she was shrieking something at him while still outside, and so loudly that I heard it from the hall."

The only person present who was not absorbed in the edifying sight of Loulou Freneau greeting her hostess and carefully taking a seat on one of the sofas was Jack. His eyes did not seem to be able to leave Diana's face.

"You must stop staring," reminded Amanda Tentrees. "I don't think my escort should spend all his time looking at someone else!"

"Sorry. You are quite right, but it is certainly obvious that you have never been in love, Miss Tentrees."

"Don't call me that. Call me Amanda, for goodness' sake. No, I suppose I have never been in love, if it means making a complete cake of oneself!"

Her laugh was a beautiful sound, and Jack smiled despite himself. At that moment Diana looked over and saw her former suitor laughing with the beautiful Amanda. She would not look in his direction again, she resolved.

Black Walter was experiencing something very like discomfort. Cama, majestic and charming, had swept up to welcome them, but he could see how the other guests were reacting. Shocking the prissy ladies of Almack's or St. James was one thing, but seeing his daughters and Drew and Jack stare at Loulou was another, he discovered. The only one who maintained absolute composure, as if Loulou were the most desirable guest in London, was Cama.

Loulou preened herself on this. Here was a famous hostess, wearing such costly emeralds in her hair, and she was so friendly to Loulou Freneau. This was the world that marriage to Black Walter would guarantee her. It was already wonderful.

Loulou's intelligence was of the crude sort and had nothing in common with the elegant deviousness of Cama's mind; but Loulou understood very well that Cama could help her a great deal, so she was on her best behavior, complimenting everything she saw.

Drew watched this ballet with great interest.

"Something peculiar in this," he muttered to Diana and Mariotta. "Cama is being awfully nice. Too nice."

"She told us she wanted Loulou to feel at home," said Mariotta.

"I should think that would be the very last thing anyone would want! Imagine what Miss Freneau is like when she is comfortable. . . ."

Diana watched Cama. "Yes, I agree with Drew. She has got that very calm expression on, and that often means that she's up to something, or so I've noticed."

Black Walter did not think along these lines. He was simply grateful. Cama had managed to soothe Loulou's bad mood immediately. On the way over she had been at her worst, and he had feared that she might leave after making a scene. But Cama had complimented Loulou on that awful gown, saying it set off her coloring to perfection.

He was only able to breathe easily when Cama took Loulou off to meet the twins. He took himself a large glass of port and walked over to talk with Jack and Drew, who had cravenly deserted the twins as soon as he saw Cama bearing down with the stepmother-to-be in tow.

"Women can ruin a fellow," said Black Walter by way of greeting.

"Oh, yes," said Jack absently, looking at the ladies gathered around the sofa.

"I quite like them," announced Drew, who was looking in the same direction as Jack, but at a different twin.

"I notice they have different shawls. Surely a good thing for us, Drew."

Black Walter quickly understood the drift of these strange remarks, and snorted derisively at these besotted fellows. But he could not let down his guard. Loulou was behaving so far, but he had absolutely no confidence that the evening would end as well as it had started. Cama was a genius, but it would require something more than that to insure it. Quite unconsciously he had shifted from thinking of Loulou as his pawn, and now she seemed just as much a threatening queen as those ladies at Almack's; whereas he thought of Cama as being on his side.

The company was summoned into the dining room, with Cama leading the way, on Lord Candelford's arm. The guests murmured their appreciation at the sight of her dining room, especially refurbished for her first dinner in months.

A large cut-glass chandelier hung over the vast mahogany table, which was set with the soup course, a *madrilène*, served in a beautiful Worcester service. But it was the decoration of the room rather than the table which had prompted the comments. The walls were hung with blue silk damask, dyed to match the rare Kuba carpets which lay on the shining wood floor. A Canaletto scene—one of his English pictures—hung over the marble fireplace, giving the room an air of lightness and gaiety. On the other walls were French mirrors, reflecting the chandelier. The long windows, which opened onto a small enclosed garden, were hung with raw silk ruched curtains, of a very pale blue.

The most vehement admirer of all this good taste and luxury was Miss Loulou Freneau.

"Now this is *my* sort of room, Walter! When we are married, I should love the dining room to be done in this style. Lady Green, where did you ever find these carpets?"

"I did not find them. One of my uncles brought them back from the Caucasus—southern Russia—some eighty years ago."

"Why don't you have uncles like that, Walter!" This was said archly, as if it were the wittiest remark in the world.

Several members of the party exchanged looks at this, but were distracted by a late arrival, the explanation for the empty seat by Cama.

Cama swept to the door and put out her hand to be kissed.

"Dear Corin! I am so glad you were able to come. You must be famished. Here, this is your place, we are just about to begin."

She turned to the company and told them that this young man was Corin West, the well-known Drury Lane actor who had played Mercutio to great acclaim the previous spring.

Mariotta committed the social sin of leaning across Drew to whisper to Diana.

"Did you ever see anything so gorgeous! Like Byron, but better. Blond hair, green eyes! So handsome . . ."

"Yes," whispered Diana, "and I wonder what he's doing here. I don't believe for a minute that Cama's really taken him up, unless, of course, he is a truly great actor. It's not at all in her line."

Diana could not continue this, because her father was sitting on her right, and she did not wish him to hear anything. She talked to him a little, and kept her eye on Corin West, who was talking a very little to the lady on his right, Mrs. Sarton, and a lot to the lady on his left, Loulou Freneau. So that was it. Diana involuntarily smiled, and moved her glance slightly to the left and met the intense blue eyes of Jack Campbell. His look was so direct and naked that it went through her like a knife. She quickly turned to Drew and began to ask him about Gerald, but she did not hear his answers. All she could think of was Jack. How could he look at her like that, when the beautiful Amanda was sitting next to him?

After dinner, the ladies moved to the drawing room, and the gentlemen were free to smoke if they wished.

In the drawing room, the conversation centered about Corin West.

"He is truly a magnificent actor," pronounced Loulou. "I saw him act in Scotland, that was two years ago, and even then! Such power!" She shuddered at the memory. Her listeners felt that there was more to her interest than pure appreciation of another actor. She tried to imply that he and she were in the same profession, though she had been nothing more than an opera dancer before her marriage to a wealthy Parisian.

Cama blandly encouraged her along these lines.

"But of course, it is really too bad, Loulou—I may call you Loulou?—that you will have to give up your career at this point. Many actresses only begin their prime after twenty-five. But Walter would never stand for it, and indeed, we live in such a narrow-minded society—you would never be received anywhere should you go on the professional stage for one performance, even."

This was not strictly true, but certainly people like Loulou, who were without a shred of talent, were not generally accepted in the ton.

Loulou looked very thoughtful after these remarks. She had not, apparently, really given the matter of her theater career much thought. Cama thought she must have assumed that she would continue. Of course Walter would have been all for it—the more scandal the better. But Loulou, Cama perceived, wanted acceptance of some kind. And not in the way Walter had planned.

The first gentlemen to come into the drawing room were Lord Candelford and Corin West. By subtle maneuvers, Corin managed to sit alone in the corner with Loulou, ostensibly discussing old times at the Drury Lane, where she had once been briefly employed. Cama seemed not to notice this improper behavior.

The others turned to the piano, insisting that Mr. Jeffrey Sarton, an old friend of Cama's and a good amateur musician, play them something they might sing to.

Amanda had a lovely soprano, so she was picked first to perform. Cama watched as the two young men immediately went to sit by the twins. All was going well. But five minutes later, as Lord Candelford had begun a touching ballad, she was not so happy. The twins and their would-be suitors did not seem able to talk to each other. They were in very stiff attitudes, which proclaimed that the conversations were strained. Cama did not know how many misunderstandings had developed over these weeks, but she could see how they might hamper communication. Something would have to be devised; this was really the last chance. Jack would be going off to Scotland for months; Drew would give up if he did not immediately get some encouragement. . . .

She told the girls to follow her upstairs, one of her flounces was torn.

They did as they were bid and were surprised to find out that nothing was wrong with Cama's dress.

"My dears, I want you to help me play a joke on William Candelford. It will be so amusing! He assures me that he can tell you apart now, even when you are wearing the same dresses. But I am convinced that he cannot. What I should like you to do is exchange shawls and jewelry. It will only take a moment, and it will be a real test for him."

So it was that when they returned to the drawing room, Mariotta was wearing the silver shawl and Diana the blue. The pearl necklace and earrings had also been switched. To help

Cama in her deception they began to consciously act a little like each other as well.

The result was as Cama had foreseen. Jack took Diana's arm and led her to a game table, and Drew asked Mariotta to join him on the sofa, where he was demonstrating card tricks.

Amanda was conversing in a most animated style with Corin and Loulou Freneau, as Black Walter watched in obvious boredom. Jeffrey Sarton and Lord Candelford were telling Cama a great many funny things about recent parliamentary problems, but she could not keep her mind on them at all.

The suspense was simply too much for her; she would have to do something to distract herself, and her present companions were absolutely useless in this regard. She caught Black Walter's eye and beckoned him over. It was time to let him in on the plan.

He seemed happy to escape the theatrical talk of Loulou and Corin, which, however, had entirely enraptured Amanda. He thought it a great bore, and all concerned incredibly self-centered.

Cama led him to the window recess, where there was some quiet and two comfortable chairs.

"Now, Walter, I have been keeping things from you, because I was not certain of them. But now I am, and I think you should know what I have done."

She proceeded to tell him about Drew and Jack, and their problems with his daughters. He began to smile—Cama was a true *intrigante*, and obviously very good at it, too. The two of them began to build castles, imagining what would happen if the twins married these gentlemen who so clearly deserved them. It was a very pleasant business, and served to distract them both from what was happening in another part of the room.

Corin West had thoroughly enchanted Loulou. She saw that

no matter how seductive the charms of society, the theater was her first love. He told her that she belonged in the play he was rehearsing now, *A Trip to Scarborough*, indeed, there was a part which was perfect for her . . . but, obviously, she was deserting the theater. . . .

Amanda Tentrees quickly saw that she was in the way, and drifted off to brighten the lives of Lord Candelford and Jeffrey Sarton, casually telling them the worst secrets of her family.

Corin used his intense green eyes to convey an unmistakable message to Loulou, a message which she understood immediately. The struggle was brief. In the final analysis, she knew quite well that Black Walter did not really love her; he merely admired her beauty. And she would never be able to tolerate the boredom of propriety, and in the end, no matter what he said, that would be his requirement of a wife.

All of this went through her mind in a flash, as she was smiling her answer to Corin West. His eyes mesmerized her. She followed him out into the hall, unsure of what he wanted from her at that minute.

"Here. Your cloak. You are coming with me, aren't you, my beautiful Loulou?"

She did not answer, but merely looked at him, amazed.

"You want to leave right now, without saying goodbye?"

Corin could not very well say that those had been his instructions, but he knew what words would accomplish this.

"Yes. That is, if you wish to come with me, and resume your career . . . and other things, as well."

He was so intense, so masterful, he swept her up in his arms, despite the shocked looks of the butler and footmen. She could not deny him, and he carried her out the door, into the waiting carriage, which had been there all evening.

The butler went into the drawing room, to inform his

mistress. The whispered account of recent events drew nothing but a sigh from Lady Green.

"Oh, I hope they didn't put you to too much trouble, Crawford. I should not like that. You needn't worry, I expected this, or something like it."

The butler went away, struck once again by the sagacity of the lady he served.

Cama turned to Black Walter, her fine dark eyes expressing deep compassion, and reluctance to see him hurt.

"Miss Freneau has left, it appears, with that odious Corin West! I am so sorry. I am completely to blame. How could I have thought he would behave! I must have been mad!"

At first Walter was simply stunned by this news, but then he felt a strong sensation of something very like relief. He could not quite admit it to himself at first—he began a quiet tirade against Loulou, but it quickly trailed off into silence. Then he could be seen to smile ever so slightly.

"Ah, no fool like an old fool, Cama! Suppose I deserved it! But what a wonderful scandal for all the tabbies to lap up."

"Oh, no, I shouldn't think so. My butler is very discreet; all my servants are. I shall tell them to be very careful. And no one else here need know. We shall say that Miss Freneau was ill, and Mr. West took her home. It will be seen as odd, but they will forget about it. They all have other things on their minds, I think.

"But Walter, I am worried. You will begin to feel very bad about this. I want you to come with me to the Fanes' country house next week. A few days there would do you good. And Nick has some wonderful horses. Two of them are going to be raced this year, and I'm sure he would love your opinion."

This was a stroke of genius, and Cama well knew it. Black Walter knew a vast amount about horses, and loved them almost more than women. These years of insufficient funds had left him unable to have his own thoroughbreds, but he was always interested in anything concerning them. And Nick Fane, that was a drawing card as well, since he was known to be choosy about his company, and invitations to his house were rare.

All in all, Black Walter began to think that he would survive the loss of his fiancée quite well. . . .

On the sofa, Drew was showing Mariotta various card tricks, but without his usual panache.

"What is the matter, Drew? You seem a little low tonight."

"Oh, Diana, if only I could tell you."

"You can, I am your friend, am I not?"

"But it concerns Mariotta."

"I am no less your friend for being her sister. . . ."

She gave him a frank smile, inviting confidences with its indication of sympathy for him.

He distractedly pushed the unruly lock off his forehead, in a gesture she found endearing every time she saw it. She thought of his kiss, for the thousandth time, and wondered how she could be such a traitor to Gerald. With a shock she heard his words, about Gerald:

"And how can I tell her that Gerald has chosen Leila, and is even now gone down to Cornwall after her. It is very likely that they will even be married within a week or two. He has written Mariotta a letter, but I am afraid to give it to her."

Mariotta's eyes were bright and hard. In a trice she passed through anger and disappointment and finally felt contempt.

"Why? She will very quickly understand what sort of man he was, and will hardly regret him for an instant. Besides . . . I think Mariotta was not really in love with him any more. . . . She didn't know very much about love. She thought it was just liking a handsome face. . . ."

Drew looked very sad. "I know. I was always sure she didn't

belong with him. . . . Oh, Diana, I am too old for her! How can I go to her and tell her how I love her? She will think me a ridiculous old fool."

"And what would you tell her if you could," said Mariotta, not able to look into his eyes. She felt a sort of shaking begin deep within herself.

"I would tell her that I cannot imagine life without her. And I would tell her that even Gerald never appreciated her true beauty, as I do, the beauty of her spirit. And what do you think she would answer, Diana?"

Here he tilted her chin up and looked in her shining eyes.

"I think she would say yes, yes, yes, and how did you know it was me, Drew?"

"It would take more than a change of shawls to deceive me, Mariotta." He had to content himself with kissing her hand, since they were in a room with other people, but he looked at her so hungrily that she began to blush. They quickly found an excuse to go into the billiard room, where they found the privacy they needed to say everything they had wanted to say for so long, and to enjoy the kisses they had been denied.

Diana and Jack saw them go; one of them guessed at the reason, and the other did not. Jack was taken in by Diana's performance as her sister, chiefly because he had been doing most of the talking, about his political plans. When that subject was exhausted, Diana asked him if he were going to marry Amanda.

"Don't be ridiculous, Mariotta! I thought you would certainly see through that charade. That was all for Diana's benefit. Cama seemed to think that Diana would only begin to realize what she felt for me if she thought I were interested in someone else. It was an old, old ploy, and in this case, it didn't work. I begin to think Diana really does not care for me, that I was mistaken.

Funny, you think you understand women, and one comes along . . . Oh, I'd like to tell her, after I shook her a little, how much I think about her, how nothing seems to have any flavor unless she is around . . . but she is the most obstinate, most impossibly complicated wretch! How can I tell her I love her to distraction anyway?"

He looked down, expecting to see Mariotta's humorous expression, and instead saw gray eyes filled with tears.

"I think you already have told her, Jack."

Since the billiard room was occupied, they had to content themselves with the little sitting room. But they were not there very long, and were in the middle of a passionate kiss, when the door was opened by a very haughty Cama.

"What is this? What is this improper behavior? Are we barbarians that we desert our guests and hide with gentlemen in darkened rooms? I am truly shocked, Walter, that your daughters should be so lost to a sense of propriety!"

"We are to be married, Cama, as soon as I find a way to break off with Trelawny," announced Diana shyly.

"Oh, you don't have to worry. I have already seen to *that*. He lied about a sick friend, and went to Castle Tarborough, like the little worm he is, to lick the boots of the duke. You need only say that you cannot marry a liar. That will do."

The same scene was repeated in the billiard room, but Drew knew very well how to put Cama in her place.

"I would be ashamed if you hadn't arranged the entire thing! There was nothing the matter with your hem, confess it! *You* are the deceiver, not we poor lovers. Now you will just come off your high horse and admit your delight, or I shall refuse to ever give you credit for the entire success of this campaign!"

Cama could only smile at that, and they rejoined the company, all of whom seemed happy for the newly engaged couples.

"But," said Amanda, "do you think it is catching? Shall I at last fall in love?"

"I shouldn't be surprised," said Cama. "It all has a great deal to do with propinquity in general. One doesn't usually go across half the world to find someone to love, one simply looks around one's own neighborhood."

That Cama meant something specific by this, no one had any doubt, but they could not imagine what. Yet another mystery from the Queen of Mystery.

"I wish I didn't know that you're up to something again," said Drew as he left.

"Don't be silly, Drew. I simply let matters take their course."

"Don't see you as a fatalist, Lady Green." Jack pronounced.

"Oh, you silly young gentlemen will never understand the subtle twists and turns of the female mind. Go on home and dream of your weddings!"

CHAPTER TWENTY-THREE

It was a very modest wedding in many ways, but no one was disappointed. After the brief ceremony, the two couples and those invited to the wedding supper drove from the church to Lady Green's house on Jermyn Street.

Among those expressly not invited to the supper were Lady Chalford, Lady Quennel, Mr. Richard Trelawny and Miss Caroline Trelawny. They had all been present at the ceremony, however, chiefly out of curiosity.

Lady Chalford had actually been invited to the wedding, since her granddaughters felt it only proper to do so. She used this occasion to boast to anyone who would listen that it was all her own doing, and to cast aspersions on the looks and intelligence of both her son and her former daughter-in-law.

Caroline and Lady Quennel were interested to see how those other newly marrieds, the Huntingtons, would behave. They were disappointed to see that the former Cecily Abingdon looked happy and well, and that Edmund Huntington could not stop beaming.

Richard Trelawny had been dragged along by his sister, and found nothing in the ceremony to make him in the least happy.

But those gathered at the supper, with few exceptions,

were very happy indeed, and drank many toasts to the two couples.

The only troublesome aspect of everything, for the twins at least, was the potentially embarrassing meeting of their parents, who had not seen each other in twenty years.

"Mariotta! Is that your father?" asked Cecily in astonished accents. "He looks dreadfully *old*!"

For his part, Black Walter told Cama that he was stunned by the changes time had wrought in Cecily.

"She looks well enough, but I heard her talking to the new husband, and you will not believe what their conversation was about. Plants!"

Cama was amused by the disparaging comments each side was making, and told the twins that it was a miracle their parents' marriage had lasted a year, never mind two.

Mariotta and Diana were so happy that they were on the edge of tears throughout the supper, and they kept telling each other that it was the most wonderful day of their lives. But Drew and Jack kept reminding them that there were many other wonderful days ahead.

The company, which numbered some fifty persons, was fed well, on eight courses of Cama's best food, and their glasses were refilled with French champagne. By the fifth course, therefore, the mood was one of relaxed gaiety all around.

Cama chose this moment to tap on her glass with a fork.

The company grew silent, expecting yet another wedding toast. But Black Walter stood up, a look of bright anticipation on his face.

"I have an announcement to make. We are celebrating a double wedding. But there is a third wedding that I should wish you to celebrate. My friends, I give you my wife, Camilla Chalford!"

Knives and forks clattered to the table, glasses froze in midair. It was an announcement that required a few moments to absorb. And then Drew stood and proposed a toast to them.

"Cama, you sly creature," said Diana. "Why did you do it? How did you do it?"

Cama was not in the slightest bit offended.

"Well, really, someone had to take care of him. And you know, I was just the slightest bit tired of my life. Walter is rather bracing you know. As for how, I told him that if he wanted to marry for money, he might as well marry me!"

Black Walter beamed, obviously proud of the fact that his marriage had produced the greatest sensation at this supper.

The guests watched the beautiful brides and the handsome bridegrooms, and everyone seemed to agree: there was something about a double wedding which cast an ordinary wedding into the shade. But everyone admitted that they would have given their eyeteeth to see Camilla Green marry Black Walter.

ABOUT THE AUTHOR

Alix Melbourne is an admirer of both Jane Austen and Georgette Heyer and wrote her novels as an homage to these two women.

ALIX MELBOURNE

FROM OPEN ROAD MEDIA

OPEN ROAD

INTEGRATED MEDIA

www.ingramcontent.com/pod-product-compliance
Lightning Source LLC
Chambersburg PA
CBHW030357020726
47493CB00003B/850